The Wanderers

by Vincent Tanner

PublishAmerica
Baltimore

© 2005 by Vincent Tanner.
All rights reserved. No part of this book may be reproduced, stored in a retrieval system or transmitted in any form or by any means without the prior written permission of the publishers, except by a reviewer who may quote brief passages in a review to be printed in a newspaper, magazine or journal.

First printing

ISBN: 1-4137-7423-7
PUBLISHED BY PUBLISHAMERICA, LLLP
www.publishamerica.com
Baltimore

Printed in the United States of America

To the memory of

Virgil I. "Gus" Grissom,

Edward White II

and

Roger Chaffee,

*the first of many American astronauts to give their lives
in the quest to reach for the stars.*

Foreword

When I was growing up, every kid wanted to be a cowboy, but, living in an urban environment, that proved to be impractical. We turned our life's intentions toward becoming police officers or firefighters, doctors or lawyers. Then the space race of the '60s began. Suddenly, everyone my age wanted to be an astronaut. I would envision myself perched on top of a rocket, blasting into outer space. 10, 9, 8…

I never made it to the "Astronaut Corps," instead I became a firefighter. Others in the same pool went on to become accountants, lawyers, janitors, construction workers, etc. Although none of us ever became cowboys, we all held on to that vision of space travel. Every one of us would give anything to reach for the stars and leave everything behind just to speed deep into the cosmos, seeking new discoveries.

Buck Rogers at the Saturday cinema matinees and later television fueled the dreams of space travel. We would "Reach for the Stars," if only in our imagination.

Now, man has been to the moon, and plans are in the works to explore farther out into the solar system. First will be Mars, and then…who knows. The ultimate goals humankind will be able to attain in even this short lifetime are beyond anything we have yet imagined.

I wish to give special thanks to my good friend of over thirty-five years, without whose prodding this book might never have been written. Thank you, Tom!

*"A journey of a thousand miles
begins with a single step."*
—Confucius

*"A journey of many light years begins
with the collective steps of a whole world."*
—Commander John Correy

Chapter 1

A golden leaf gently cascades to the forest floor—making nary a sound—settling ever so softly—resting on the others preceding it. The autumn traveler gently glides in among the pile. If you remain perfectly still, not moving a muscle, holding your breath, you just might be able to hear the quiet rustle the moment it lands, calmly resting where it drops until the gusty autumn wind decides to move it farther on. The air is filled with the lingering sweet smells of a warm fall day, slowly drifting into the crisp stillness of the coming evening.

How I love to walk through the woods alone—alone with my thoughts, especially at this time of year. I am at peace with my heart, my mind, my self. I take in the beauty of the forest surrounding me, I feel at one with the spirit of the deep woods. The trees shed the last remnants of their lush green summer garments, which have now turned to vivid hues of red and gold, yellow and brown. Each one delicately plucked from their branches one at a time, or often in large groups—the gentle breeze pulling at their fragile fastenings. The season is growing colder.

A gray squirrel splits the quiet autumn air with his chattering. Hidden from my view by a tangle of tree branches, he spots me long before I could ever hope to see where he is hiding among the many boughs. With his unceasing chippering, he is letting all the rest of the woods know exactly where I am. Out of the corner of my eye, I catch the flashing red flutter of a cardinal darting from one tree branch to another, alerted to my presence by the fluffy-tailed sentry's alarm.

The velvety gray watchman chatters on, following me along the path I tread. His steel colored body hopping from limb to limb alongside my path for a considerable distance. Leaping from one tree to another, he trails after me. He becomes silent only when I move a far enough distance from his home territory where he no longer feels threatened by my intrusion.

The young saplings sprouting along the wooded path struggle to get a hold on life. My foot tangles in some of this year's new root growth. The musty smell of last year's leaves wafts up—assaulting my nostrils with the aroma of decaying vegetation. I pull my foot free—pausing for only a moment to adjust my shoe. I spot a young yearling doe off to my right, grazing on some of the last greenery she will see for some months to come. I know there is sure to be a buck somewhere close by. The young female deer are never alone in the forest at this time of year. Their antlered counterparts are continuously in pursuit, gathering the does together into a harem. Still unseen, I hear his snort from behind me the moment he catches my scent—the doe, ears twitching, bounds away. I watch her leap over the underbrush, soon joined by the cunning master of the herd. They flee away together into the shelter of the deep forest cover.

Far off in the distance I hear the muffled drumming of a ruffled grouse. More than likely, he is perched prominently on an old tree stump somewhere in the dark forest. The majestic fowl is forcefully thumping his wings against his breast. The slow, accelerating rhythm with its increasing tempo repeats at intervals.

The drumming of his wings echo and reverberate through the quiet woods. His territorial call resounds through the entire glen. "Here I am!" he is letting the world know. "This is my domain, my part of the forest, my patch of ground! Unless you desire to be my mate—keep out!"

I continue to dream of walking along through the forest hollow, my mind begins to recall the wind and rains of spring and the heat of summer. I am thankful they are now long past and no longer a bother. I find the fall season by comparison much more enjoyable. I dread the thought of the deep chill of winter fast on its way, when the sheer thought of even moving around becomes a chore. Winter is not something I even wish to consider thinking about on such a beautiful day as this. Winter can wait. Now it is the fall season!

Autumn is such a wonderful time of year! There is a slight chill in the fresh, clear air. It is not yet cold enough to be uncomfortable or cause me to shiver. I take a deep breath of the brisk, lingering scent of the woods. Instead of chilling me, it fills me with a sense of being alive—a sense of being free.

The gentle breeze whisks a few more remaining leaves from their branches one by one. Slowly they tumble down, forming a new layer on top of those already on the ground. I continue onward, my feet brushing through the leaves lying on the pathway, crinkling under my shoes with each step. In my mind, I inhale the fragrance of the newly fallen leaves mingled with the musty aroma of decaying matter from all the previous years. Only in my thoughts, I continue to walk along the wooded path—in deep reflection—listening to the soothing, crunching sound of the leaves under my feet.

How I wish I could go back to Earth, back to those almost forgotten wonderful days of autumn, when there were once lush forests and an abundance of leaves to tread through. How I long for the tranquil sounds of the woods instead of the resounding metallic clang of the crew members' magnetic gravity boots striking the steel mesh decking surrounding me. How I long for the quiet flutter of leaves instead of the clatter their boot-laden feet make, holding them in place one step at a time.

It has been almost a year since we left Arilias-6, and almost eleven years since I last heard the soothing sound of crisp leaves under my feet on Earth. Eleven years enduring the sterility of space. Our travels are seemingly unending—broken up only one time by our brief sojourn on the surface of the one planet that came so very close to resembling what we remember life being like on our long-dead world.

Chapter 2

Ship Time: Year 10, Month 9, Day 17
Post-Earth equivalent year: 2078

My name is Commander John Correy of the North American States Air Force; first officer in command of the Multinational Astronomical Base for Universal Studies. The M.A.B.U.S. platform—our star traveler and only home for many years, and will be for many more years to come.

M.A.B.U.S. is an aging Earth orbital observation station painstakingly converted to an immense interstellar vessel—transporting the small segment of what remains of the Earth's people to the distant stars. Our mission is to seek out a suitable planet to call our own. I cannot help but think about the lost, dead planet we left behind so long ago and dream about the beauty it once held. I especially miss the short seasonal interlude between the hot insect-laden summer days and the icy frigid winter snows. I did enjoy autumn so very much.

The events that occurred after we landed on the first suitable new planet we found have reduced our number to less than half what we were when we originally set foot on Arilias-6 more than nine and a half months ago. Now, back in our wormhole, we must press onward—"Always looking forward and never back." There is nothing left to look back to, and only uncertainty ahead! Earth is gone, and Arilias-6 was far too hostile for us to remain on its surface any longer. We press on....

Right now, along with four other crew members, I am sitting at the main command console of our massive transport. I must force myself to put my reminiscent daydreaming aside and return to monitoring the flight path of our platform through a wormhole—continually tracking our forward progress on computerized holographic displays, since there are no windows. Even if there were—when traveling through a wormhole there is nothing to see. Straight out ahead of us is nothing—behind us more nothing—all around us—nothing. We are traveling at a speed 4.61 times faster than the speed of light—858,000 miles pass for every second we remain in this wormhole. Millions and millions of miles disappear behind us with each passing hour.

Inside the wormhole we are free from the confining physical laws of space and time. The speed of light is no longer the maximum attainable speed. We have far exceeded what was known until a few decades ago as the limits of space travel. Within the wormhole there is no friction, no inertia, no G-forces, and by all physical description, no mass. We are outside the realm of physical space and time.

We wait with great anticipation for news from our remaining three piggyback probes as they race toward our next destination. These probes were dispatched into wormholes created parallel to ours as soon as we cleared the Arilias star system. Earlier two- and three-stage exploration probes were sent out from our orbit around Arilias-6 when it became clear we could no longer remain on the planet. One by one they reported back with negative findings—except for the very last of a set of seven planet seekers. It reported finding two planets capable of supporting human life. Both were located in the same solar system, which still lies trillions of miles ahead of us.

These probes, each measuring between ten and eighteen meters in length, depending on the number of booster stages making up their propulsion systems, and each with a diameter of four meters, were sent out at regular intervals.

The boosters, housing only an e-matter drive with the associated equipment are jettisoned with the activation of each successive stage's drive engine. The main exploration capsule of each probe contains a complex array of scanners, sensors, mini-probes and two small mobile landing craft for gathering information. In addition to the e-Matter drive, each probe is also equipped with conventional thrusters necessary for slowing the exploration probe to sub-light speed while still inside the confines of the wormhole.

The wormholes originally created by each of the two- or three-stage exploration probes we launched en route to our destination are now gone, but we encounter new ones as we travel along. As each additional booster activates, it destroys the old one and forms a new wormhole running parallel to the one we are in ourselves. The fact the wormholes are even there is comforting. This gives us a bit of reassurance the probes are still functioning out there ahead of us in the vast reaches of space. If they were to suddenly cease functioning and their wormholes vanish, we could very well be heading for the same fate.

The separation of the two stages and firing of the second e-matter drive propels the main probe to twice the terminal velocity of the original configuration. Twice the speed at which we ourselves are traveling, destroying the trailing end of the original wormhole, and creating a new one in its place. At the same time propelling the probe forward to an even greater velocity, almost four times the speed it had been traveling before release.

When an explorer probe is jettisoned behind the M.A.B.U.S platform, there is a short burst from their conventional thrusters, slowing the capsules. The explorer begins decelerating behind us, falling farther and farther back from the M.A.B.U.S. station until the piggyback probe is safely a few hundred thousand miles to our stern.

At the precise moment the probe is safely far enough behind the main platform, the main e-matter engine on the booster is fired, destroying the trailing end of our wormhole and creating a new one of its own parallel to ours. This initial firing of eleven e-matter pulses nearly doubles the velocity of the exploration probe to over nine times the speed of light, twice our speed and the probe is instantly millions of miles ahead of us.

Two or more wormholes cannot exist with one inside the other, but will form outside the primary trajectory and bond in a parallel configuration, forming a separate wormhole for each probe following the same passage as the M.A.B.U.S. platform's original flight path. Our sensors are able to detect the other holes as they continue to parallel us.

At a safe distance of two to three conventional light-years in front of us, the second stage e-matter drive on each probe is brought into play. The exploration capsule moves out at nearly eighteen times light speed, vaporizing its original wormhole and possibly causing disruption to the leading edge of our own. The probe creates a completely new passage it will follow into the outer reaches of the cosmos. This new wormhole extends both forward and back to infinity, again paralleling our own.

Calculating our progress in time instead of miles, our chief navigator holds a constant vigil, watching for slight curves in our wormhole, alerting him if we are approaching a black hole or a very massive galaxy. He also keeps a close eye out for any adverse changes to our wormhole caused by the severe energy released when the first and second stages of each probe returns to physical space at over nine and again at eighteen times the speed of light. The sudden eruption of physical matter traveling at such speed back into real space and time must be a remarkable sight to see. The booster is instantly vaporized into individual atoms, which in turn are split apart as the wormhole protecting them disintegrates.

The amount of energy released by each booster as it returns to physical space is more than all the explosions; from the smallest firecracker to all the largest nuclear and conventional detonations ever taking place on the planet Earth throughout all history combined. This massive release of energy occurs at such a tremendous distance from us, and we have calculated the expended force should have completely dissipated before we arrive at the location of breakout. So far we have been correct in our assumptions.

Our main propulsion coordinator must keep a close eye on the status of our e-matter drives and the containment periphery inside the wormhole. A constant balance needs to be maintained between the e-matter we have stored in the gamma-flux magnetic chambers and the e-matter keeping us within the wormhole. If the e-matter enveloping the platform is lost or ever varies out of phase, the M.A.B.U.S platform would return to physical space and time at over four and one-half times the speed of light and vaporize in the same manner as the exploratory probe boosters.

Our fuel reserve for the conventional thrusters is now running below 50 percent. The shuttle craft ferrying personnel and supplies back and forth between the M.A.B.U.S. station and our ground base on Arilias-6 used up a great part of our reserves. We used fuel at a rate three times faster than we could manufacture new hydrogen to replace the fuel used by the shuttles.

We were not overwhelmed by the need to set up a secondary fuel facility immediately on the surface when we first reached the planet; there were plenty of natural resources to manufacture more shuttle fuel when needed. For the time being, the platform could continue to synthesize the necessary thrust, producing liquid hydrogen.

We were sure we would be able to construct a fuel plant on the surface within the confines of the main ground base long before we passed the point of having to curtail flights to conserve our reserves. If we had more time before we were forced to leave the surface of Arilias-6, the partially constructed fuel plant would have been completed and supplies totally replenished.

Our primary concern when we first arrived on the surface of the planet was with lodging and the survival of our 1,800 people. The simple task of breaking water down into hydrogen and oxygen would have given us all the fuel necessary. Although we do have the ability onboard to accomplish this task using our drinking water, it is energy-intensive, and our supply of water is much too precious to use at this time. Lieutenant Farmington, our main propulsion coordinator, estimates we can successfully break and accelerate three more times if necessary before having to resort to manufacturing additional hydrogen while in flight.

On first thought, you might consider with so much free hydrogen and oxygen, M.A.B.U.S. would be nothing more than a stellar gas bomb waiting for a leak or accident. To the contrary, the hydrogen and oxygen are contained in the same manner as the e-matter—within magnetic-flux containment bubbles. The precious gas is concentrated and condensed to a liquid within a magnetic field. With old technology, the gas had to be compressed under very low temperatures and then the pressure removed, causing the resultant heat loss to chill the remaining gas further, causing it to liquefy. The liquid had to be stored at extremely low temperatures for it to remain stable.

Before the separation of the two gases, hydrogen and oxygen, the water is infused with additional oxygen. It is converted from H_2O to H_2O_2— Good old hydrogen peroxide.

The magnetic flux exerts such tremendous pressure that upon separation, the gases are turned instantly into stable liquids, separate yet confined together. If there ever were a major failure in the storage systems, the resulting re-combining of the hydrogen and oxygen would leave us awash in very cold hydrogen peroxide. Probably bleaching all of us snow white for the rest of our lives.

The other two crew members on the bridge are our life support specialist and our logistics officer. They are deeply involved in a discussion as to possible ways of increasing the nutritional output of our shipboard-grown plants. The hydroponics garden onboard ship has produced some very unusual looking hybrids after so many years in the weightlessness of space. Our chief medical officer, a brilliant physician from the Georgian province of the former Soviet Union, steps onto the command deck.

Captain Stephenalagorphy Vladisconifskoski, whose name is so difficult to pronounce we just refer to him as Doctor Stephski, or simply Doc, interrupts their ponderous conversation. "Dr. Madeira, I will need your assistance reviewing the list of crew members due to be awakened from hyper-sleep tomorrow."

Some of the "New Walkers," as we affectionately call them, will replace several of the standing crew and undertake their own scheduled ninety-day tour of duty. The rest will return to hyper-sleep, along with the relieved crew members, in three days. "With our reduced number, the people with the proper fields of specialization to insure the continued function of the ship must be awakened first."

Although the number of surviving crew members is now down to less than half our original number, a serious drain had been placed on the ship's resources during the time we attempted to establish our colony on Arilias-6. At that time, all personnel were awake from hyper-sleep for the entire time we were on the surface of the seemingly docile, but ultimately extremely hostile, planet.

In the ensuing battles in and around our planet base camp, we were fortunate enough to be able to fortify our landing zone, forcing us to abandon very little on the surface when we finally did have to leave. However, we were given no choice but to abandon many valuable seed sources, especially those from the new plantings, which were just beginning to sprout in the fields we had so carefully tended.

This new leg of our long journey is estimated to take another 14.2 ship's years, even at this tremendous speed. It will take an additional number of weeks to get everything and everyone ready before we begin our final breaking and at last exit the wormhole. Once back in physical space we can again switch over completely to the e-matter drive, and we will be able to collect even more of the e-matter, which is absent in the wormhole, to supply the drives as we go along. By using the e-matter drives exclusively after we are back in physical space, there will be no need to rely on our precious hydrogen fuel. However, that is still many years away.

For now we are heading into the deepest reaches of space, on our way to the next two nearest planets determined to be capable of supporting life as we know it. One of these yet unnamed worlds, located in a star system we are designating as Alpha, is where we hope to make our new home.

It is now six weeks and two days into my three-month tour of duty on this part of our voyage. A voyage having its beginning in a laboratory in the Midwestern United North American States more than forty Earth years ago.

Chapter 3
The Discovery

April 27, 2035

The solar research lab is quiet on this sunny spring afternoon. Robert Jensin sits stroking quietly at his holographic keyboard, comparing the new data he has just received from three other observatories around the globe with the figures from the previous week's solar observations. He quickly combines the new information with the stored data collected over the past several months.

His fingers deftly glide over the projected keys. He enters the latest information, his hands sheathed inside a pair of virtual gloves. He suddenly freezes motionless, staring at the hologram displayed in front of him.

"This can't be possible!" he says aloud to himself. His fingers, making no sound, begin typing feverishly, re-calling records from several weeks prior, comparing the information and transmitting each new batch for celluloid printouts. The farther back he searches in the database, the more frantically he types.

"Georgia, look at this! You're not going to believe what I've just uncovered! Look at the playback and check the printouts. Please tell me I'm having a really bad dream!" He keys in the necessary commands to create the virtual model stored in his data.

Georgia Simone, Jensin's immediate supervisor, walks over behind him and leans on the back of his chair. After scanning what is on his holographic display for several seconds, she stands bolt upright.

"Are you playing some kind of a game, Robert? This can't be right! Where did you get the information to come up with something this absurd? If this is your idea of a joke? I'll…" The brightly lit display shows a constant increase in the sun's circumference, almost undetectable in the earlier readings, but there is definitely a constant change. The display is sped up exponentially, taking into consideration normal variables and adding future predictions for coming solar events.

"Look at the printouts if you don't believe what you're seeing!" he interrupts. "It's all there! Every bit of what I have found so far! I know…I know I still need to do more checking, but it doesn't look good! Damn! This does not look good at all!"

She leafs through the immense pile of celluloid data sheets he has put together for her to check. With a catch in her voice, she tells Bob Jensin, "Go over it all again, right now, in front of me! I want to see how you came up with this. You have to have made an error someplace!"

Jensin re-enters the data from the original observation. From his original starting point, he enters the remaining compilation of information, one step and date at a time. Georgia Simone's eyes widen, watching the data progression bear out what Jensin has just called to her attention.

"Oh my god!" she exclaims. "We have to alert Dr. Murdock about this right away!"

"Not yet," Jensin pleads. "I need to get more readouts. This information is from only four observatory stations with only a few hundred miles separating them. There still might be an error in the data or something I am overlooking. This could turn out to be nothing at all. I'll have to retrieve info from several of the other outposts to confirm what I have found so far."

"Do whatever you have to on this, Bob," she says, placing her hand on his shoulder, patting gently. "Don't leave anything out or assume a reading is unimportant, but be very careful! We don't want to leak out any information that is going to start a panic. You can contact all the other observatories, but be extremely cautious about what you ask for. Just ask for the data you need, and for heaven's sake, do not answer any direct questions. If you are asked, just say you're checking out something to do with those recent solar storms. I'll cover your butt until it's time to tell Murdock."

Chapter 4

July 14, 2035

"Sir! Sir! Dr. Murdock! Please, sir, you must look at these celluloids." Robert Jensin hurries down the long corridor, desperate to intercept Dr. Roy Murdock before he has a chance to pass behind the solid oak doors blocking the solar technician's access to the head administrator of the headquarters of the North American division of the M.A.B.U.S. team.

It has been almost three months since Jensin first made the fateful discovery. He put off revealing his findings to Murdock for far too long. A lot longer than he had wanted, but he knew he must be sure. He had to be sure there was no mistake. Would it have been any worse if he and Georgia Simone had informed Murdock of his findings three months ago? Probably not, but he needed to be positively sure. There had to be no doubt left in his mind that what he discovered is correct, no matter how terrible this finding turns out to be. Now he was sure. Dead sure!

"Can't this wait, Jensin? I'm on my way to a very important budget meeting."

"I'm afraid this can't wait any longer, sir. I wish to God I was wrong about this, but you must look at these data sheets now. You must look at this immediately!"

Dr. Roy Murdock, head of the astrophysics lab at the North American M.A.B.U.S. complex, gathered a growing impatience with the young upstart in front of him. All around him celluloids were dropping to the floor from his overburdened arms—his glasses sliding down the bridge of his nose every time he spoke or moved. Jensin developed a continuing reflex to push them constantly back up after every second or third word. He could have the need for glasses done away with in only an afternoon's visit to the base's eye doctor, but Bob Jensin will have none of it. He has worn glasses all his life—no sense in changing now!

Jensin's uncombed hair and traces of whatever it was he had for lunch spattered all over his lab coat only adds more to Dr. Murdock's irritation of being interrupted on his way to a crucial finance meeting. If Robert Jensin was not a certified genius, graduating magna cum laude from MIT at the tender age of seventeen, and if he had not proven himself to be right more times than not, Murdock would have gladly passed over this sudden confrontation.

"What the hell is it that's so damn important?" he demands.

"This, sir. The sun is going to expand outward and destroy the solar system!"

Murdock, growing more irritated, begins to fume. "Jensin, where have you been? For almost a century, scientists have known an event like the one you mention will ultimately take place. In about five billion years the sun is going to swell into a red giant, vaporizing all the inner planets, including the Earth. It will destroy most of the rest, if not all, of the solar system."

"Yes, sir! No, sir! But sir, they're wrong, it's going to happen in my lifetime, in your lifetime, look at the data." He hands the top section of his massive pile of celluloids to Dr. Murdock, picking a few additional ones he needs from the floor. Murdock reads over what Jensin has handed him while the young solar scientist expounds further on his findings.

"The sun is expanding as we speak! It is starting to grow outward, pulsating at an ever-increasing rate. It will still be years before we notice any distinct climatic changes, but it is happening right now! Dr. Murdock, the sun is going to explode!"

"Are you sure about this?" he asks, pouring over more of the celluloids Jensin holds out to him. "Absolutely sure?"

"Positive, sir. I no longer harbor any doubts! The sun is definitely expanding! It's starting to grow outward toward us."

"You have checked this out thoroughly?" Murdock asks. "This is not an off-the-cuff hypotheses? A problem with one of the scopes at the observatory or whatever?"

"It's been checked, double-checked and rechecked again! It is happening now!" Jensin fidgets, preparing to inform Murdock of the fact he has known about this development for three months, but now he cannot find the courage to tell the head of the complex.

Flustering for a few seconds, Jensin states, "I noticed an anomaly in the coronal fluctuation and centered my attention on the increase in sunspot activity. At first I hoped there was a misalignment in the main observatory. We checked everything out and it came up negative, so I did extensive calculations and all the data indicates the sun is pulsating beyond any previously known perimeters. Everything, all the data and all the observations, points to the same conclusion. We are approaching a celestial event of apocalyptic proportions."

Murdock grows increasingly unnerved, no longer because of the shoddy appearance of the young man before him; he had come to trust whatever Robert Jensin said as fact. However, the information Jensin just handed him made the hair on the back of his neck bristle. The more he read, the more upset he was becoming. "What time frame have you come up with?" he asks, wiping his neck with his handkerchief, which was only moments before resting neatly folded in his suit coat breast pocket. He can feel the sweat begin to build over his entire body, running down his skin in rivulets.

"Our best estimate at this time is thirty-eight to forty-two years," replied Jensin. "We need more information before we can pin down an exact time frame, but most life as we know it will probably be gone more than ten years before that particular time comes."

"When the surface of the sun reaches the orbit of Mercury, the oceans on Earth will have boiled away, the subsequent continuous solar winds will sweep away much of what remains of the Earth's atmosphere."

"The intense heat will cause the surface of the Earth to become totally parched and fuse together like glass. When the outer surface of the sun reaches the orbit of Venus, the Earth will be nothing more than a molten ball of magma waiting to be absorbed into the fiery hell of the sun itself."

"Twenty to thirty years left for life on Earth!" Murdock said aloud. In his mind the thought, "My god! What? Oh my god! Jannene, Linda, Lois! How do I tell them?"

Dr. Murdock's deep thoughts immediately go to his family—to his wife Jannene and their two daughters, Linda and Lois, both around the same age as Jensin. His youngest, Lois, had been married only last year, and Linda and her husband are expecting their own daughter in just four months. How is he going to tell them about this horrible development?

Marjory Laythrop, Dr. Murdock's personal secretary, stands in the middle of the hallway with her mouth half-open, visibly trembling, dumbstruck by the news she just heard. She appears to be almost in a state of shock. Murdock shakes her arm to get her attention. "Miss Laythrop! Miss Laythrop! Marjory!" Murdock now shakes her roughly by both arms.

Visible beads of perspiration creep down from under the bangs of her perfectly styled hair. She looks at Roy Murdock in bewilderment. She has never known Bob Jensin to be wrong, and what she just heard paralyzes her with fear. If Robert Jensin said the sky would turn purple on Tuesday and it would rain soup, Tuesday morning she would be outside wearing complimentary colors and carrying a spoon. Now she has just heard him tell Dr. Murdock the world is going to end and they are all going to die a horrible death in the not-too-distant future.

There were so many things she planned to do in her life. Now, all of what she planned was going to be left undone. She always hoped to marry—have children—and maybe someday, grandchildren. Her dream has always been to spend the waning years of her life spoiling her own children's children, as grandparents are obliged to do.

For many years she also had a deep desire to travel the world—to see the great wonders all around the globe. Now, with what she has just learned, she would probably never have any children—and she and all the others in this world will be gone long before there was ever a chance to have any grandchildren. There would be no time left to take in the earthly wonders as the world threw itself into turmoil and dissolved into the fiery belly of the sun.

"Marjory, did you hear me?" She turns to Roy Murdock with a tear running down her smooth cheek. Still is hoping she did not really hear what she just heard!

"Y-yes, sir!"

"Cancel this afternoon's meeting and set up a video conference with the world chiefs of staff for sixteen hundred hours. It is priority one: urgent. You, Jensin, I want in my office STAT! Bring all, and I do mean all, of your data and have Simone come with you. Keep this quiet for now. We cannot afford having something of this magnitude flapping around the complex until we have all the facts. For now this is totally hush-hush! Marjory, are you still with us?"

Marjory Laythrop, finally snapping back to reality but still disconcerted by the news she has just experienced, answers, "Yes, Dr. Murdock," and hurries down the corridor to affect her supervisor's directives. Her professionalism overshadowing her personal feelings and fears, she sets about her assigned task.

Murdock stands in the middle of the hall, watching Jensin heading back to his lab, having to constantly stop and pick up celluloids from the floor that keep slipping from his laden arms.

Marjory heads off in the opposite direction, toward his office complex. "This is a real mess, a real damn mess!" he says aloud to the walls. His thoughts return once more to his family. He knows what the consequences of an expanding sun will be and the total devastation resulting once the changes in the Earth's climate begin to occur.

He thinks about his unborn granddaughter. He trembles at the thought of how she will have to grow up in a world full of strife, with no future and no hope. Jannene, his lovely wife and companion for thirty-seven years, and their two daughters will perish along with the rest of the populace long before their time.

"How do I tell them?' he asks himself. "How do I tell them? My wife, my children! How am I going to tell them they are all going to die in a short time? My god!" The extreme settles in on him. "How will the rest of the world react when they learn of this? This is not something to be ignored or kept hidden while people go about their daily business. People are going to see things as the changes begin to occur, and will hear all sorts of rumors!"

If Jensin is right, there are going to be catastrophic changes all over the globe in the matter of several short years. You cannot hide something like this from the rest of the world! They are going to see! They would have to be blind not to notice the ocean is now in their backyard, even though they live twenty miles inland!"

He turns and walks slowly back in the direction he came. Although he is completely surrounded by other people, he has never felt so alone in his entire life. Never so much alone as he feels this very minute.

Roy Murdock brushes a hand through his gray hair. At seventy-three he has a receding hair line, not so much as to say he is balding. Meticulously he replaces the damp handkerchief in the breast pocket of his impeccable three-piece suit—a direct contrast to the attire of Robert Jensin.

Murdock has come to be a major part of the personnel overseeing the Multinational Astronomical Base for Universal Studies. It was nineteen years ago, as senior astrophysics consultant for the infant space platform program, when he first came on site.

Even as a senior consultant, he was not someone who was afraid to get his hands dirty. He spent two years aboard the newly constructed satellite overseeing the work on the new astronomical laboratories that would eventually house the three gigantic telescopes now fully operational on the space station.

The original construction of the M.A.B.U.S. platform began in June of 2017. It had its humble beginning as a small orbiting laboratory, and for the next several years its dimensions were a paltry fifty-seven meters long with a diameter of twelve meters.

As the year 2026 approached, M.A.B.U.S. had grown in size to more than nine hundred meters in length, with numerous modules supporting the multitude of laboratories above, below and on both sides of the main platform. The M.A.B.U.S. platform continued to increase in size as more and more laboratories were added to its structure over the years, until it was now almost a quarter of a kilometer in diameter and more than seventeen hundred meters long.

The three large observatories located one at each end with the largest of the three stationed in the middle of the platform are the center of all activities aboard the satellite. Although the three massive telescopes are located only five hundred meters apart, when all or any two are focused with the same resolution on a relatively near object such as an asteroid, the combined enhanced image is rendered three-dimensional.

Murdock was instrumental in having the immense space station moved to the stationary orbit it now occupies. The task of moving a complex object more than fifty-two hundred feet long and almost a quarter of a mile in diameter and keeping it from breaking apart was not something for the fainthearted. Total reinforcement of the entire platform had to be undertaken, with new struts added throughout the structure to eliminate any flexing under thrust, and a completely enclosing outer skin with deflector plates was constructed to protect the delicate observation platforms as well as the rest of the interior from space debris.

M.A.B.U.S. became an enclosed capsule of titanic size. The outer skin, working in conjunction with the new reinforcing struts, adds a tremendous amount of new area and volume to the orbiting giant. The cavernous outer plates opening up much needed space for storage and for the smaller laboratories needing the weightlessness of space, but not requiring direct access to the vacuum of the outer universe. M.A.B.U.S. looks something like a gigantic elongated football.

A completely new propulsion system was installed in order to move something as enormous as M.A.B.U.S. into an orbit reaching the farthest influences of Earth's gravity. The e-matter pulse drive was determined to be the safest and most efficient means of moving such a mammoth structure as the M.A.B.U.S. platform.

The platform was ever so delicately nudged into a higher, ever-increased orbit. Eventually its speed through space matched the velocity of the Earth's orbit around the sun, placing it in perpetual darkness on the night side of the world, providing a constant nocturnal view of the universe, protected from the solar glare by the Earth's shadow.

The ever-changing daily vista of the heavenly skies drifts past the platform, renewing every three hundred and sixty-five and one quarter nights. M.A.B.U.S. became a permanent fixture in the night sky. Large enough to be discerned with the naked eye as one of the brightest stars if it was not in the constant shadow of the planet below, no sunlight ever reaches the platform to reflect from it. The space station is in a perpetual total solar eclipse.

Life supporting energy for the space station is derived from the controlled release of minuscule amounts of e-matter, released out of phase into deep space. Reacting with the cosmos provides more than enough energy to supply a large city and fuels the platform with all the power it needs in the deep blackness on the dark side of the Earth.

"Had the M.A.B.U.S. platform not been moved as I directed, would the expansion of the sun been detected any earlier?" he thought. "It doesn't matter. Even if it had, there is nothing anyone could do about it. The sun is still expanding. Whatever we say now makes no difference. We are all dead!"

Arriving at his office door, he notices his hand shaking when he reaches for the handle to his sanctum. "Jensin, I hope you are wrong. God, I pray you are wrong. For once in your data-intensive, weigh-all-the-facts, leave-nothing-to-chance life, Bob, please be wrong!" Murdock sits down at his desk, placing his head in his hands. He covers his face and sighs.

Thinking of his unborn granddaughter, Sharon, to be named after his own mother, he begins to weep quietly to himself. She should not have to come into a world destined for destruction—a world that will not be here long enough to let her learn to love, to care, to do anything else but fight for her own survival. A fight she and all the rest of the world will ultimately lose. Murdock massages the bridge of his nose with his thumb and index finger. Alone at his desk, he silently, yet tearlessly, wept more.

Chapter 5
Political Conflict

Year 2023

At a time when Robert Jensin was just a young teenager at MIT, the world was not as it should be. This was a time when politics was undergoing many changes since the near nuclear holocaust of 2015. At this perilous time in our history, all the nations of the world were on the brink of self-destruction. Virtually every country on Earth possessed a growing nuclear arsenal.

During any given period of time, saber rattling was heard in a dozen different locations around the planet. Fortunately for humanity, common sense somehow managed to prevail—preventing anyone from ultimately "pushing the button." The concept of starting a snowball rolling that would be much too large to ever be stopped was the only sane thought that allowed the world to survive. Most of the world's diplomats worked hard and long hours to keep the various heated situations from escalating into total annihilation.

Beginning with the terrorist attacks on the city of New York, things got worse. Alliances broke down, allies separated, the world was on a downhill spiral headed for total destruction. Ethnic groups from one faction did not feel safe in the presence of another counter group.

Tempers flared, violence broke out. Innocents died by the thousands because of unfounded hate. Sanity showed its head amid the insanity. The people of the world grew tired of the bloodshed. This was the one time in human history when the people, not the governments, decided that they had enough. Nevertheless, there was more to come....

One by one, all the nations came into unison. Not the governments, but the people themselves. Something had to be done to put the brakes on the direction the world was headed. The people put pressure on the leaders, and soon universal global disarmament was accomplished after years of negotiations. Unfortunately, this was precipitated by catastrophic events in the years of the early twenty-first century, brought on by political and religious extremists.

The atmosphere of sociologic and economic differences throughout the world was growing increasingly tense. The mutual distrust among all nations caused by racial, ethnic and economic as well as religious differences had been escalating tensions throughout the globe. Nuclear weapon technology had been acquired by almost every nation on the planet. Even so-called third world countries had the ability to deliver a limited nuclear first strike.

A low yield device could be smuggled into a neighboring country or province in a suitcase or even built into the undercarriage of an automobile or other transport. Tensions were highest in the Middle East, where the newly recognized Imam of Iran was becoming an ever-increasing threat to all the neighboring countries and to those far removed.

Terrorist activities had escalated to previously unheard-of proportions. The Imam's attempt to start a second holy war was defused in the eyes of the world when he used a small, particularly dirty low yield device attached to a school bus full of children as a means of delivering an attack on a neighboring province. When it detonated, it vaporized all the children aboard the bus as well as killing thousands of other innocent people, thus rendering the region unfit for human habitation for many decades to come.

The major nations of the world felt they could no longer stand idly by. Putting their differences aside for the time being, they banded together to attempt to stop this mad man. Diplomacy, negotiations and pseudo-concessions bought precious time to set up strategic defenses. The talks broke down, as was expected when dealing with a fanatic, and missiles were launched from Iran. All the missiles launched except one were intercepted and destroyed before reaching their targets.

One multi-warhead missile made it through the defenses, annihilating millions of people and devastating a two hundred square mile area.

Baghdad, one of the world's oldest cities, was no more, and ruin extended to beyond the Turkish border. Nations who were previously adversaries had banded together to try to stop a mad man—doing their best to put an end to his tyranny. This was the concluding result. Millions of innocent people, gone forever. Where would this all end?

The world governments had to pause at this monumental time in our history and look seriously and somberly at what the nations of the world were becoming. Nation against nation, country against country, family against family, brother against brother. It had to stop. Had this happened between any two superpowers, there would have been no way to prevent retaliation upon retaliation, escalating the conflict to the point of no return.

The world scientific community, supported by the general populace, voiced loud and clear the disturbing fact that the human race was fast on the road to self-destruction. National and political differences had long since been discarded by this small but vocal group in favor of a unified effort to increase knowledge and to seek the betterment of all humanity as a whole and not for just the rich and powerful.

The World Scientific Conference convened in August of 2027; the unanimous consensus being the entire globe must put aside its petty differences and begin to work together as a single unit if humanity was to survive at all. They called for a cessation of all hostilities worldwide, and total global disarmament. At first their pleas were ignored, but seeing what was happening around them, the people of the world began to listen to what was being presented by this small but vociferous group. They began to question the wisdom of their own governments. There was an out-cry from the world's populace. "Enough!"

Progress was slow in the beginning, but soon many of the major nation's military forces were joining with the common people, fearing it better to face the consequences of not obeying orders than face total annihilation at the whims of politicians. The world slowly began to open its eyes. A worldwide strike was initiated, shutting down all aspects of commerce and government.

The WSC, even at that time under threats of arrest, convened meetings, eventually gaining recognition from the heads of state in all major and many smaller nations. Conferences were initiated and convened with the governments of all nations. Some were fruitful immediately; some after an extended period of time; others completely in vain. Now, at last, the people of the world were letting those in power know they were tired of war, and it was time for their leaders to stop and finally listen to them.

There was much hardship caused by the strike—those who ceased producing the electrical power for industry were without electricity themselves. Those who stopped producing the food found they could not obtain the necessary sustenance for their families. The people of all nations suffered the consequences of the shutdown, but still they continued to stand together in complete unity. A unity welding them together into one common people that had never before been seen in history.

The world governments at first felt they could outlast the general strike. There was no way the poor starving people could long endure this shutdown before they buckled under! Yet, this time the people had been pushed too far. They did not give in and did not give up.

Support in favor of the action was growing stronger by the hour. Soon, many members of the governing bodies, out of fear of falling more out of favor, were starting to side with the strikers. The cards had been laid face up on the table by the WSC, backed now by the people of the entire world. Stop fighting and start talking, or the strike would become total! There would be no backing down this time!

Many of the staunch politicians clamored to find patriots to support them, but their cries fell upon deaf ears. Patriotism was not dead, but it was no longer aligning to their side. The cry had changed from, "My country, or my nation!" to become, "My world!" This solidifying idea is now what the people were willing to fight for, even die for, and many did. Never before in the history of humanity had the common people of the world banded together with such great resolve, strength and unity.

Over the previous many years there had been such a great divergence across national borders by peoples and cultures that the political and ethnical differences, which once separated and originally drew the lines between nations, had all but vanished. The people of the world were echoing the voice of the WSC. They were fed up with of the political strife dictating whom they were to hate and whom they were to embrace.

With regard to the Imam, if one madman could cause so much devastation and carnage, how long would it be before there was another incident and then another? Retaliation brought about by one nation against the next—ongoing repeatedly until there was nothing short of full-scale escalation. In a short time we would be back in the Stone Age—if there were any survivors left at all.

The people of the world were forced to stop where they were and ask, "Where will this end?" Fortunately, it would end in a unity never before seen in the history of man.

The day of the common man had finally come. Streets were filled with people. There was now only one voice, and it was a voice that rang loud and clear. "Let us live in peace and let all others live with us in peace! Do not order us to fight each other just because you want more. Share what you already have with those who have given it to you. Put an end to war now!" The Imam's own people turned against him, his blue turban trampled under the feet of his own followers. His still-living body torn to shreds at the hands of angry protesters.

The entire world merged into a common line with one sentiment: "Why should the few in power decide that I must kill my neighbor or my neighbor kill me because he doesn't agree with what my rulers dictate is popular in today's political environment?"

The WSC was persistent in their quest, backed by the entire world population, and managed to bring first the major nations and eventually all nations to the bargaining tables.

Everyone knew this would not be easy or one-sided, with the wealthy nations helping or taking advantage of the poorer countries. The less fortunate nations had much to offer in the way of culture, art and resources. The world needed now more than ever to band together as one people, without regard to wealth. The rich would still be rich and the poor would still be poor, but at least we would not be killing each other over petty political differences.

Through years of talks, multilateral disarmament was eventually achieved. There were scores of arguments, demands and concessions, but although the governments of the various nations were arguing, at least they were not fighting. World peace had finally become a reality.

Economic concerns gave rise to the uniting of formerly smaller, antagonistic countries into single, larger components. Many of the former boundaries disappeared, leaving larger, more productive, nations living in peace.

There was still strife, but it was worked out with diplomacy instead of armed conflict. The world was at last at peace. One world government, although discussed at length, was determined to be unfeasible. Many of the smaller nations joined with the larger ones to form new solidly united entities.

Between the United States and Canada, the longest unfortified border in the world disappeared, along with the border of Mexico and the U.S., forming the North American States. Japan and China, for centuries antagonists, merged into one nation along with India and Australia. Joining this union were most of the Pacific Island nations.

What was once the Soviet Union, the largest single nation in the world, had become totally and politically fragmented. The eastern portion drifted away and joined with the Sino-Japanese Alliance, while the western regions merged with the European and Balkan countries, forming the Eurasian Commonwealth.

Africa finally united into one nation, as did South America, forming the African National Confederacy and the South American Union. All five multinational organizations often butt heads while governing in cooperation with each other. There were still differences, but they were worked out with discussion instead of fist shaking and threats, and there was no more armed conflict for the rest of history.

Now, with this latest development, Roy Murdock is thinking maybe it would have been better in the long run to have let things continue down the original path of destruction and to have blown ourselves into oblivion in one fell swoop than to face what is to come. "A war at that time would have ended human life in a matter of weeks. Now we will have to wait thirty years for what we know is definitely coming. Instead of giving up our lives to immediate bombs of which we would know not their origin—coming at us from wherever—we now are faced with the prospect of having to just sit and wait, watching the sun grow ever larger—rising and setting each day before we die. Day after day, each of us slowly dying in our hearts. "Would it have been better to annihilate each other quickly than to face the slow hell of the now expanding sun?"

Chapter 6
The Joint Chiefs of Staff

Jensin and Georgia Simone, a nine-year M.A.B.U.S. veteran, enter Dr. Murdock's office, carrying two large containers of data sheets. "This is most of the more important information," said Jensin.

"I said I wanted it all, Robert!" bellowed Murdock. "I can't go before the joint chiefs with only part of the information!"

"The rest is on the way up, Dr. Murdock. There are a few last-minute reports being digitized, and this was about all we could carry anyways. The rest will be here in a few minutes."

"Sorry, Bob. I'm a bit on edge. For the last couple of hours I've been going over the celluloids you gave me earlier, and needless to say it's…it's…shall we say a bit upsetting. Georgia, do you concur with Bob's findings?"

"Yes, Roy. Jensin first noticed something wasn't right about three months ago and…"

"Three months ago? Damn it, Robert, why did you wait so blasted long to bring something as important as this to my attention?" Murdock fumes, slamming his coffee cup down on his desk. Rivulets of dark liquid splash across the tabletop and onto the celluloids scattered over the surface.

Bob Jensin sheepishly stammers in front of the man in charge. "We…we have had the whole lab working on this day and night to confirm it. We have had observatories all over the globe sending us new data continuously. At first I hoped I was wrong, and when I was sure I was not, I still needed to get additional confirming figures before I...I...I didn't want to be accused of crying wolf, but right now I'd give anything...if...all the other labs I've contacted bear out what we've found," stammered Jensin, skirting the issue of the three months.

Murdock grew red in the face. "You've been in contact with the other observatories about something as big as this without checking with me first? Have you lost your mind? If this gets out before we can get global cooperation, there's going to be world-wide panic!" he roared. The head of the division wiped his brow in frustration.

Georgia Simone tries to calm him, stating, "We asked them only for specific data on certain observations. No one else that we know of has put two and two together, or we would definitely have heard something by now. There were not even any out of the ordinary questions asked either. They just confirmed or discounted what we asked for. As far as Bob's findings, there is no doubt he's right."

"Damn! Three months! You still took an awful chance going outside this base without proper clearance," said Murdock. "But that's water under the bridge now. Again, why did you wait three whole months?"

"I'm afraid that was my fault." Being true to her word, Georgia Simone began to cover for Jensin, who sheepishly stood looking at the floor. "There was a lot of data to sift through—much of it had to be checked and rechecked at each turn. We didn't want to rush into anything without being..."

"No!" The room fell silent. "No, it was all my fault," Jensin interrupts, pushing his glasses back up his nose. "I had to be absolutely positive. I hate mistakes and was hoping I made one in my calculations. I kept looking for an error somewhere, hoping I would find one and rid myself of this nightmare once and for all. I kept insisting to Georgia—to Ms. Simone—that I needed more time. I wanted to recheck everything. I just kept putting it off—rechecking, putting it off—rechecking. I wanted to find out I was wrong. God, I wanted to be wrong! But, I'm sorry!"

All right, Robert, there's nothing we can do about that now." Murdock changed the subject back to the matter at hand. "Let's see what you have there with you and meanwhile call down to your lab and speed up the rest of the data."

Roy Murdock sits at his desk with his fingers massaging his temples, eyes closed. The reams of information he has just gone through all point to one unmistakable fact—Jensin is right. Now the hard part—getting cooperation from the joint chiefs for a full global study. News of this magnitude cannot be made public until it is proven one hundred and ten percent accurate. Leaving no doubt—none whatsoever.

Jensin and Simone leave Murdock's office to transmit the huge amount of records, accompanied by Murdock's report to the offices of each of the joint chiefs. The joint chiefs will not have much time to absorb the immense quantity of information before the scheduled meeting in less than an hour. Murdock thought how ironic it was that the meeting he had canceled earlier this afternoon was to discuss the upcoming budget. If and when this is proven, money is going to be the least of anyone's worries.

At 1530 hours, five of the twelve monitor screens across the room from his desk flash to life displaying the seal and name of each of the joint chiefs indicating communications with each of their offices had been established. Marjory has done her job well. All have been notified, and the conformation that they will attend the meeting is indicated by a scrolling message at the base of each screen.

During the next thirty minutes, communication system and security checks will be performed. Priority Level 1 involves the highest degree of security with total encryption. Although he is one of the major directors of the world scientific community, Murdock still had better have a good reason to declare such a short notice urgent meeting with the head leaders of the world. He believes he does indeed.

One by one, the seal of each joint chief is replaced by a still video image of the person whose name had previously been projected on the screen. In a few minutes, the actual people would be speaking face to face with Murdock. He and all the others would be visible on the screens in each office.

Being in the same proximity time zone, the first on line was J.C. Randolph Lockmere of the United North American States, giving Murdock a few precious moments to confer with the leader of his country on handling the others. "This is a real nightmare, Roy," is about all Lockmere had time to communicate before the other screens began flashing to life in quick succession.

The video image of J.C. Miranda Diswego of the South American Union flashed on the screen, followed by J. C. Bagumba Logala of the African National Confederacy.

J. C. Herishito Shimoto of the Sino-Japanese Alliance, and finally J. C. Roger Fieldling of the Eurasian Commonwealth, quickly followed. No introductions were necessary since all had met numerous times before, but courteous acknowledgments were made all around.

Dr. Murdock apologized to those he was forced to roust from their beds, and began to explain the seriousness of the matter. "Madame, gentlemen, I need to confirm that each of you is in possession of the information transmitted to your offices earlier today. I realize that you have not had much time to go over this material in its entirety, but trust you have read my summary report that accompanied it."

Each of the joint chiefs confirms the receipt of the data, and Murdock commences to fill them in with a bit more detailed layout of what had been determined before dumping the whole ball of wax in their laps.

"Are you absolutely sure this is not just some sort of an elaborate hoax?" asks J.C. Fieldling of the Eurasian Commonwealth. "We wouldn't want to get all in a huff about a fly-by-night theory?"

"Of that I am positive! I have complete confidence and trust in the staff here. They have presented me with all the information they have thus far been able to obtain, copies which have been sent to each of you. I have never been faced with so great a compilation of confirming data to substantiate a situation than I have with the one I present to you now," Murdock replies.

"I am sure that after you've had sufficient time to review all the data in your possession, and confirm it to be accurate, you will agree that an immediate full global study is warranted. Once you've had the opportunity to go over all the data we sent you today, and the subsequent information that is to follow, as it is compiled, I am sure you will realize, as I have," he concludes, "that we have a very serious problem!" "One that is definitely not going to go away."

Chapter 7
News Flash

September 9, 2023

Several weeks and countless meetings later, the findings of lab technician Robert A. Jensin are totally substantiated and documented by the hundreds of other observatories around the globe, as well as the four more far-reaching science labs based in lunar colonies. His findings have been proven to the letter; there is no longer the slightest doubt. He is totally, as he said, dead sure! And so now is the rest of the world!

The world leaders now must decide how they are going to deal with the problem currently facing them. How do they release this news to the public? It will have to be done very carefully, and also very soon! It will not be long before the changes in the Earth's climate begin to reveal themselves—in devastating measures.

Inevitably, rumors of the forthcoming disaster manage to leak out. Too many people know about the impending calamity now. There is, at first, sporadic panic in various regions around the globe. Different areas react with varying degrees of unrest to the rumors of the impending cataclysm. The entire united world governments decide they can no longer delay the release of this devastating news. It is now time for a press conference to alert the world of the pending dilemma and put to rest the rampant rumors that are fast spreading throughout the globe.

The "powers that be" decide to hold a press briefing to be broadcast worldwide simultaneously on all media. The hope in everyone's mind with this news release is it will put a halt to the hysteria that is fast developing and put an end to the general consensus of an immediate impending doom.

The people of the world do have the right to be alerted, and they need to be provided with the truth that it will still be many years before even the first signs of change will be taking place. The sun will continue to rise each morning, shine all day and set in the evening, just as always, and for many more years to come. The time to be concerned is still far off, but when that time finally arrives, who knows!

The task of delivering this devastating news inevitably falls on the shoulders of Joint Chief Randolph Lockmere of the United North American States. After all, his people discovered the problem the rest of the world must now face, an expanding sun, and he should be the one to inform the world's people. All the other joint chiefs will be backing him in total unison.

At the prearranged moment, all broadcast stations brake into their transmissions in progress with a special bulletin.

"We interrupt the regularly scheduled programming to bring you a special announcement from the world chiefs of staff. We now go live to the headquarters of the World Scientific Committee." All broadcast stations, both audio and video, simultaneously are switched to the auditorium at the committee center. All eyes are on Lockmere.

Accompanied by the other four world leaders, he approaches the podium to deliver the prepared statement destined to change the world forever. The broadcast will be transmitted consecutively in all languages.

There is a short pause as the auditorium falls silent and Joint Chief Randolph Lockmere begins.

"People of the world, it is with heavy hearts that the governments of all nations and the entire scientific community come before you with this information. There have been many rumors circulating concerning the sun, and we are here today to confirm what was discovered on July 14 of this year and to hopefully dispel all other false information.

"We were forced to delay the release of this news in light of certain definitive facts that needed to be confirmed beyond any shadow of doubt. It was necessary for all the information to be completely verified, and an exact time frame calculated concerning the coming events that will befall this planet. All data needed to be confirmed before we were able to release this devastating news and make it public.

"First, our sun is indeed dying. This has been completely substantiated." There is a sudden rise in the level of murmuring from those in attendance. "Please, may I have your attention so I may continue? Yes, the sun is dying; however, I beg your patience as I make this one fact perfectly clear—it will be many, many years before any changes in the Earth or its climate begin to manifest themselves.

"It is true that the sun is beginning to expand outward and will continue to do so at an ever-increasing rate until it envelops the Earth. If this expansion continues at the calculated rate, and we believe it will, there will be no indications of any change for the next twelve to fifteen years. The first signs will be minor changes in the global climate. These alterations will be very gradual at first and then increasing in magnitude as the sun continues to expand outward.

"Eventually, earthquakes will also accompany these climate fluctuations as the expansion of the sun increases toward our planet. There will be substantial tremors first felt in quake-prone regions, and later on there will be small tremors in regions all over the world where there has never been any movement before. The activities in the Earth's crust will also increase in frequency and magnitude as the gravitational effect of the expanding sun pulls more and more on the Earth's tectonic plates. There is nothing anyone can do to prevent these movements of the Earth's surface. This is going to be something we will have to learn to endure for many years."

"An orderly evacuation of those regions that are extremely earthquake-prone is in the planning stages for when the time of increased seismic activity will occur."

"Again, I wish to repeat. It will be twelve to fifteen years before our expanding sun begins to have any affect whatsoever on the Earth. There is no need for panic."

"There is nothing at this time we are aware of that can be done to stop the sun's expansion. We have resigned ourselves to the fact that all life on Earth, as we know it, will cease in approximately thirty-two to thirty-five years from now. In the meantime, your government and all the governments of all nations are working in full cooperation with each other along with the scientific community to address the problems we all are going to have to face in the coming years. It is not going to be easy, but…" he paused in despair, clearing his parched throat.

"We are all, every one of us, going to have to work together to make the time we have left on this planet as safe and as comfortable as possible. If a solution to this problem should surface, we will endeavor to follow up completely on any new paths, or…" He was forced to clear his throat again. "Any avenues which may surface. We ask all of you to remain calm and work with us to assure the continued peace as we see this through together. When the end does come, it is predicted to be swift. Again, we must emphasize these changes are not going to even begin to appear for several more years, and the end time is more than three decades away. We still have much time together and even more work to accomplish. May God have mercy on us all."

Lockmere's statement was re-broadcasting every hour for the remaining part of the week, as well as repeated in every form of printed media. The newly released news had the exact consequences that were most feared by the government. Panic, rioting, looting and suicides by the thousands were occurring. Martial law was declared in an effort to keep order. The panic soon subsided into feelings of helplessness and despair.

The constant run on grocery establishments diminished, as did those on various sources of survival supplies. The many people who fled away from the cities in fear were now at last returning to their homes. The people throughout the world settled back into the routine of everyday life, finally realizing there was nowhere to run. There was nowhere in the hills to go to escape from what was surely to come on the whole Earth. Martial law was lifted. Life continued. That is, for now.

Chapter 8
The Solution

January 4, 2024

"Dr. Murdock, is it true there might be a chance for the people of the world to escape from the expanding sun?" the chairperson of the World Scientific Conference asks.

"The population of this world will not be able to leave or escape, but there is an outside chance that a very small number of people might be able to travel out of the solar system before the sun finally explodes," states Murdock, leaning toward the microphone on the podium. "But there is no chance whatsoever for us all to leave before the sun envelopes us."

"Wouldn't that outside chance to save even a small number of mankind entail building a massive spaceship and equip it for interstellar flight?" asks the chair. "The construction and testing alone will take most of what little time we have left to accomplish it, and then even if we are successful in building such a space craft and the small selection of people do manage to travel into deep space—after that, where would they go?"

"I will answer the second part of your question first," Murdock began. "Equipping and testing a large-enough vessel for long-term space travel is going to be a monumental task. Much still needs to be worked out and determined. As far as having to actually build such a ship brings me to the first part of your question, which is much simpler to answer. We already have such a massive craft, and it is in orbit right now, the M.A.B.U.S. platform." Murdock continues. "It can be retrofitted and modified in a fraction of the time it would take to construct any new vessel, and the platform has already proven its space worthiness for almost thirty years.

"Any sections now remaining on the platform that would not serve specific purposes for the long space flight can be jettisoned, converted and scavenged for materials for reconstruction. M.A.B.U.S is already equipped with e-matter pulse drives that can and will be easily upgraded to a larger, more powerful version. We will, however, need to install hyper-sleep chambers and redesign many of the sections to make the station totally and completely self-sufficient, enabling it to endure the years of space travel the crew will be forced to endure. As far as where the space platform will ultimately travel is as of yet still to be determined and at this time is being researched."

"Who will be the ones to go when it is time, and who will decide who will leave and who stays behind?" is the next question.

"We'll work on the problem of who will go at a much later date," Murdock replies. "Right now our first priority is to set out on the path of developing a way for anyone at all to leave this dying planet in the first place. After that is accomplished, we will turn our full attention to figuring out where they intend to go, if and when they do attempt to escape the expanding sun. Research is already being done to find a plausible destination."

There is a great amount of murmuring among the attendees present. Murdock continues, "A lot of ifs and maybes are still in the equation. As of now, there are eleven different star systems that we know of at this moment that are indicative of having orbiting planets. There are eleven separate solar systems within the reach of our earliest probes, which as we speak are speeding through space inside wormholes. We hope to find one or more planets that have a suitable atmosphere and also surface conditions capable of sustaining human life.

"Until the results of the preliminary exploratory probes are in and any findings of subsequent probes come to light, we must focus our attention and efforts on the significant task of re-designing M.A.B.U.S. so that the platform can carry as many people as possible. All governments are in total agreement involving this project and have given their complete consent to proceed without regard to manpower or expenditures."

"Plans have already been set in motion, and work has begun dismantling the sections of the platform we have determined are definitely not going to be of any use on a long space voyage. The next step is to scavenge those modules of all usable materials to complete the required modifications. It is much more practical and economical, both fuel-wise and time-wise, to take advantage of what we already have up there in space than to cart additional needed materials into high Earth obit and begin any new construction. At this time, orbiting shuttles are collecting every useless piece of hardware man has launched into space—everything they can find drifting aimlessly in orbit—and docking their gathered cargo alongside the M.A.B.U.S. platform for use as needed. There are hundreds of tons of outdated satellites and materials drifting in space that can once more be put to good use. As head administrator of this project, I will personally be returning to M.A.B.U.S. to oversee much of the work—work proceeding as we now speak."

A lot of muted and loudly voiced conjectures are stirring among the crowd, but before any further questions are raised Murdock adds, "There is still a multitude of problems to overcome and a lot more questions facing us at this time than we have answers for right now. Every scientist and engineer in the entire world is working night and day to find those sought-after answers—answers we desperately need before the ship moves a single millimeter from where it is now located. It will take years of hard work, but if we work together we might find a way. Yes, in answer to the question on all your minds, we feel it will be possible to save a very small segment of the human race before this is all over.

"In answer to the last part of your question, as far as those who will be leaving on the M.A.B.U.S. *Star Traveler* when and if it does depart—that particular decision is many years down the road. However, it is very clear, considering the future time frame, that those we do decide to send on this voyage will out of necessity be much younger and stronger than any of us discussing this problem. Much younger, to be able to survive such a long journey. Those future star travelers are only infants and small children at this present time. We can safely state, unequivocally, without question, that none of us here now within this room will be leaving when the time comes for M.A.B.U.S. to depart for the stars. We will need to turn the future over to a much younger generation."

Gathering his notes, he closes by saying, "Thank you, ladies and gentlemen, and I will keep you posted on any new developments."

Chapter 9
Exotic Matter

"The universe if full of the wonderful, the mysterious, the magical!" a poet once wrote. "Countless strange things the mind cannot even begin to fathom."

The universe is truly full of the strange and the wonderful. Much of it mysterious, and to the untrained eye many physical aspects and events appear to be magical. One of the strangest of these wonders is a newly encountered form of matter. Although it has been present since the creation of the cosmos, its existence was unknown until the early part of the twenty-first century.

Two groups of scientists working independently of each other discovered exotic matter in the year 2016, while collaborating with each other on whatever information they gathered. One team was from the North American States Science Federation, the second group involved the Sino-Japanese Scientific Committee. The two independent teams were soon to make a number of discoveries destined to change the course of mankind.

Working separately, the two teams simultaneously uncovered a previously unknown type of matter that defied all current laws of physics, completely unique from anything before encountered in the exploration of the cosmos.

This new form of matter, exotic matter, or e-matter, as they chose to refer to it—was truly mysterious and did indeed appear to be magical. In opposition to anti-matter, which when it contacts physical matter destroys a mass equal to the negative mass of the anti-matter. E-matter instead combines with physical matter and cancels out the physical properties, including its mass, without affecting the fundamental characteristics of the matter itself.

E-matter essentially combines with or, for a better description, coats, and surrounds each atom of the existing physical matter, completely engulfing it and causing it to cease to exist within the realm of time and space that encompasses everything we can see and touch.

The teams discovered, after years of study, that the electrons of the e-matter atoms all orbit their nuclei in perfect synchronization—each individual electron in the atom of e-matter perfectly aligned to all other electrons orbiting the nucleus of the captured bit of matter. The rotation of these electrons, it demonstrated, could be slowed, accelerated, stopped and even reversed—leading to the development of reversed ionization. Using this new process of reversed ionization, the electron orbit of the e-matter atoms was indeed slowed, stopped and then reversed, causing the e-matter to be repelled by the physical matter, making the e-matter flee back into its own separate negative mass as it separated from the physical matter. The physical matter instantly returned to the same state it was in before joining with e-matter.

Although the initial reactions in early experiments were not on a grand scale, the resulting push as the e-matter separates from physical matter is equal to the mass of the physical matter it encompasses—Newton's Law: for every action there is an equal and opposite reaction. E-matter, having no mass and therefore no physical properties, such as inertia, remains in place. The physical matter is in fact forced away from the e-matter—leading the scientists to the development of the e-matter pulse drive engine.

The amount of thrust is directly proportional to the speed of the reverse ionization and the amount of physical matter contacted by e-matter. When the e-matter separates from physical matter, the reverse push away from the physical matter is at the speed of light. The force exerted on the physical matter is equal to the mass of the physical object and in the opposite direction from the static e-matter. The amount of thrust is tremendous for any given mass.

Some additional interesting facts discovered about e-matter were it has no physical weight. Massive quantities can easily be lifted, limited only by the weight of the magnetic containment vessel apparatus needed to encapsulate this unusual matter, which can easily be controlled by surrounding it with a synchronized gamma-flux magnetic field. The surrounding magnetic field causes the e-matter to rotate rapidly around itself in a perfectly spherical mass. When it is reverse ionized using the gamma-flux magnetic field, the e-matter clings to itself and at the same time it is repelled by all physical matter. It could almost be kept in a canning jar if you could seal the containment vessel down to the atomic level.

It was also discovered that when e-matter is held in gamma flux containment, it compresses in on itself to an astronomical degree, allowing massive amounts of it to be contained in a very small volume. It does, however, occupy a physical space, as does any other matter, physical or otherwise. The extent of compression would be equal to condensing the area of a football field one hundred yards in depth into just a sewing thimble of volume.

Physical matter, when combined with e-matter, is also weightless. It has no inertia, is not affected by gravity, and when accelerated, produces no g-forces.

E-matter cannot be manufactured by any known means, but is readily abundant throughout the universe. After years of research, in the early twenty-first century a primitive magnetic collector was designed and constructed to attract e-matter. It was discovered that this strange atom is extremely abundant throughout the entire universe in quantities of approximately one atom of e-matter per 100×10^{22} cubic meters of outer space.

One e-matter atom collected and then held in reverse flux would immediately attract a second; those two would attract two more, the four would attract four, etc. The atoms move through the universe at the speed of light, allowing the need for the apparatus to be activated for only a few seconds to collect billions of e-matter atoms in an instant.

E-matter is never found on Earth in its natural state due to the presence of physical matter. When e-matter atoms enter the Earth's atmosphere, they instantly bond with physical matter atoms and mutually vanish. This was determined to be the true cause of the large ozone hole in the Earth's atmosphere over the Antarctic continent discovered in the late twentieth century. The magnetic pole of the Earth offered a clue to the means of attracting and controlling this intriguing form of matter.

When e-matter is held in a gamma-flux magnetic field, it is totally inert. Released from the field, everything it contacts vanishes. Return it to the field and all the physical matter reappears just as it was before. The avenues for experimentation this discovery opened up were endless. So were the problems in dealing with this new form of matter, as well as the limitless questions accompanying it.

The foremost was—where does the physical matter go when it disappears? It still exists, but where? If it were destroyed, it would not be able to return when separated from the e-matter. What happens to something when it combines with e-matter?

The answer to these and many other questions concerning e-matter were soon to be answered. Scientists working at the North American Science Institute, as well as their Asian counterparts who were also conducting experiments with e-matter, were about to open a whole new realm of discoveries. Some of which would later prove to be the only hope for humankind.

The experimentation with e-matter continued over the next several years, and so did work on the new pulse drive engine, in hopes of being able to send deep space probes beyond the reaches of conventional rocket engines and at much greater speeds, approaching that of light. In the fall of 2033, during a series of e-matter experiments, they made a startling discovery. There is a dimension outside of our own. A second dimension completely separated from space and time.

Chapter 10
Worm Holes

Held in a magnetic chamber is a pristine cube of polymyceric acetate, a long chain polymer composed of a completely transparent plastic, making up a module totally unaffected by ultraviolet rays, extreme temperature changes, impact, abrasion, stress or torque. This small, square cube is virtually indestructible, possessing a zero refractive as well as reflective index. Light passes through it undisturbed from any angle or plane. To the eye it is not even there. Nothing this perfect, symmetrically or chemically, has ever been produced before.

The ten-by-ten-centimeter cube is meticulously examined, every square micron of it recorded. Its molecular makeup, right down to its atomic structure, is painstakingly converted into computer data. From the moment of its manufacture, it has been untouched by human or mechanical hands. It is moved about and manipulated with magnetic-flux forceps. It is kept at a constant temperature, untouched and unblemished, each surface is in exact geometric alignment with all the others. Not one single atom of the most perfect, flawless object ever created by man, and is now about to be sent into oblivion, is out of alignment.

"Ready on the e-matter influx." The cube, held in its magnetic containment chamber is virtually invisible, the perfection of its composition and surfaces render it difficult, if not impossible, to discern with the naked eye.

Totally non-reflective and non-refractive, it is equally invisible from every angle, like a perfect diamond in a glass of crystal clear water. You have an object sitting right in front of you that you are positive is there, but it is so transparent you have difficulty seeing it, even though it is stationed directly before your eyes.

"Start countdown to e-matter influx." The cube of perfect plastic, suspended in the magnetic field, made visible only by gridlines superimposed on it by a computer imager, is about to join with e-matter. "On my mark, influx e-matter. 5, 4, 3, 2, 1…influx!" The cube is gone. The computer with its massive bank of sensors cannot locate anything within the magnetic vacuum chamber. It detects no matter present. The cube is completely gone!

"Begin reverse ionization process on my mark. 5, 4, 3, 2, 1." The cube is back—as pristine as before. Measurements and evaluation begin immediately. There is no change whatsoever in the cube's molecular makeup or, even more importantly, its atomic structure. It is the first physical object ever to move beyond this realm of time and space and to return intact.

The sending of an inert, totally un-reactive object into another dimension was a complete success. At this point, the only thing known for certain is e-matter effectively neutralizes physical matter and could be again separated from physical matter, returning the physical matter to this realm of time and space. Where the matter went is not yet known.

After numerous successful inert matter transfers and retrievals, it is decided to send a probe of much more complexity into the "unknown" and record anything in this region, where matter seemed to disappear. Something capable of accurately recording what was on the other side of this dimension, a self-contained recording probe, was laboriously constructed, possessing video, audio and sensory capabilities. The initial probe contained no moving parts, only sensors to record data for later retrieval.

"On my mark, influx e-matter. 5, 4, 3, 2, 1." The probe was gone. The first object comprised of more than one type of matter is sent to who knows where. If it comes back intact, what will it tell us? "Begin reversed ionization. 3, 2, 1."

"We have the probe!"

The data from the probe left everyone in a state of amazement. Its tactile sensors could contact nothing. The positional equipment placed the probe exactly where it originated, but now in the center of a tube only molecularly larger than the diameter of the probe itself. No sound, no movement, no contact.

The tube was totally silent. Only the sound of the hum of the probe's own electronic switching modes was recorded on the digital audio. The video retrieved by the probe is what spun the heads of everyone around. Extending forward and aft, in a perfectly straight line, was a tunnel or a tube, a wormhole in space.

When e-matter reacts with physical matter, the resulting combination causes the physical mass to cease to exist in this realm of time and space—it enters a wormhole. When e-matter bonds with physical matter, a wormhole the size and shape of the object plus the mass of the e-matter surrounding it is created. The length of the wormhole theoretically extends to infinity in two opposite directions, running in a straight line, curving only with the curvature of space. The direction of the wormhole is determined by the atomic clock of the e-matter atoms. The alignment of the electrons in the e-matter atoms determines the ultimate direction of the wormhole.

The direction of a wormhole in space and time could be manipulated by calculating the precise alignment of the e-matter electrons at the instant of combining with physical matter. By precisely timing the joining of e-matter and physical matter, the wormhole would form perpendicular to the electron alignment in any of an infinite number of directions.

Further experiments discovered that when the physical matter moved within the wormhole and then separated from e-matter, it would reappear in a place other than where it first joined with the e-matter. This displacement is in direct relation to how far it has moved in the wormhole.

It was also discovered that the wormholes always form in a straight line, independent of the physical universe. Wormholes being outside the realm of space and time pass directly through solid objects such as walls or buildings, even people, making for some very interesting early experiments inside and out of the labs.

With the discovery of e-matter, a new form of propulsion was perfected. It was observed that if the polarity of a small mass of e-matter was reversed while it was in phase with the rest of the mass of e-matter, the matter that became reverse polarized would repel itself away from the remaining mass at the speed of light.

The remaining mass still encompassing the physical matter would accelerate in the opposite direction at a speed proportional to the amount of force the ejected e-matter produced.

By timing the polarization change to occur at set intervals, a powerful new engine came into being, the e-matter pulse drive. In a short time, speeds approaching that of light were attained with unmanned probes in physical space.

Using this principle in the confines of a wormhole, which is outside the restrictions of time, space and with inertia playing no physical part, resulted in speeds many times that of light? The distance light travels in one entire year could be covered by a craft in a wormhole in less than three Earth months.

The e-matter pulse drive does have some severe drawbacks. In physical space, there are g-forces and inertia. Physical objects would inevitably be encountered while traveling at near light speed. At such an enormous velocity, there is no possible means of detecting an object in the path of a spacecraft or probe until it is too late to do anything about it.

Space is not as empty as many people have come to believe. At speeds near that of light, even a minute particle of cosmic dust can have a devastating effect on a space vehicle. Many of the earlier deep space probes, which were sent out using this new form of propulsion, simply disintegrated after striking some small piece of space rubble that happened to be crossing its path.

Using the e-matter pulse drive inside a wormhole gave birth to a whole new set of problems. Although there was nothing to collide with inside a wormhole, and you could attain unprecedented speeds, you still had to be able to slow down when you reached your destination.

Essentially, with the release of un-bonded e-matter to propel a ship forward, you destroy the one thing separating you from physical time and space. The released e-matter is attracted to the boundaries of the wormhole, effectively canceling it out.

Inside the wormhole, conventional thrust engines can be used to propel a spacecraft to speeds near that of light, due to the absence of inertia and craft having a neutral mass. The same thrusters can also be used to slow the spacecraft. However, this uses a considerable amount of fuel—which is difficult to replace in the far reaches of space.

Within the confines of the wormhole, speeds at or above 160,000 miles per second are easily attained. When that velocity is reached, the e-matter pulse drive can be engaged and will immediately accelerate the spacecraft to well past the speed of light.

As you release e-matter behind you, propelling you forward, you destroy the trailing wormhole behind you at the same time. Advancing toward you from the rear at the speed of light is physical space. If it overtook you, it would be like being slammed from behind by a solid granite wall at more than 186,000 miles per second.

It is therefore necessary for the e-matter drive to accelerate the craft to speeds much greater than that of light for it to remain within the wormhole. Developing such speed is not a difficulty, since there is no mass and no inertia to overcome.

Inside a wormhole, even a vessel the size of the M.A.B.U.S. *Star Traveler* could be moved to tremendous speeds by the flick of a single finger. Small thruster engines using a minimal amount of fuel could accelerate the ship to remarkable speeds in seconds. Once near the speed of light, the e-drive would take over, immediately accelerating the ship to almost one and a half times light speed with the first pulse.

When engaging the e-drive, the consequences of a miscalculation or system failure would be foremost in everyone's thoughts. Each pulse of the drive sends the ship on its way through the wormhole at an ever-increasing rate.

When the pulse drive is first engaged and the speed of the ship jumps from 160,000 miles per second to 253,000 miles per second. The wormhole behind you has been destroyed, and the encroaching end is less than 67,000 miles away.

The drive is again engaged, and the speed increases to 343,000 miles per second, 3,000 miles per second less than the first pulse, but it is a tremendous increase in speed compared to what the ship was initially traveling. This firing of the drive has created a new end to the wormhole, as it will with each pulse. Fortunately, the new end is much farther behind because of the ship's speed. A respectable 157,000 miles behind you.

With the next engagement of the e-drive, the speed approaches half a million miles per second. With each successive pulse, the acceleration rate decreases by approximately 1,000 miles per second less than the pulse before, until a maximum speed of 858,000 miles per second or 4.61 times the speed of light is reached. In all, the drive is engaged eleven times in as many seconds, and there is no more speed to be gained. The ship has reached terminal velocity.

You can breathe easier now. At this speed in an hour, the trailing end of the wormhole will be almost three and one half billion miles behind you.

The biggest problem now facing you is: What do you do to slow down an object traveling at more than four and a half times faster than the speed of light to less than light speed without destroying it or the wormhole separating you and it from physical space? Again, conventional thrusters would come into play.

Without any inertia, and now possessing a neutral mass, there is no sensation of breaking. The spacecraft simply begins to decelerate at an astonishing rate. In a matter of minutes the craft will drop below light speed and continue to slow.

Once the velocity has reduced to about one-half the speed of light, the e-matter drive, this time directed forward, can be brought into play for the final deceleration, slowing the craft even more while opening up the wormhole in front of the ship, returning it to physical space. Timing and calculations must be precise or you might find yourself materializing inside the middle of some giant distant star or planet.

Returning to physical time and space, even at the greatly reduced speed of half that of light, is not a very pleasant experience for anyone. After spending much time in an environment of no inertia and no g-forces, it is difficult to maintain equilibrium, especially in the weightlessness of deep space.

Further experiments brought to light that a bank or piggyback series of e-matter pulse drives could be used in stages to increase the speed of a vessel even greater. A ship or probe could have a second and even a third stage booster array. If each stage is contained in separate, individual e-matter envelopes or "bubbles," the maximum speed is increased exponentially. With the firing of each successive e-matter pulse drive, the craft would accelerate to twice the terminal velocity of the original booster as it separates from the first or second stage. It reaches speeds over nine times the speed of light as it separated from the first stage. The same could theoretically be said for each of the additional stages. Reaching speeds of over eighteen times that of light is about as fast as could be safely be achieved and still be able to have sufficient fuel reserves on board to slow the craft enough to be able to exit the wormhole.

The pulse drive engines are quite simple in construction. The actual drive components are shaped very much like parabolic satellite communication antennas. The necessary equipment to control the e-matter makes up the bulk of the engine. The gamma flux generators have been reduced remarkably in size over the years to the point where the apparatus needed to propel a medium-sized space craft is about as large as an office desk. Work continued over the years with much success on efforts to reduce the size of the generators even more.

The actual pulse drive dish is divided into two distinct areas. The e-matter is held in flux in the central part of the disk, controlled by the obverse magnetic field in the outer ring, circling the dish itself.

When the polarity of part of the e-matter is reversed, the resulting pulse propels the remaining e-matter in the opposite direction. The quantity of e-matter lost is quickly replenished. A second pulse followed by additional pulses accelerates the craft even faster—far beyond the speed of light.

Chapter 11
The Way We Speak

"How's everything going, Georgia?" Murdock asks, entering the solar lab.

"As well as can be expected, Dr. Murdock," she says, setting aside the celluloids she has been thumbing through. "When are you leaving for the M.A.B.U.S. platform?" She watches Murdock pace from one data station to the next, making his way around the perimeter of the entire solar lab.

"On the Thursday afternoon shuttle, if everything goes as planned." He returns to her desk. She places the stack of printouts in a neat pile, rising to greet him.

Shaking her extended hand, he explains the reason for his visit to the frantically busy solar lab. "Is Jensin around?" he asks, continuing to glance at the individual stations, looking for the young man who first discovered this whole mess. "I need his input on a communications problem we've been having." Dr. Roy Murdock would just as soon forgo any dealings with the unkempt lab technician who had the unconscious ability to crawl under his skin with each and every move and statement whenever their paths crossed.

"If I know Robert, he went down to the commissary to get something to eat again," answers Georgia. "I swear that kid has a hollow leg! If I ate half what he does I would have to live in the zero gravity of space for the rest of my life just to be able to handle my own weight. Is there anything I can do for you, Doctor?" she asks.

"I have something I want you and your people—especially Jensin—to work on," Murdock begins in all seriousness. "We have come up against a brick wall—a major communications problem. Frankly, we are at a complete dead end. Right now we are totally stumped and don't know which way to turn. We need to come up with a way to communicate with a spacecraft inside a wormhole. Regular radio transmissions are not able to penetrate the boundaries of the hole any more than light or any other energy source. Before we dare send M.A.B.U.S. into a wormhole for its first test, we need to have a way to maintain contact with the platform in case there are any problems."

"Quantum teleportation," Jensin's voice came from behind them. "You could try montum melemormaton," he says again, through a mouthful of food as he was stuffing the last of his snack into his mouth.

Murdock and Georgia Simone turn in the direction the words emanated from. Both utter in unison, "What?" In the doorway stands Robert Jensin, wiping his mouth on the sleeve of his lab coat. The mere sight of him makes Murdock's skin crawl.

Finished wiping his mouth and swallowing his morsel, Jensin repeats, "Quantum teleportation."

"Quantum teleportation? That form of communication hasn't been used for almost a quarter century," says Murdock with a snort. "It's right up there with the old Morse code."

"Maybe so," says Bob Jensin, "but in theory it should work." The lab technician unconsciously flapped his arms down at his sides to rid them of any lingering crumbs before approaching the other two in front of Georgia's desk. "Distance and the vacuum of space never hindered the operation of the system in the past. It just might be able to penetrate beyond this dimension."

"I don't know if there are still any transponders in existence, and if there are—if there are, can they even still function or be made to function again." Murdock is perplexed and looks at Jensin. "And how do you know anything about that? That's supposed to be a piece of classified military hardware!" he states.

"Was classified," Bob replies, tearing open another packaged synthetic treat, stuffing the morsel into his eager mouth. "The military de-classified it when I was a young kid," he mumbles through his chewing. "We used to build our own versions to play challenge games back and forth after bedtime so we wouldn't be heard by our parents."

"I knew there was something untrustworthy about you, Bob." Georgia Simone laughs. Jensin coughs at her statement.

"You really built one of those as a kid?" asks Murdock.

"Quite a few, actually. They had to be built in pairs because other singles or pairs couldn't work together because of the single photon polarity shift," Bob explains. "We built banks of them. Quite simple, really!"

"I can't believe kids were constructing replicas of military hardware such as those less than twenty years ago!"

"Not replicas, working units," Bob smugly adds.

"Where did you get the isolated photons?" asks Murdock.

"Mail order at first," Bob replies. "We would split them using the school equipment. That was, until I learned how to isolate individual photons and constructed the apparatus I needed to split them on my own."

"That's something I wouldn't put past you, Robert!" Murdock laughs. "I'm assuming you would have no trouble putting a few sets together in this late day and age?"

"I might be a little rusty, but with a few minutes of research to check out any new developments along that line and to track down a hardware list—I think it can be arranged in short order," replies Jensin. "Maybe an hour or two at most."

"We have nothing to lose by giving it a shot," adds Murdock, looking over at the young man with a slightly greater degree of respect.

"Huh?" quizzes Georgia. "Maybe I've led too sheltered a life or something, but I did study engineering and physics. What the hell are the two of you talking about?"

"You explain it, Bob," says Murdock. "You probably know more about the damn thing than the people who originally developed it, and definitely more than I do. I've only read about it, but you say you've actually built a number of them from scratch when you were a kid."

Bob Jensin picks up the marker from the tray of the white board across the lab from where Georgia Simone and Dr. Murdock are standing; their attention riveted on his every move. Approaching the center of the large white panel, he commences to draw a circle, bisecting it from top to bottom. Placing a plus sign in one half and a minus sign in the other, he steps back to admire his artwork and turns to Georgia Simone and starts to explain.

"Here we have a photon, or what is supposed to resemble a model of a photon, not drawn to scale, of course, or…"

"Get on with it, Bob, this isn't an elementary school class!" chides Murdock. "And there's nobody here to impress that you haven't already overly impressed."

"Uh, yeah, right," he continues. "When you split a photon you have the two halves, a negative half and a positive half. Keep the two halves separate and nothing happens. The photon decays and is gone. Bring the two halves close enough together and they rejoin. The negative attracting the positive and the positive attracted to the negative. Simple physics."

"If you time it just right, bringing the two halves just close enough to each other that they begin to attract each other, they will align in opposite polarity. You have less than a nanosecond to do this, but if you manage to separate them again once the halves have aligned, but before the two halves rejoin, you have the basis for the quantum teleportation communications system. If you don't succeed on the first try, you can use the original rejoined photon over and over again until the separated halves align before rejoining. That is, unless you mess up and the photon decays. Then you have to start all over again with a new one."

"I still don't understand," Georgia states. "We have two half photons in polarity alignment but kept separated. How do you communicate with those?"

Bob continues, "Once the two halves have been re-aligned, they will remain stable indefinitely and will not decay. As long as they are kept apart, they try to seek out the other half to re-join. You have two halves sitting there in their own containment apparatus, mutually attracted to each other but separated by whatever distance you choose."

"Change the polarity of one half of the photon and the polarity of the other half instantly switches to the opposite of what it was to be able to continue to attract its counterpart. By changing the polarity of one half, the other half reciprocates, unhindered by distance, like turning a light switch on and off to blink your message. The Army even used it to communicate between Earth and the early military complexes on the moon."

"Now I see!" exclaims Georgia. "A simple binary code, plus or minus, 1 or 0, on or off. Amazing! We'll have to put a set of these together and test them in a wormhole as soon as you can get them assembled Robert."

Murdock notes, "I'm leaving for M.A.B.U.S. in two days to oversee the dismantling of two of the three major observatories. We'll be doing calculations on the mass and material density of the station to determine the amount of e-matter we will need to keep onboard and how often we will have to break and disperse the wormhole to collect additional e-matter. Get to work on your theory and let me know as soon as possible when we might have some operational sets of transmitters."

"I think I'll be able to have several sets ready before you leave, Dr. Murdock. I did a lot of tinkering with quantum teleportation in my adolescent years and made some considerable improvements on the old Army version. I think I'll be able to recall what I changed and improved on if given just a little time. I might be able to add a few new tweaks to the older system."

"I'm sure you will, Robert! Take whatever time you need, but don't drag your feet. A means of communication is vital to the project, and time is of the essence," Murdock states, leaving the solar lab.

Bob Jensin immediately takes his place in front of his computer station. Donning his virtual gloves, he immediately begins entering requests for data into the computer. Murdock, upon leaving the core of the lab complex, mutters with fragile confidence to himself, "I know you will find a way, Robert. If anyone can. God, I hope you will find a way!"

"Bob," Georgia asks, "why do you need several sets to start? I am sure Murdock would be happy to have even only one before his departure. I'm still a little in the dark about this! How big is something like what we were talking about, and what do we do with it once you've made it?"

"As I mentioned," Jensin continues, "these transmitters only work using the identical halves from the same split photon. If you bring halves from different photons too close together, they obliterate each other. That was one of the main reasons the military abandoned and unclassified the research on quantum teleportation.

"Whenever the government tries to do anything, there are always those who look for shortcuts so they don't have to do any extra work. If one set of transponders had a problem, instead of dismantling the apparatus, they insisted on trying to pair it with another set that also malfunctioned. The results were stockpiles of useless equipment that cost billions.

"With the ones that did function properly, it was great for command-post-to-command-post communication, but you needed two separate units for every two locations that wanted to keep in contact. If one of the two was destroyed or disabled for any reason, the other was rendered useless. The rogue half photon would begin to rotate at an increasing rate of speed until it was spinning faster than could be measured. Unable to slow, stabilize or remove the gyrating half photon, the remaining equipment was rendered useless until the dying photon half decayed.

"We didn't have that problem with the sets we built as kids. If we had any difficulties, we just dumped the photons and started over again. We even got a kick out of ejecting a rogue photon from the transmitter. Each one was like watching a miniature fireworks display. The military never recycles anything. That would be too easy. They just build everything new all over again using the same defective plans until eventually they scrapped the whole deal.

"At that time, the military was trying to develop a communication system that could not be intercepted or falsified, and they thought they found one, but it was too limited. The original equipment with the needed computers at the time was about as large as an automobile. By the time I was able to start fooling around with it, the size was about that of an old laptop computer. As a matter of fact, that's what I used with the first ones I made.

"Now I think we might be able to shrink each unit down to the size of the mini-calculator in your lab coat pocket. We should be able to bank several systems together with proper shielding and send and receive huge amounts of data in a fraction of the time my old ones did."

Georgia Simone stood gazing in wonderment at this young man, who so matter-of-factly dismissed the blunderings of the government establishment with a confidence, revealing he had the answer to the most important communications problem to ever face mankind. In addition, his answer was nothing more than a child's toy. "Let's get to work on this right away," Georgia excitedly states. "I want to see this thing work, even if it won't work in a wormhole!"

"I really believe it will work, Georgia," Bob Jensin states. "I do believe we can make it work."

Chapter 12
The QT Probe

"You know, Bob, maybe simple communication might not be enough," Simone says to Jensin. "How about if we see if we can make up something in the way of a probe that will actually be able to execute commands as well as receive information. I think we should try to do more than just communicate to something inside a wormhole. The probes we will be sending out in the near future will have to have the ability to receive new instructions that might change after they are well on their way to who knows where, and then let us know if they are in fact doing what they were told to do. We both know how important establishing a link between M.A.B.U.S. and the outside world is, but I don't see why we can't combine the two endeavors into one experiment."

Jensin agrees. He begins retrieving what little data is still available concerning the now archaic quantum teleportation communication systems. He found obscure files buried within millions of electronic documents of declassified military information.

Georgia Simone sets about gathering and assigning the people who are to assemble the small module they will use to test their first apparatus.

"I don't need anything very sophisticated. Just a simple piece of equipment that can follow a few straightforward commands and not break down right in the middle of it," she orders. "We need something that will record input and follow clear-cut instructions."

Georgia continues to fill her people in on exactly what she needs the probe to do and the specific perimeters where they will need to concentrate their efforts.

Jensin is the first one finished. His task of collecting the massive amount of needed information at last over and done with, he makes his way into Georgia Simone's office. The first of several chairs he makes contact with skitters across the floor. Dropped pages of celluloids flitter behind him. "I've been over every bit of available data on QT, and I feel the toys we built as kids surpass what the military first developed or anything anyone else has come up with since." He bangs another chair, sending it slowly spinning out of his path. More printouts drop behind him.

"Why am I not surprised!" mutters Georgia. "Can you build one now? One that we can use on a small probe?"

"No sweat." The remaining stack of his celluloids spill over on to her desk. "I can get on it right away."

Jensin begins compiling a list of materials he will need as well as working out the specific dimensions of the new QT transponder.

Georgia Simone flashes requisitions throughout the compound to obtain the necessary materials. "I don't want to have to wait, I want these supplies yesterday!"

Several hours pass before the design team bursts into her office unannounced—carrying an ominous looking piece of machinery.

"Take a look at this, Georgia!" the senior designer exclaims. "I think we've built just what you're looking for." Pushing aside the celluloids on her desk—much of it cascading to the floor, the head of the design department slides a conglomerate of machinery in front of her. "This small probe will record digital information as well as process specific commands."

The strange object sitting in front of her on the desk is about eighteen inches long with a diameter of ten inches. It looks like a toaster that had an unexpected run-in with a blender.

"It ain't pretty, but it does everything you asked!" The design coordinator adds, "I think we've left enough room inside for Jensin's receiving equipment, based on the stats he gave us."

On the top of the probe, under a protective glassine shield, is a bank of twelve LED lights, six green and six red. Inside, above the recording apparatus, is a simple, small round disk attached to a servomotor. One side is white and the other black—illuminated by a separate light source and monitored by a photocell positioned directly below the disk.

"You send commands to the unit for whatever sequence you want. All green lights, all red, or any pattern you choose. Send the command and the lights change to the sequence you request. The by-colored disk is designed to flip from white to black on command also. The digital recorder will store all information sent to the probe for playback later—displaying whatever sequences you sent—and it will also record the responses of the probe to the commands it receives." The design coordinator was running the probe through its paces when suddenly they were interrupted by a voice from behind.

"Here it is, Georgia, one pair of QT transponders to go!" Jensin announces. He stops dead in his tracks. His eyes focus on the mishmash of hardware sitting on the desk in front of his supervisor. "What the heck is that?"

Georgia Simone smiles at his obvious consternation. She chuckles. Bob Jensin stands there staring at the probe with his mouth open. "Do you think you can get your gizmo married to our new probe before we leave here today?" Georgia inquires.

Flabbergasted, and plopping his precious cargo on the desk beside the probe with the blinking lights and flipping black and white disk, Jensin sputters, "What paradigm sequence was used to configure the matrix?" His eyes are still fixed on the probe.

"Plus or minus nine nanos, as you requested," the head designer states, checking his notes one more time.

"Standard 408DLA configuration?" Jensin asks, moving closer to examine this strangely complex yet simple instrument sitting on Georgia's desk.

"Only what we were sure would work based on the narrow window you asked for," the head designer adds. "We tried to keep it as simple as possible."

Scratching his fingers through the unkempt mop on top his head, Jensin lets out an audible *whoosh*. "I think we might be able to have this…whatever it is…up and running in less than half an hour or so!" With diminished confidence and building doubts, he sets about plugging in cables and attaching interface clips to strategic points on the exposed circuit boards.

Two long hours pass before the boy genius is ready to relinquish his work to the others. "OK, Robert. Let's see if your QT thingamabob really works," says Simone, filled with apprehension.

Jensin sends the first commands to the probe. Each bank of six LED lamps switches from green to red, and the white disk changes to black. What has been recorded is printed out on the main computer display, confirming each command.

More commands are sent. Various patterns of lights emerge. The disk switches back to white and again returning to black. Back and forth, first white then black. Then black turning over to the white side, red to green, green to red and a mixture of both. Repeatedly obeying every command, the display confirms each command as correctly executed. There is no question—QT works! But will it work in a wormhole?

"Notify the e-matter facility. I want them to be at our total disposal as of 0800 tomorrow. No delay or excuses!" Simone hollers with excitement. She grabs Jensin, spinning him around and giving him a motherly hug. "Robert! Robert, you've done it!"

"I hope so," he says, slowly turning back toward the ugly probe. "Let's just hope this thing works as well inside a wormhole as it did here today." He bends back over the hunk of experimental machinery sitting on the table and wiggles wires and clips.

The early morning finds the e-matter lab buzzing with activity. Tests are being run on the influx procedures to make sure there are no last-minute bugs in the system before the first testing with the probe. Various standard test items are sent into a wormhole and retrieved without any hitches. All final tests are at last completed. They are ready for the probe.

Full magnetic flux simulations in close proximity with the probe and additional influxes completely enveloping this ugly object are initiated to determine if there are any adverse effects caused by the high intensity magnetic field on the QT receivers and any of the mechanical parts tightly compacted in its interior. All systems appear to react as designed, and everything is fully operational. It is time to send the QT probe into a wormhole for the first full-scale test.

"Stand by to influx e-matter on my mark!" a voice echoes over the intercom. The e-matter coordinator inputs commands to the virtual terminal. The probe is instantly suspended in the center of the clean room, held in levitation by the surrounding magnetic field several inches above a mass of gridlines laid out on the base surface.

A massive bank of computers superimposes three-dimensional holographic grids on the probe itself—which are visible from all sides—tracking the position of the probe right down to its molecular level. The probe is slowly rotated while still held within its containment field—after being given a three hundred and sixty degree sweep—the floating object is returned to its original starting position.

"The probe is stable, matrix is aligned. Anytime you are set we're ready for a go!"

"5, 4, 3, 2, 1. Influx e-matter!" The probe at first shimmers, then vanishes.

"OK, Bob, it's all yours now!" Georgia Simone wipes the perspiration from her forehead. "Let's see if this thing will work as well as we all hope."

Jensin, smiling at her, begins sending the first of a series of commands to the probe—commands that are simultaneously recorded on the master computer for later verification. Georgia stares intently at the graphic display, the only connection to the vanished probe. The grid lines show where the probe is supposed to be, but there is only empty space—nothing is visible except the intersecting grid lines. More commands follow. The probe has now been in the wormhole for seventeen minutes.

"Reverse ionization on my mark! 5, 4, 3, 2, 1. Reverse ionization!" No probe! Nothing but emptiness in the clean room. The probe did not re-materialize. It is gone!

"Do we still have influx?"

"Negative! All systems are at normal!"

"I…I don't know what happened, Ms. Simone. It didn't come back! This is the first time we've ever sent something into the hole that didn't come back!" the chief e-matter coordinator stammers. "Run a full systems check," he orders. "The probe has to be somewhere! Find it!" Minutes pass like hours—data is checked and re-checked.

All hands are diligently combing over every bit of accumulated data when the door to the lab abruptly flies open. "Hey, you people know anything about this?"

John Fleming, the administrative assistant to the shuttle flight coordinator, bursts into the control room with the damaged probe in his arms. He pushes past several bustling technicians in the passageway. "This thing just blew a two-foot hole in the wall of my office and knocked over two file cabinets." He stands there, holding the QT probe in his hands, the front of the piece of hardware is slightly caved in from the impact with the back of the large stack of steel drawers.

"THE PROBE!" everyone instantly exclaims. It is immediately snatched from Fleming's arms, nearly ripping his shirt sleeves away with it. Fortunately there is nothing in the forward section of the probe that cannot easily be replaced. The brunt of the impact was absorbed by the titanium-shielded servo motor package—simple hardware is all that is damaged. The important parts—the data collecting sections—appear to be intact.

The probe materialized some eighty feet away from where it was launched into the wormhole. More than 25 meters from where it originally vanished, it reformed back into physical matter from within the wormhole, moved back into real space, but instead of hovering in the clean room—it appeared inside the structure of the distant office wall and behind a metal filing cabinet. The e-matter vaporized the wall that surrounded the probe as it returned to this dimension, but the probe was moving when it reappeared, and at a considerable speed so it seems, knocking over two heavily loaded steel file cabinets.

"How could I have been so stupid!" Jensin exclaims smacking, himself on his forehead with his palm.

"What are you babbling about?" asks Simone.

"Atomic polarity shift counter reaction!" he exclaims.

"What are you on about now?" Georgia queries.

"Don't you see," explains Jensin, "when you change the polarity of the photon in a wormhole, there is nothing to resist the change. If you give it a plus charge, it will move in one direction. Give it a minus charge and the polarity shift will cancel out the previous push and it stops. Give it another minus and it will reverse direction."

"Think of it as right and left. You start at zero. One plus and it moves to the right at an unknown velocity. Give it a minus and it stops," he explains. "Give it another minus and it will now proceed toward the left at the same speed. We just changed the polarity of the photon thousands of times in the last fifteen minutes or so! We may have sent this thing all over the cosmos without realizing it!" He excitedly adds, "I can't wait to get into the data banks and find out how far this thing wandered before we got it back—and we're lucky we got it back at all!

"I do know one thing, we have to send the QT receivers out in pairs with opposing polarity or we may never get another probe back again! One set starts out positive and the second set negative with duality of transmission. That way they will cancel each other out as far as APSCR." He pauses, thinking. "No, wait! That won't work either," he says aloud to himself. "That would be like two motors on a boat, one going forward and the other back. That will only cause the probe to rotate. We need to send these out in a rotating quad array mounted in an axial configuration if we want to keep the damn thing stable."

Georgia Simone, not understanding anything Jensin was going on about, just shook her head in amazed confusion, stating, "Whatever you say, Bob. Just make it work!"

There was nothing—no hardware and no software on board the probe to indicate there was any movement at all or how far and in what direction the probe had moved, let alone the answers to the question how fast? How far? Where?

The lost probe, now returned to its point of origin and at last interfaced with the main-frame computer, commenced the process of re-transmitting the commands originally sent to it. Every command had been executed as directed—red to green, green to red, white to black, black to white! Over and over, over and over. For the seventeen minutes the probe was inside the hole, traveling beyond the reaches of this universe, it did as it was commanded, all the while shifting back and forth within the confines of the wormhole, but where?

"We need to let Murdock know what we've found," Simone said to Jensin, the two walking back to her office. Georgia is in elation—Jensin is deep in thought.

"Yeah, we can let him know QT works, but we need to do a lot more experimenting before we let the cat all the way out of the bag!" Jensin replied. "We need to make sure we can hold a probe stable inside a wormhole. Can you imagine if something the size of M.A.B.U.S. started to move on its own and there was no way to control it?"

This sobering thought suddenly struck home to both of them. Jensin walked on a bit more before speaking. "We need to have a lot more control over any inanimate probes before we can release this Pandora's Box on the platform. It's just too..." They walked on in silence.

After several pregnant moments, Jensin stops in the middle of the hall. "Give me just a little more time to think on this, and in the meantime, let's see if we can come up with a probe that can communicate to us from inside the wormhole. While the lab works on that, I'll try to come up with some kind of configuration that will keep the probe stable and stationary!"

Georgia Simone agrees with Robert Jensin completely. Stopping just outside the door of her office, Georgia returns to the pondering lab technician and places her hand on his thin shoulder. "Now that we know what we are up against, it shouldn't take us too long to design and reconfigure a probe that can transmit as well as receive. If I know you, it will be one we can be pretty well assured, based on what you have explained to me, is going to materialize at least in the same general region of the cosmos we send it from."

Next day, the work begins in earnest. Much of the original probe is scavenged, modified and reconstructed to new specifications to house the hardware necessary to conduct two-way communication. Jensin busies himself constructing the paired transmitters and receivers to be installed in the new probe—along with the rotational array needed to hold the entire configuration together. Rotating quadrality should prevent any unexpected motion inside the wormhole.

Synchronization is crucial at this point. Phase misalignment—even down at the atomic level—will cause unwanted movement of the probe within the confines of the portal. All paired components must be perfectly aligned or the probe may never be recovered—traveling endlessly in an unknown direction inside the wormhole—forever traversing the cosmos.

Chapter 13
Hello in There!

The new probe is ready, somewhat larger than the first, but just as uncomely—if not more so. The final tests are run and everything appears to be in order. All systems check out in A-1 condition. Jensin programs the probe to transmit a series of binary sequences on command. Sets of pluses and minuses, 0's and 1's, to be read in simple binary code by the probe's miniature onboard computer and then transmitted back out from the wormhole. The four banks of transmitters and receivers are set in motion, rapidly rotating around each other, each set consisting of a pair of transponders working perfectly in unison. All is ready. The e-matter lab is put on standby.

"What're you planning for our first trial?" asks Georgia Simone. "I hope it's not something that's gonna blow another hole in a wall somewhere."

Jensin, still wrapped up in the last minute details of the program for the probe, replies, "We already know the probe can receive." His fingers are flying over the virtual keyboard. "So the first command we send is going to order it to transmit." He pauses, feverishly checking the last of his figures on the celluloids. "What was it you asked me? Oh yeah, I'll order it to transmit a predetermined set of binary numbers back out to us from inside the wormhole."

"If we receive any data from the probe, then I'll send in a series of commands for a set of simple calculations the probe is designed to execute on its own, and it should transmit the results back to us. Except for the initial response triggered by the first set of commands, none of the data I will be sending is stored in the probe's onboard computer, so it will have to work independently of any outside influence or information."

"You sure you're not going too fast?" she questions. "Seems like a lot of steps to hit on all at once!"

"Dr. Murdock said he desperately needs this communications setup, and I promised to give it to him as fast as possible," Bob replies.

Let's keep our fingers crossed," Georgia Simone remarks. "You about ready to set this thing in motion?"

"Just putting the finishing touches on our new baby," Jensin answers. "I just need a little more time to run the last of the program checks."

Finishing the task, Jensin and Simone lift the probe from the worktable, place it onto a transport cart, and begin to make their way to the exotic matter transfer lab. "I'm sorry we couldn't have this up and running before Murdock left for M.A.B.U.S. yesterday," Simone utters.

"At least the boss knows the QT transponder works," Jensin adds. "And if this part of the experiment is successful, we can contact him with the news together. That should make his day." They both fall silent. Delicately and deliberately, they push the cart with their precious cargo down the long corridor.

Everything is at full readiness in the e-matter lab. The probe is ushered in, positioned in its place of distinction at the center of the grid lines on the magna-flux platform. The room is cleared. "Engage magnetic flux." The probe, engulfed in the magnetic field, rises up several inches to the center of the magnetic containment vessel. "Probe is stable, matrix is aligned."

"Stand by to influx e-matter on my mark."

"I hope this works," sighs Simone. Bob nods. The command to influx the e-matter is received from the coordinator. As before, the probe shimmers and then vanishes. The probe is now within the wormhole. The e-matter lab falls silent.

Bob Jensin sends the first of a very long series of commands to the second invisible machine sent out of this realm of time and space. He fingers the send command with the virtual gloves. Suddenly the computer screens flash to life with a sequence of ones and zeros.

"Decode!" Simone orders excitedly. The binary numbers are instantly replaced with letters. On the display, the words, "HAPPY BIRTHDAY, GEORGIA," can be seen.

"What? My birthday isn't for three months."

Jensin perks up. "I wanted to send something that would show us there was no mistake in the probe's receiving commands or in our decoding the subsequent transmission. No one but I knew what the reply to my first commands to the probe should be. I stored the information for that response in the onboard computer, but the probe had to do the calculations to be able to search out and retrieve the hidden information based on the commands I sent. If even one byte of data was not correctly received, we would not have gotten that birthday wish."

"Well, it may not be my birthday, but it sure as hell made me happy!" Georgia adds. "But, I'll kill you if you ever tell anyone my actual age," she whispers to him.

"Let's get on with the rest of the program," she continues. "See what else this thing can do." Jensin feverishly sends command after command. Instantaneously, the probe responds. Commands are completed to the letter. Every calculation is exact. "OK, lets bring 'er home!" Simone orders. "If we can find it!" she whispers to herself.

"Standby for reversed ionization, on my mark. 5, 4, 3, 2, 1. Reverse!" The room shimmers and the probe reappears, in the same spot where it was before. It is exactly where it was when it first disappeared.

"Robert, it's here, it's here! Simone exclaims, wrapping her arm around the thin figure next to her. "Now we really have something to present to Murdock and the rest of the scientific community!"

The e-matter lab is alive with activity. Technicians scurry in every direction. Jensin stands staring at the probe in silence. In all the activity, Jensin's eyes remain fixed on the newly materialized probe. "What's the matter, Bob?" Georgia asks.

"Something's wrong!" Jensin replies. "There's something wrong, but I can't put my finger on it! It's just not righ…"

"Don't touch it!" he suddenly shouts! "Nobody touch the probe!" He hollers over the intercom, "Everybody! Everybody get away from the probe! Out! Everybody out! Full magna-flux containment! Now, damn it! Now! Clear the room!"

"Matrix on!" the command comes and the probe is again contained within a magnetic field strong enough to confine the energy of a hundred and fifty pounds of C-4 plastic high explosive.

The probe rises to its pre-assigned position within the grid lines of the containment field, held motionless a few inches above the grid plate. All eyes shift from the probe to Bob Jensin and back again. Seconds tick by like hours. At first there is no change in the probe. It floats within the magnetic containment field, still and stable. "Readings?" Jensin shouts.

"Negative. Everything is stable."

"What is it, Bob? What's wrong?" Simone asks.

Jensin continues to stare at the probe, moving from side to side. "I…I'm not…I don't know for sure!" He turns back toward the coordinator. "What do you have now?" The supervisor looks puzzled and stares back at Bob with confusion showing in his eyes.

"These readings don't make sense!"

Jensin turns back to Georgia. "The polarity indicators were way out of sync—the figures didn't add up and it didn't feel right. It just didn't feel right! Something is…wait a minute…there's…holy shit!"

A sudden change in the ambient light surrounding the probe draws everyone's attention in that direction. Undulating at an increasing rate, the probe begins to implode in on itself. There is millisecond of a silent, blinding flash and the probe is gone.

"What the—! Shit! Where'd it go?" Simone exclaims. "Bob, what the hell just happened?"

"I'm not positive, but I have a couple of hunches. I'll know more once I've checked the data banks," Jensin replies. "Murdock's not going to be too happy about this, and I don't like it very much either." Robert Jensin turns his attention to retrieving the information recorded in the lab computers from the start of the experiment until the probe's final self-destruction.

A few hours later, Jensin walks into Georgia's office and plops a massive pile of celluloids on the desk in front of her with a look of seriousness on his face that she was unused to seeing. "I think I've found where the 'curly hair on the soap' came from!" he states.

"You can be disgusting sometimes, Robert!" she says in revulsion. Her thoughts were not on the gravity of the situation but on his off-the-cuff, crass statement. "Couldn't you say something like you found the 'fly in the ointment' or something like that?"

"Sorry!" he apologizes. "But I think I know what went wrong. No one is to blame, and it's nothing that anyone could have possibly predicted."

"What did you find?" she asks, shuddering at the lingering thought of his previous statement.

"Anti-matter."

"Anti-matter? From where?" she asks.

"From the probe itself!" he continues. "I noticed the polarity indicators were not at the settings where they should have been. Actually, they were a full one hundred and eighty degrees out of sync. Then there was the difference in the light around the probe. I've seen it before, doing anti-matter experiments as an undergraduate student at MIT. It has a strange iridescent glow just before going critical. I didn't see it at first in all the excitement, but I caught it out of the corner of my eye when I wasn't looking directly at the probe under the bright lights of the lab."

"How did the probe become anti-matter?" she questions.

"Exactly how I don't know yet, but I think I know why." Jensin starts to explain, "The probe's photons were undergoing a continuous barrage of atomic shifting while receiving commands and carrying out orders. Additional shifting occurred as it transmitted the results back out to us.

"This change in atomic alignment was transferred to all the atoms surrounding the photons. Essentially, the entire probe shifted in structural composition with the transceivers, switching from matter to anti-matter and back again millions of times as we sent it commands."

"What about the first probe?" she asks. "Why wasn't that anti-matter also?"

"We were lucky on that one in more ways than one," he says. "We were up against a 50/50 chance with the first probe in that it only had the one transponder. It was going to end up either being matter or anti-matter. It came back as solid physical matter. Fleming down the hall in shuttle flight can attest to that. If it came back as anti-matter, we would be constructing a whole new building wing instead of replacing a file cabinet and patching up a wall."

"And the second probe, why didn't that just destroy this whole complex when it materialized?" she asks. "Why did it sit there, seemingly stable for so long without any problem, if it was composed of anti-matter?"

"The e-matter itself played a significant part," Jensin says. "E-matter in reversed ionization is repelled by physical matter, but on the other hand it is attracted to anti-matter. The probe was held temporarily in a cocoon of fragile reverse-phase e-matter that was rapidly decaying. Its outer layers were in contact with physical matter and slowly deteriorating. As the atomic layers dissipated away, I noticed the change in appearance of the probe. That's why I called for it to be contained in the flux field. Checking all the data revealed that an amount of e-matter equal to the mass of the probe was lost somewhere. It was not recovered with the rest of the e-matter, as it should have been. It turns out it combined with the air molecules in the lab once the flux field was disengaged. We had a few vital minutes of a tremendous tug of war between matter and anti-matter that resulted in what you saw. We walked a hair-thin line in the lab today. A few seconds more and the balance would have been upset. We would have lost the protection of the small amount of reversed phase e-matter separating us from several kilos of anti-matter, enough to level this entire complex and leave a crater tens of meters deep."

"My god, Robert! That thing could have killed more than a thousand people, you and me included!" Georgia injects. "What the hell are we going to tell Murdock?"

"First let's worry about finding a way to make this thing safe, and alert all the other labs that are working along these same lines before someone gets in real trouble playing around with this unpredictable substance. We can tell Murdock later. We have to get on the horn and warn all the others. There are a large number of labs all around the globe working on the same hypothesis we are. Word needs to get to them immediately concerning what happened here today. I hope we will be in time to prevent a tragedy."

Several hours later, after contacting all the other facilities working on the communications dilemma, Simone and Jensin sit at the desk in her office. The hour is quite late, but every lab had been notified of the problem. The most difficult message sent is the one they send to Roy Murdock aboard the M.A.B.U.S. platform.

The two sit in silence for quite a while. "OK, Bob, what can we do about this? Any ideas?"

"I've got a few things I'm working on. One is so old you might laugh, but it might be worth a try," he says.

"At this point I'm willing to try gargling peanut butter!" Georgia says in anticipation. "What little surprise do you have up your sleeve now?"

"Do you remember Dr. Murdock's statement about QT being archaic like the old Morse code?" Jensin asks. "Well, that got me thinking. It is so simple it might just work."

"What, damn it? What might work?" she irritably asks, her fatigue starting to show.

"The stop," he says.

"The stop? What the hell are you talking about? What stop?"

"The stop at the end of each line of a telegram. It was to let the telegraph office know when to start a new sentence. We can program in a stop at the end of each command so the transponders will revert to their original configuration. Always returning to matter instead of anti-matter."

Georgia jumps from her seat. "Bob!" she exclaims. "It just might work, damn it. It just might at that! That just might be the answer."

"How soon can this be incorporated into the program?" Georgia paces quickly back and forth. "Can you actually get this into the program with built-in failsafes so everything will remain normal?"

"Doing that's a piece of cake. Which reminds me, I haven't had anything to eat for several hours and that potted plant on your windowsill would make for a nice salad."

"Come on, I'll buy." She smiles at Jensin. "But, I don't make as much as you might think, and I already know how much you can eat, so go easy on my purse."

Chapter 14
Return to M.A.B.U.S.

Murdock's shuttle approaches the M.A.B.U.S. platform after a considerable delay in the flight schedule. "The damn world's going to hell in a handbasket, and I still have to wait for a ride up to the only bus that's going in a different direction!" he mutters under his breath. "Life on this planet is going to come to a screeching halt, and those bastards running the show still can't overcome the everyday delays that are making every task more difficult for everyone. You would think by now they might put aside the unnecessary bureaucratic red tape and let the ones who are trying to accomplish what needs to be done get on with it, but no! They've been making things even worse. The fat cats still have to keep their fingers in everything, afraid they will miss an opportunity to take a little more and further pad their purses. The damn politicians figure they won't be alive in twenty or thirty years anyway, so they are trying to grab what they can now and the hell with the rest of the human race. I am glad none of those bastards will be able to leave when or if we ever do get this thing operational. I hope the small group of travelers in the future will be able get underway without having to put up with this kind of bullshit!"

The shuttle settles gently on the hanger deck of the M.A.B.U.S. platform. The gantry in position at the outside cabin hatch re-compresses the airlock connecting the two.

"Welcome aboard, Dr. Murdock. I'm Ensign Morgan." An extremely attractive junior officer in a well-fitted jumpsuit greets him. "I'll show you to your quarters. There is an 'eyes only' communication from the surface waiting for you in your stateroom. It just arrived moments ago, so I thought you might want to head there first."

"Thank you, Ensign, nice to make your acquaintance. I will check in with command after I see what the lab back on the surface has to say. I'll follow your lead; just let me get my gear."

Is there anything I can help you with?" she asks.

"No. I have everything in hand." His few satchels float weightless in the airlock, tethered together by their straps. Venturing out behind his new guide, he clips the lead strap to his belt, freeing both his hands.

The ensign is compelled to slow her pace a bit, as Murdock plods on behind her. He is out of practice. It has been many years since he wore the magnetic gravity boots designed to keep a person's feet in contact with the steel decking. He forces his way along, one laboring step at a time, behind his attractive chaperone.

Wearing gravity boots is like having extremely sticky feet. More like your feet are sunk in a couple of inches of soft mud. You must push down with one foot while you pull up on the other to break the magnetic attraction of the boot on the steel floor. Balance is not a problem in the weightlessness of space, since you cannot fall over. You might sway back and forth a bit as you prepare to place your next foot in contact with the decking, but there is no down to which you can fall. As a matter of fact, if both of your feet managed to separate from the steel decking, you would float motionless until your boots again made contact with the steel grid.

This strange way of having to walk accentuates the shapely Ensign's already enticing natural wiggle. "Oh, to be young again!" Murdock says to himself, following behind her. He is a captive audience, but he is enjoying every minute of the view immensely.

Arriving at his quarters, Ensign Morgan ushers him inside. Giving him a quick "cook's tour" and powering up his communications equipment, she states with a smile, "If there is anything you need, I'll be at your beck and call." Pointing to a button on his console, she says, "You can reach me over the intercom, day or night, but here it's always night."

"Very good, Ensign Morgan, the quarters will suit me just fine," he states, scanning both her and his new surroundings. "I think I can find my way around. If I do need you, I will page you, Ensign Morgan."

"You can call me Susan. We're very informal up here. Official rank protocol only comes into play when we are working on a crucial project or there is a problem somewhere. The rest of the time we're like one big happy family."

"Thank you, Morgan. I mean Susan. I let you know if there is anything I need." He watches her leave and thinks once more to himself, "Oh, to be young again!" Feeling a little embarrassed and somewhat ashamed of himself, he whispers, "If Jannene knew what you've been thinking, the side of your head would be greeted with a frying pan." He turns his attention to the message folder clipped to his desk.

Breaking the seal on the packet edge, he proceeds to digest the information sent to him by Georgia Simone concerning the setbacks at the e-matter lab.

"Well, Jensin, the ball's back in your court once again! Work your magic, Bob. Make that damn thing work. We're going to need it, and very soon," he says aloud to himself. "We can only go so far without a solid communications system." He prepares his reply, confirming the receipt of Simone's message, and adds his hopes and encouragement for their success.

The communication station in his stateroom has a direct link to the main communication center. His personal station enables him to have direct access to sending and receiving non-secure messages as well as direct voice and digital links to anywhere on the ship. Any communication involving encryption, or of a type requiring even more strict security, would have to be taken to the communications center personally. The message he now sends is not of any security risk, so he can send it over normal open channels.

That chore accomplished, Roy Murdock begins carefully unpacking the few precious possessions he brought with him to this weightless environment set in deep space. Busily humming, he removes each individual item and sets about storing every one in their proper compartments; his thoughts drift again to the lovely Susan Morgan. He can still see her in his mind's eye. The smooth, round curve of her hips—watching her walk ahead of him in the passageway. The delicate rise and fall of her pert breasts in the weightlessness of space each time she breathed. He pictures her lustrous chestnut hair floating unrestrained in zero G's, and her almond-shaped, deep brown eyes. He remains fascinated by the delightful way she would arch one light brown eyebrow whenever he commented on some insignificant change in the M.A.B.U.S. platform in his effort to make innocent conversation with her. He could still envision her smile and her supple, moist lips.

The task of stowing the few meager items brought with him takes much more time than he anticipated in the zero gravity confines of his stateroom. Nothing can be left lying around, as on Earth. Every single item must be placed in lockers, under hold-down straps, or in some other way anchored, or it will float around on its own and become a hazard.

That job completed, he feels confident in the delusion he still remembers his way around the space station, and after a quick scan of the ship's layout on the view screen, heads out to find the main command center to check in with the ship's commander. He promptly discovers he is hopelessly lost. M.A.B.U.S has changed extensively since he was last aboard six years ago.

There are new passageways and hatches where there were none before. Corridors that were there the last time he was aboard have been moved or removed. Bulkheads are now in places where there used to be open passage, passageways where once there were solid walls. Many new labs have been added and an equal number of others removed. Locating an intercom station, he sheepishly calls for Ensign Morgan to come and rescue him.

"What a way to make a first impression," he says aloud to himself. "The man in charge gets lost in his own house!"

"Have no fear, Susan's here!" came a coy voice from behind him. "Don't feel so bad, Dr. Murdock. This happens to everyone up here all the time. With all the many changes constantly being made, even the people who have been here the longest still get misplaced."

"I feel like a total idiot," he utters. "I glanced at the station diagram and thought I still remembered my way around. I guess I…"

"The route we have to take now will probably change before the week is up, or even before we get there. That's why we put in these station locators." Suddenly she realizes she was remiss in one of her duties. "Oh, I am so sorry, Dr. Murdock! This is entirely my fault. I neglected to tell you about them. We use them so often these days that we take them for granted," she apologizes, pointing to the screen in front of them on the bulkhead.

"Each intercom station has a holographic heads-up display. It gives you your precise location and the shortest route to where you want to go. Here, I'll show you."

She leads Murdock to the display panel to the right of the intercom. He again notices her delicate figure. "Key in 'locate' with this button, and that's us right there." Pointing to the illuminated red dot on the holography screen displaying the three dimensional layout of the M.A.B.U.S platform, she continues. "Each station is code numbered so you always know exactly where you are. They are also located only about a hundred feet apart, so you don't need to go very far to find one. The stations are situated along all the passageways, and there is an additional one located at every turn or level change. They are shown by these yellow spots here." Murdock is looking at her, not at the display.

"You enter where you want to go, and it shows you the quickest route. The primary route is illuminated in red for the first five direction or level changes. It's a good idea to re-check your route at that last point because by the time you get there, with all this work going on, your route might have already changed. The remaining mapped route and secondary routes are lit in blue." She notices his gaze.

He stammers, "This beats having to send out a search party to find those 'little lost astrophysicists' who are too proud to ask for directions." He chuckles, a bit embarrassed. "And by the way, how did you find me so fast? Were you following me?"

"No, but fortunately I wasn't too far away. Only one level down, or up, depending on what plane you are on at the time. I've been assigned as your liaison while you're here, so anytime you need assistance they contact me and I'll come running, so to speak."

Lucky me! he thought. "That's a lot better than dropping bread crumbs to find my way home." He says. "But please show me the way to the command deck, if you would. I'm still a confused and lost administrator!"

"This way, Dr. Murdock." She gestures in the direction indicated on the monitor.

"You can call me Roy," he boyishly stammers, blushing inside if not outwardly.

"OK." She giggles. "This way, Dr. Roy. Just follow me." Again, he watches her tread along the steel decking, enjoying what he sees, following as close as he dares with his out-of-practice plodding.

Heading down the passageway, Murdock was wishing he could get closer to her. Close enough to catch the slightest bit of her scent. She wears no perfume. All artificial aromas such as cologne, after-shave, perfume and even fragrant soaps are banned aboard the space station for fear of contaminating the air purification systems.

He wants to get near enough to be able to sense her true fragrance. Now he finds himself wanting to hold her to him. He wants to experience the essence of this lovely woman in front of him, to touch her.

They reach the fifth turn and stop to re-check their directions. Murdock inches closer to Susan, pretending to have an intense interest in the display. He can feel the warmth of her only inches away from him. He wants to reach out and touch her, feel the heat of her body next to his, caress her smooth skin, taste her sweet lips.

"There are only three more turns before we get to the command center," she states. The sudden sound of her voice made him jump back. "Do you think you can find your way from here, or do you still need me?"

Oh, I need you all right! he thinks. "I believe you better stay with me in case I have trouble finding the rest of my way, and then trying to find the way back! So much has changed and—"

"Okay, no problem." The young, unassuming ensign who he'd met just a few short hours ago was not much older than his own daughters, and had unknowingly aroused feelings and desires in him that had long been forgotten. He wanted this woman standing next to him. He wanted her more than anything else in the world.

"Well, we're finally here," she says. "Now that wasn't so hard, was it?" She turns to leave and extends her hand, starting to say goodbye. "If you need me for your journey back to your stateroom, just give a holler."

Murdock takes her hand in his, knowing the gesture was only meant to be a polite, innocent handshake. "Susan, please stay here. I won't be very long," he states, still clutching her hand. "My work doesn't start until tomorrow. I only need to check in with the CO out of courtesy. I thought—umm—maybe you could show me the way to the mess deck. I'm sure they've moved that too." He stands facing her, still holding her hand tightly in his.

"OK," she says, gently pulling her hand free from his. "I am a little hungry myself."

"Great!" he states. "With all the delays, I haven't had anything to eat since early this morning. There wasn't anything fit for human consumption on the trip up here either. This won't take very much time, I can assure you."

Although the platform commander is well aware of his coming aboard, proper protocol dictates that he report his arrival to the commanding officer in person before assuming his position as chief administrator. Ensign Susan Morgan, with a slight degree of puzzlement, watches Dr. Roy Murdock hobble across the command deck in his cumbersome gravity boots to speak with the officer in charge.

"All set," Murdock states upon returning to where Susan is waiting. "I'm famished! I could eat just about anything at this point. Let's hope there is something better to nosh on than the cardboard rations they had on the shuttle."

"Unfortunately, you won't find the bill of fare much better up here," she informs him. "The cooks try, but there isn't much they can do in zero gravity. At least we don't gag too often." They both laugh.

"The food probably hasn't changed much since you were last up here. It never really fills you up—it just gives you the nourishment needed to keep going. It's not at all like what you are used to down on the surface. The mess deck is one level down and two sections over to starboard." She leads him back out into the main passageway. He walks in silence next to her, stealing an occasional glance at her lovely face. Meanwhile, Susan Morgan continues along with the mandatory guided tour of the soon-to-be-made-over M.A.B.U.S. platform.

Reaching the mess deck, they are immediately confronted with a bustle of activity. Crew personnel are leaving tables, others are just settling in to eat, and more wait in a line in front of the menu station. Their turn arrives, and Murdock asks the faceless machine, "Hi, honey! What's for dinner?" Susan, smiling, pushes in front of him.

"Well, let's see, we have some green stuff, some brown stuff with a little yellow goop on the side, and I don't have any idea what that oozy mess is supposed to be," she jokingly adds.

Suddenly recalling the fact the man standing next to her was on terra-firma less than twelve hours ago and was used to being a partaker of real food, she laments, "This is the best we have to offer. It's not what you're used to, but…what I would really like right at this moment is some solid food that I actually have to chew for once!" she tells Murdock with a longing in her voice. "It's been such a long time since I've used my teeth for anything more than keeping my gums apart." She turns to Murdock and states, "Why don't you go first. You're still a guest until tomorrow, so it's only fitting you should do the honors and, as such, be the first to see what we are forced to endure day after day!"

Space cuisine is in a world all its own. Solid or hard foods present various problems. It becomes too difficult to control and consume an item that will not stay on your tray. Liquids also present their own set of unique challenges. The final solution was to convert everything to a paste form, held together by a tasteless, colorless gelatin. The gelatin gives the food a certain amount of adherence to itself and your serving tray. The compartmentalized tray has a clear semi-ridged cover with a food tube you pull out from each section to allow access. It is simply a matter of using the food tubes like straws to ingest your meal. Actual liquids are combined with less gelatin to maintain more of the liquid characteristics, and are served in separate squeeze containers called soupers, clipped to the trays. These you hold to your mouth and squeeze out the contents.

The food itself is primarily vegetable-based, with vitamins and protein supplements added for nutrition. There is the occasional meat-based selection, but gelatinous beef, chicken or pork coagulates are not very popular.

After much contemplation, and their choices made, they move on to the dispensing hatches. Assembled in seconds, their selected meals are hot and ready. The light above each hatch indicates when their meal is complete and ready to be removed. Retrieving their trays from the respective hatches, the two make their way to a couple of vacant seats opposite each other.

The seats and tables are a marvel of engineering simplicity. Numerous small holes that serve several purposes cover the tabletop and each seat. A constant stream of air drawn into the holes forms a slight vacuum effect, holding the tray placed on the table by suction. It is much like placing your hand over a vacuum cleaner hose, only the vacuum table has much less suction. The vacuum effect also removes any food odors and eliminates any minute droplets of food that might escape the food tubes. The seats have the same vacuum characteristics as the tables, gently holding you in place while you eat, allowing your feet to break contact with the steel decking for a short time if you so desire.

Placing their trays on the table and sliding into their respective seats, they begin to pull the food tubes from each of the tray compartments, readying themselves to experience their culinary mysteries. Murdock watches Ensign Morgan sample first one, then another, moving on to a third of her choices. All the while, she is sitting across from him in total silence.

Finally taking the food tube from one of his tray compartments in his mouth, he takes a hearty swallow. He was about to say that it was not as bad as he had expected. He only got as far as, "Hey, it's n…" when he realized his mistake. Eating and talking at the same time in space in not a very smart thing to do. You might think your mouth is completely empty, but there is always a minuscule amount of your meal clinging to your tongue, palate, or one of your molars just awaiting release.

He watched in horror as the tiny green glob tumbled out of his mouth and floated straight at Susan. Before he could reach for it, the tabletop came to his rescue, sucking the morsel harmlessly down into one of the waiting vacuum holes.

His face now a strange shade of scarlet, he reprimands himself. How could he be so forgetful? Murdock spent years in space on numerous occasions, and now to be so absentminded—especially about such an elementary precaution. He spelled out the word sorry on the tabletop between them with his finger.

With his hopes for any pleasant dinner conversation with the gorgeous Ensign Morgan totally dashed, he resigns himself to finishing his meal in the same stone silence exhibited by the lovely ensign and all the other crew seated around them.

Their trays now empty, he watches Susan unclip a squeeze tube of synthetic coffee from her tray and place the end delicately between her lips. Murdock felt his pulse quicken just watching her. He never wanted to be a souper so bad in his entire life!

Following a quick trip to the lavatories for an after-meal clean up, he would be able to speak to her again. The cleaning apparatus located in the lavs is like a cross between a water pick and a vacuum cleaner. All remaining food particles are flushed away by a dentifrice and suctioned out. In a few seconds, the viscosity of your saliva returns and it is again safe to speak.

His first words to her were those of apology. "I am so sorry, Susan, I can't believe how much about space life I've forgotten in just six years!"

"It's like riding a bicycle." She brushed his statement aside. "Once you learn how, you never really forget. It'll all come back to you in a short time. Besides, no damage done."

"Thank heaven for the suction holes on the table or you might not think it was no big deal," he answers. "You could have had…" He lets the matter drop, and she does not pursue the topic any farther.

Leaving the mess deck, she suggests that it is time she returns him to his compartment. "We've all got a busy day tomorrow. Number 3 observatory is scheduled to be jettisoned and docked outboard from us. They are going to start dismantling it and begin scavenging it for materials in only two days," she states.

The leisurely stroll, if you could call walking in gravity boots strolling, to Murdock's stateroom was pleasant enough, but over much too quickly to suit him.

"Would you care to come in?" he asks.

"Thank you, but no. Maybe some other time. We've both had a long day, and we have another long day coming up tomorrow," Susan Morgan replies. "I'll see you bright and early in the morning."

"Breakfast?" he asked. "I promise I won't do any talking!"

"OK, breakfast," she consents. "Goodnight, Dr. Roy."

"Goodnight, Susan."

After she turned to leave, Murdock partially closed his door, holding it open just an inch or two so he could watch her proceeding down the passageway. Watching until she was no longer in his line of sight, he slowly pushed the door closed until he heard it latch.

He drifts ever so slightly in his sleeping sack, tethered to the bulkhead to keep one from floating away too far from the sack's anchorage. Gravity boots removed, he stares at the overhead illuminated by the soft glow of the emergency lights above his doorway. He wasn't thinking about M.A.B.U.S or all the work lying ahead of him. He didn't think at all about the expanding sun. Least of all, he did not think about his wife, Jannene, or his daughters, Lois and Linda. He was not even thinking about his baby granddaughter, Sharon. He just drifted there almost motionless, floating above the deck—thinking.

Dr. Roy Murdock, head of astrophysics at M.A.B.U.S., chief director of the World Scientific Community, and head administrator of the platform, could only think about one thing. That one lovely thing he watched walk down the passageway not more than fifteen minutes ago. Slowly drifting off to sleep, all he can see is Susan. Only Susan.

The metallic voice from his computerized wake up call aroused him with a start. "I hate that damn contraption," he swore under his breath. "0500. What an ungodly time to have to wake up!" He dressed and donned his gravity boots.

"Should I call her on the intercom?" he asked, himself sitting in the vacuum chair at his desk. His finger nervously approaches the intercom call button. He jumps at the sound of the knock on his cabin door.

"Dr. Roy? Are you awake?" It was Susan, gorgeous, beautiful, breathtaking Susan.

"I'll be right there!" He tries his best not to sound excited. Opening the door, he could feel his own face fall. Yes, it was the lovely Ensign Morgan, but she was not alone. Standing next to her was a young, rugged looking officer, almost a full head taller than Murdock.

"This is Lieutenant Jim Southern," she said, introducing her companion to him. "And this is the famous Dr. Roy Murdock."

Lieutenant Southern thrusts his hand forward, shaking Murdock's arm with vigor. "It's a great pleasure and an honor to finally meet you, sir!" The lieutenant continues to pump Murdock's arm.

"When Jim heard you were aboard, he was ecstatic and has been dying to meet the man who did so much of the original designing for the station," Susan injects. "He asked to come along this morning and get to meet you. I said it would be OK. It is, isn't it?" she asks.

"Sure, sure," Murdock said, feeling his gut drop inside. "The more the merrier!"

Liar! he said to himself, wishing the handsome lieutenant were at the other end of the space station.

"It's a pleasure to meet you, Lieutenant Southern."

"Call me Jim." The tall young officer is beaming.

"OK, Jim," Murdock replies as if they had known each other for ages, but deep down in his gut there is a growing dislike for this new acquaintance. The trio heads in the direction of the mess deck. "Tell me Jim, what do you do aboard this bucket of bolts?"

Chapter 15
In the Shadow of
the Wormhole

The e-matter lab is set for one more of Bob Jensin's probe experiments. Georgia stands nervously next to the young genius while he makes the last adjustments to his new creation. The probe is suspended in the magnetic flux chamber. After one final system check, they are ready for the ultimate test.

"I've got all my fingers crossed, and if I didn't need to see what I'm doing, I would cross my eyes too!" Georgia whispers to him. Robert Jensin gives her a wink and, gently nudging her aside, makes his way to the center of the command console.

Donning the virtual gloves, he states, "The video MPEG responder we installed should tell us what happens once the probe enters the wormhole, and if—" He stops speaking as he fastens the snaps on the gloves.

"If what?" Georgia asks, pressing closer to get a better view of the displayed data Jensin is about to send to the probe. She is extremely apprehensive after the last few episodes in the e-matter lab.

"If the probe goes anywhere at all once it's inside." She pushes closer to the monitors. "Run one last test on the video imaging," Jensin calls out. The probe sends its series of 1's and 0's through the transponder banks. The computers instantly translate the binary code to a video image of the far wall of the lab. "Rotate imager," Bob orders. The new images, a flickering sequence like an old movie, appears. All eyes watch the monitors, as the imager slowly rotates under its protective cover. "That's good, we're all set to go," he says. "Double check to make sure the probe is still transmitting images before you influx. This will be the first time anyone has seen what it is actually like going into a wormhole. We may only get this one shot."

"Only get this one? That's the first time I've ever heard you sound like you're not sure of yourself," Georgia adds, placing her hand on his shoulder.

"We're all entitled to get cold feet once in awhile," Jensin replies. "The last couple of disasters were just…you know, a bit humbling."

"Well…welcome to the real world, superman," she chides him, giving him a sharp jab in the ribs.

"Ouch!" He jabs back at her, but knowing what was coming, she moves out of his reach just in time. Undecipherable figures transmit from his virtual gloves and appear on the display. With a flick of his finger, the screen clears. "Cut it out or you might mess up the matrix.

"Sorry!" she says, giving him one more gentle jab to his side.

Turning back to the data monitor display, he orders, "All recorders on. Influx!"

The event is anything but anti-climactic. The entire view of the lab twisted at the instant of influx as though it was only a reflection in a piece of shiny Mylar slowly being crumpled. The scene fades to gray, flashing to blue and finally revealing the blackness of the wormhole.

"We should be getting a picture but nothing is showing on the display!"

"The external lights were on, weren't they?" was asked.

Jensin bends over for a closer look at the display screen. "Correct to true density on this view and run the recording from the moment of influx, but slow it down as much as possible." The density correction is checked, and it is already at the setting confirmed to be true. Watching the influx procedure in slow motion, Jensin stares thoughtfully at the display.

"What is it, Bob?" Georgia questions.

"It's black, but not as black as it should be if the probe is gone," he says. "Switch to a different display, but re-check the density before you switch. Then pull up full brightness but hold contrast at midpoint." They switch display monitors with the same results. "Hmm! It's more like a shadow, like the shadows you encounter behind a boulder on the lunar surface. No air there to scatter light. Black, but yet not completely black. We're going to have to chance it."

"Chance what?" Georgia asks with a bit of urgency in her voice.

THE WANDERERS

"Moving the video recorders before the motion sensors are up and running," Bob answers.

He proceeds to the control panel, takes a deep breath and sends the command to the probe to do a 360-degree pan of its surroundings. All eyes are on the view screens.

They watch and wait. If the probe is inside the wormhole, it should show something, but there is nothing visible until, like a flickering sunrise, the boundaries of the wormhole come into view.

"Just as I thought!" Jensin exclaims. "The wormhole is only molecularly larger than the probe, and when we entered it, the lens of our camera was pointed directly at the wall of the hole with only the slightest hint of external light."

The technicians in the e-matter lab gaze in awe at the display screens in front of them. Flashing from one image to the next, vista after vista, they are seeing the complete confines of the mysterious wormhole at last. The video pickup slowly rotates, taking almost five minutes to revolve 180 degrees. The images before them slowly begin to fade into the same gray-black they encountered with the first view of the inside of this new dimension. The gray-blackness begins to give way to ever-increasing brightness as the video pickup continues to rotate. They watch a surreal sunrise unfold before them for a second time. Now visible to them is the opposite passage of the wormhole. The lens continues to rotate; there is no visual indication the probe is at all moving in the slightest. It seems to be stable!

The viewing of the entire wormhole complete, Jensin gives the order to pan back to the center of the hole. "Now for the moment of truth!" he states to Georgia.

"I'm going to activate all the motion sensors and begin sending the first of our series of commands." The newly enlivened motion indicators pick up only the slight vibration of the video control servos. The probe appears motionless as the first commands are received. The QT banks and mini-computer operating as one complete the calculations in nanoseconds and transmit the results back out of the wormhole. The probe remains motionless. There is no movement along any planes; it is completely stable.

The stop command built into the programming is a complete success. Sensors indicate that the probe, surrounded by e-matter, remains physical matter. The unusual foreign object captured in the center of the wormhole remains motionless, executing command after command, never moving even the width of an atom.

"Let's bring it on home," Georgia says with excitement. "We don't want to press our luck too far until we've had a chance to go over all the data and see if there are any other bogeymen hiding in there!" The scene on the display screens is the reverse of what it was when the probe entered the wormhole.

The projection slowly unscrambles and becomes smooth as the influx chamber shimmers and the probe reappears, hanging motionless a few inches above the gridlines. The only change from when the probe was sent in is there is a different picture showing on the monitors because the angle of the video lens, which was changed numerous times once the probe was inside the wormhole. It now points at a different part of the lab. This is further proof, from the recordings and all the data, that there is another dimension.

"Hold flux until we check everything out, Jensin orders. We don't want a repeat of the last time." The collective breaths of everyone in the lab are held—the newly returned probe is scanned and re-scanned. This probe's mass far out cedes the mass of previous objects sent into the wormhole. It is doubtful whether the magnetic flux containment is strong enough to encompass this amount of mass if it happened to return as anti-matter. All test are completed, and the probe is determined to indeed be physical matter and not as was feared by many—anti-matter.

Like two children pouncing on a stack of Christmas presents, Jensin and Simone converge on the probe the instant it is released from the magna-flux containment, busying themselves with downloading the stored data from the probe's onboard computer for comparison. A large number of technicians wait impatiently for their chance to disassemble the dormant probe and examine every square millimeter of it for any change.

Simone and Jensin pour over the reams of data printouts until the wee hours of the next morning. They devour every bit of information, sorting through piles of tech reports and computer comparisons. "We have our communications link!" Georgia says with a sigh of relief, leaning back in her chair. "As soon as we get our report off to Dr. Murdock, we can call it a day."

"That's fine with me," says Jensin. "I'm bushed!" He also leans back in his seat, stretching to relieve the kinks in his neck. "Tomorrow I'll start work on a refined program for the stop command—one that I'm absolutely sure has no chance of having any bugs."

She looks at the exhausted young man and, feeling as equally worn out herself, states in an authoritative tone which leaves no room for discussion or argument, "Not tomorrow. Take the day off and sleep in. You've earned it, Robert. Besides, I want you fresh when we start on the final design for a system they can use on M.A.B.U.S." She gives him a motherly peck on his forehead and adds, "Thanks, Bob. This wouldn't have been possible without you."

"You go home now and get some sleep. I will compile my report to Murdock and send it off. Now get! Be away with you. Be gone, young upstart, and no sass!" Robert Jensin rises and laboriously trudges out of her office. Georgia Simone begins to compose her message to Dr. Roy Murdock.

Georgia Simone, just shy of age fifty for the last three years and feeling many years older after the last week and a half of rigorous experiments and testing, sits silently at her desk. The communiqué to Murdock has been sent off. She can now relax. She is twenty years Jensin's senior, slightly overweight, not unattractive, but by no means glamorous. The stylish pantsuit she wears under her lab coat looks like she slept in it. Glancing in her compact mirror, she sees her raven black hair, the few unwanted strands of gray having been rinsed away at the beautician's shop, partially hangs across her face. She brushes her hair back in place. "Oh, Robert!"

She has worked closely with Robert Jensin for the last four years. This was only the second time she had observed him working under pressure. The first time was with his discovery of our expanding sun. Although that just dealt with gathering information, she was amazed at the diligence with which he accomplished the task before him. With this latest series of developments she had gained a completely new respect for the young genius' abilities. He never wavered, keeping his mind entirely on his work. He solved each new problem with exacting precision. She could not help but marvel at his absolute dedication to the project. Totally exhausted, his thoughts still were on the next task needing his attention.

Her fondness for him had increased over the last few months. She felt with a note of sorrow that if there will ever be anymore recorded history, he would be distinguished as the man who discovered the end of the world and not for how much he toiled to try and save it. Turning off the lamp over her desk, she tiredly rose and left her office, a single tear streaming down her cheek. She also headed for home, exhausted and alone. Muttering only one thought…"Oh, Robert!"

Chapter 16
A Rose, by Any Other Name

Dr. Roy Murdock sits at the desk in his stateroom. He opens the newly arrived communiqué from Georgia Simone. A smile of elation breaks out across his face upon reading the celluloid copy of Simone's message. In his excitement, before he has a chance to remember that he is in the weightlessness confine of outer space, he pushes up from his vacuum seat with enough force to cause his gravity boots to break contact with the steel decking. Roy Murdock propelled straight toward the overhead at great speed. The resilient covering on the ceiling of his stateroom is sufficient to prevent any serious injury from such an unintended impact.

Murdock, with the wind knocked out of him, is now propelled back again in the direction of the unprotected steel deck. Grabbing the side of his desk, passing only inches from it, he slows and finally stops his descent.

Regaining his footing and composure, he says aloud to himself, "I have been away from space too damn long! I've got to stop thinking like I'm still back on Earth and remember to make every move deliberate before I seriously injure or even kill myself!"

Reestablishing his equanimity and his breath, he collects the remaining free-floating sheets of celluloid from the various areas of the stateroom, re-securing them in their folder. He places the folder as well as a few other stray documents that have begun to drift around under the spring clip on his desk. He sits back down in his vacuum seat and, still smiling, wipes the sweat from his face with his hand.

"It works! Damn it! It works! I knew you could do it, Robert!" Murdock had to fight the urge to jump off the decking once more. "If there was anybody in the world who could find a way to communicate in and out of a wormhole, it would be you! You with your silly child's toy! You! Probably the only person in the world who would remember something as simple as the old quantum teleportation!"

With this news, they could now forge ahead! The project could at last move forward! They now have a source of communication that really works! If the testing proves what Robert Jensin had discovered and the communication system will operate reliably on long-distance probes—the observatories and other complexes around the world will soon be able to search for somewhere to send the M.A.B.U.S. platform. Deep space probes will soon be sent to the far reaches of the cosmos. The search would—with this new breakthrough—begin almost immediately. There could be a search for some distant planet where a small number of people might be able to survive. A planet to replace the doomed one…

Once the platform is reconfigured and ready, all testing complete, all calculations checked and re-checked, they would at last be able to send M.A.B.U.S. into a wormhole and perform all the necessary final testing and be able to communicate in and out of this other dimension. They could all the while still be assured of having the M.A.B.U.S. platform remain where it was when they first enter a wormhole, thanks to a young lab technician by the name of Robert A. Jensin.

Settling down at his desk, he drums his fingers rhythmically on the hard surface before him. The elation caused by this message still floods his mind. "Robert, you did it! You actually did it!"

Finally regaining his composure, Murdock begins to put his thoughts in order. "First I need to get a directive out to the home base immediately," Murdock thinks. "I want to make sure the base provides Jensin and Simone with anything and everything they need to pursue this thing all the way without any complications." He again erupts in joy. "I knew you'd come through, Robert! I really believed you would! And you, too, Georgia. I am so glad you had the confidence in him—confidence I lacked. If you had let him give up after the earlier setbacks, we wouldn't have this breakthrough now." Roy Murdock begins to formulate his orders in his mind and then to words inscribed on celluloid to be transmitted.

Reaching for the switch on his intercom, he pauses for a few seconds. He needs to compose himself after receiving this report. "This is Dr. Murdock," the chief administrator announces over the command intercom. "There will be a mandatory staff meeting at 1300 hours. All command personnel are to be present, with no exceptions. He clicks off and sets about compiling his message to M.A.B.U.S. central command.

With his reply in hand, he heads for the communications center to personally transmit his urgent priority message. He gave the order before leaving his stateroom to clear all channels for this important transmission. There is to be no delay in the sending of these directives. In his mind tumble thoughts of all the men and women working on the QT project along with Jensin and Simone. He was saying to himself, "Keep at it, people! Do what you have to to give the world what it needs to see this through to the end!" The self-sealing hatches on the command deck open at his approach. All eyes turn in his direction.

Murdock enters the communications center and a hush falls over the control room. The boss is here to send his message! Murdock never wanted to present that semblance, but the image had followed him up from Earth. Back on the surface, he was only one of many major heads of the scientific community. Now, up on the M.A.B.U.S. platform, he has absolute authority.

"Hello, Dr. Murdock." It was Lieutenant Southern. "We're just about ready to release module number three. Will you be staying here for the jettison procedure? All preliminary work has been accomplished and we are just waiting on your final word."

"No, Jim, right now I'm only here to send off an urgent message. Later on I'll be going down to the docking bay and boarding one of the shuttles to oversee the release of the module from outboard," Murdock replies, feeling uneasy around the tall lieutenant—his features resembling those from ancient Greek statues—the epitome of manly excellence. "I'm going to postpone the separation of the observatory until after this afternoon's meeting. I received some very interesting and uplifting information concerning the ongoing modifications, and, more important, the communications problems we have been experiencing—which is what this reply is about, and this afternoon's meeting must take precedence over all else."

"Sorry I can't be there," Lieutenant Southern says mournfully. "I have to remain on station. The observatory is sitting in a very precarious state at this time. There are only eight explosive bolts holding it to M.A.B.U.S. right now. Besides, as a lowly lieutenant, I'm not yet included within the command staff designation. I hope you will bring me up to date later on. I would really like to know what you're planning for this 'gracious old gal.' She's been my home for almost two years now."

"I'll get back to you as soon as the last of the details are worked out," Murdock replies. "I have to get this communiqué out and what's going to be happening soon definitely concerns the job you do here in the communications center. I can't tell you any more than that right now or at least not until after the briefing, but it is right up your alley. I'll see you later; meanwhile, keep up the good work."

He was glad to get away from Lieutenant Southern. The young officer has been nothing less than extremely pleasant, cordial and professional during their first and subsequent meetings. His demeanor borders on hero worship for Dr. Murdock. Still, Roy Murdock feels robbed of the personal time he might have spent alone with Ensign Susan Morgan, if Lieutenant Jim Southern had not been there so many times. He did not know when or if he would get another chance to be alone with her again. He could call for her on the intercom, but how many times could he get away with pretending to be lost before....

"Whoa, slow down! Oh, hello, Susan!" Ensign Morgan rounds the corner of the passageway, almost smashing into him.

She is on her way to the communications center to join Lieutenant Southern. She's rushing there to be with him when things start to get hairy, Murdock thinks. He is beginning to dislike the tall, handsome lieutenant even more.

"There you are, Dr. Roy! I've been looking all over the platform for you. You weren't in your cabin, so I figured you might be up here in the communications center. I know I don't qualify as command staff, but I thought I might be of some assistance to you at this afternoon's meeting. I know this station as well as anybody aboard, and probably better than most. I might be able to supply you with information concerning the ongoing changes and modifications, as well as those that have already been completed. Would you like me to accompany you to the meeting?" she asks, looking up at him with her brown eyes.

Control yourself, you dumb fool! he thinks, fighting the urge to reach out and clutch her to him. "That's a wonderful idea," he says, gazing back into her eyes. "I'm still not sure where everything onboard has been moved to, and heaven knows—I'm sure you will be of great help." Putting aside the compulsion to take hold of her hand, he instead offers his arm to her and says, "As the Lone Ranger used to say, 'Lead on, oh trusted, faithful Indian companion.'"

"This way, kemosabe," she says, smiling back at him. He almost stopped dead in his tracks, stunned by her reply. He was amazed that this young woman, no older than his own daughters, would in the blink of imagination possibly remember such an inconsequential morsel so deeply buried in the folklore of the distant past. As a matter of fact, they were both surprised that she would remember something as insignificant as this reply from the yarns of so long past and almost forgotten in the by-gone stories of Earth. Taking his arm with one delicate hand, she leads him down the passageway toward the conference deck.

Murdock wishes they could walk slower, but this important meeting is already running late, and he was the one who ordered it in the first place. She shyly removes her hand from his arm once they enter the conference cabin together. All personnel come to immediate attention. Murdock proceeds through the door, followed closely behind by Ensign Susan Morgan.

"As you were," he orders.

"This is my liaison officer, Ensign Morgan," he says, turning back toward the woman following him into the briefing room. "She will be assisting me with additional information throughout this meeting. I have been away from this station for more than six years, as all of you know, and much has changed. I have been back aboard for only a couple of days, and Ensign Morgan has been invaluable in helping me re-orient myself to the layout of this platform and to the continuous modifications to M.A.B.U.S. I will be calling upon the ensign at different times during this meeting. She will provide me with any clarifications as to the disposition of the various sections of the space platform that are undergoing extensive modifications and those scheduled for revamping. Ensign Morgan knows much more about the present state of the platform than I do at this time, and I trust you will afford her the same consideration you would me.

"First, I wish to thank all of you for your prompt attendance at this short notice meeting. In addition, I wish to offer a special thanks to Ensign Morgan for directing me along the shortest path here from the communication center. Without her knowledge of the platform, you might still be waiting for me to arrive for quite a while to come. She is a very competent guide, and I am sure by now that all of you have heard the amusing stories about how I became totally lost in the first few hours I was back aboard. Ensign Morgan has saved me from several hours of aimless wandering, trying to find my way to whereever I happened to be heading." There were several audible chuckles before he continued, "But, now, let's get down to business."

"As you all know, until now, we have had a communications stalemate. The only way we could possibly move M.A.B.U.S. beyond our solar system and on to another star system is to place the platform inside a wormhole. We did not dare send the station into the next dimension until we had a way to communicate into a wormhole and back out again. In laboratory experiments with small objects, we were able to control all aspects of the experiment from the outside of a wormhole. With something as massive as the M.A.B.U.S. platform, the control of the whole operation would have to be from on board M.A.B.U.S. and thus, within the confines of the wormhole itself. In the labs, the e-matter used came from an external containment field. With M.A.B.U.S., the e-matter will have to come from the e-matter storage vessels on the platform itself. This presented a completely new set of problems, although not insurmountable. The greatest test was communication. Without communication in and out of the wormhole, nothing can be certain. Communication is therefore vital. There are hundreds, possibly thousands of tests that will need to be done in complete unison and strict synchronization—from inside the wormhole and from the outside.

"Today, I bring you the good news that the communication barrier has been broken. We now have the means to connect our transmissions between the two dimensions. Our labs on the surface have overcome the obstacles we have been facing. Prototype systems are being assembled and will be sent up to us for experimentation."

There is a burst of murmurings. "These prototypes are being put together as we speak. Once installed, testing will begin. All data retrieved will be relayed back to the main labs and used to perfect the final communications apparatus we will then install on the M.A.B.U.S. *Star Traveler*. We are ready to move forward! No more looking back. From here on, we only look forward. Once we have a solid working communication system installed, the next step will be to move M.A.B.U.S. into a wormhole."

Murdock continues to explain the news about the quantum teleportation communication system to the command staff. Susan Morgan, listening and watching his every move, stares at him wide-eyed. Dr. Murdock caught her by surprise when he suddenly asks her about the location of an obscure section of the platform. She became so wrapped up in his description of the new communication apparatus and his extensive explanations of the complexities that she was caught completely off guard and had to pause for a moment and search her memory in order to recall what it was he needed. She and Murdock were both glad the information was something she was able to remember immediately.

Although, to her embarrassment, it seemed like hours instead of seconds before she recalled it, no one else noticed the hesitation. The rest of the meeting went forward a lot better for her. She was ready and waiting the next time Dr. Roy Murdock needed some information about the location of a number of various sections of the space station. He was also careful not to catch her by surprise again for fear of embarrassing her any further. She was not about to let it happen again either. The meeting lasted a little over two hours. After a lengthy question-and-answer session, which left everyone with more questions than answers, Murdock decides to end the meeting.

"I believe it is time we adjourned this discussion," Murdock says in closing. "This meeting has gone on far longer than I anticipated, and I assume by now the command deck must be getting very nervous about having more than 270,000 metric tons of observatory held in place by only eight bolts not much larger around than my wrist."

There was a sudden, distant scraping sound followed by a distinct thud about three seconds later. No one gave the sounds much thought. With all the disassembling, construction, demolition and reconstruction going on, M.A.B.U.S. was full of unusual sounds.

"That will be all for today," Roy Murdock states, gathering the celluloids he brought with him. "I will keep you posted on any new developments as they become known. It is now time we return to the work facing us—work that has been delayed much longer than it should have been. Please return to your stations. It's time to separate module number three from the main platform."

The meeting thus closed, Murdock and Susan Morgan leave the conference deck. "I'm sorry," she says.

"Sorry for what?" he asks.

"I let you down. I became so engrossed in what you were imparting concerning the new communications system that I wasn't ready when you needed me."

"Nonsense!" he reassures her. "You wouldn't believe the mess of confusion this quantum teleportation communications has caused back on earth. Don't even give it another thought. By the way, I'm about to board one of the shuttles and observe the separation from outside. Want to come along?"

"I don't have the clearance," she states.

"You have the clearance now as the liaison officer officially assigned to the chief administrator." Murdock smiles.

"I guess I do, at that! Don't I?" She giggles.

Dr. Roy and his liaison begin their long walk aft to the waiting shuttles on the hanger deck.

"Dr. Murdock! Dr. Murdock! Your presence is required on the command deck immediately!" a voice blares over the ship's intercom. "Dr. Murdock! Dr. Murdock!"

"Murdock here," he says, answering from the nearest intercom station with the help of Susan Morgan. "What's happening? Is there something wrong?"

"I can not disclose over an open channel," the agitated voice of the officer in command of the bridge replies. "Please report to the command center as quickly as possible, sir! We need you here at once!"

"I'm on my way!" he barks back into the intercom.

"Sorry, Susan, but I've got to fly," Murdock states to her disappointedly. He really wanted to spend more time with her, but now he is needed elsewhere.

"It sounds serious!" she says. "And fly you will, if you promise not to have me grounded for showing you this." She steps back a pace from him.

"What we are about to do is against all regulations, but a lot of us do it quite often when we have to cover long distances very quickly. This seems to be one of those times. If you will just trust me, we can be at the center in a fraction of the time it would take by plodding along on the deck. Just do what I do."

Grasping an electrical conduit along the bulkhead, Susan lifts first one gravity boot and then the second from the deck. Murdock watches her, now floating weightless in the passageway. "Now you," she says. Murdock copies her.

"Now grab one of the pipes and push yourself along. Keep your eyes to the front. We're going to start moving pretty fast. If you find you have to stop quick, just push your feet back down to the deck and the gravity boots will do the rest."

Grasping one of the many conduits on the bulkhead, Dr. Murdock lifts his feet off the decking and then pushes off, accelerating at an enormous rate of speed. He finds himself starting to tumble. "Oh, shit!" he exclaims. Susan grabs the back of his jumpsuit to steady him while they both propel down the long passageway.

"Start putting your feet down now," she tells him. "We have to make a turn to starboard up ahead." Their gravity boots regain magnetic contact with the decking, bringing them to a sudden halt, rocking back and forth like two cartoon characters. "If we were walking, we'd still be a quarter of a kilometer back that way," she says.

"Stand by for phase two!" Again pulling themselves free from the deck, they are off in another direction. "I'm glad all the hatches open inward instead of outward into the passageways," she remarks. "It could get very interesting if someone suddenly opened a door in front of us."

The two continue streaking down the long passageway. "You still have to be on the alert for somebody stepping out into the hall ahead of you. Most of us have learned to look first and be ready to duck each time we leave a compartment. You never know who might be passing by at great speed."

"We're ready to stop again," she says, tightening her grip on his jumpsuit. "Start to put you feet down now!" she says. "I guess we have to walk from here on. There's not enough room to play Peter Pan anymore," she jests. Murdock shakes his head, contemplating the vast distance he and Susan had just covered in a matter of minutes.

Just my luck, he thought jokingly to himself. *I'm getting mixed up with a fast woman, one who really likes to fly—literally!*

He and Susan Morgan enter the command center. The control deck central is a beehive of activity. What's the problem?" Murdock asks, approaching the main console. Officers and technicians are working feverishly at the controls. They occupy the five seats in front of the main console—alternately firing thrusters on module number three in a vain attempt to stabilize the massive observatory undulating almost out of control.

"We've taken a meteor hit! A bad one," the CO informs him.

"When?" Murdock asks. He moves to a position that enables him to view all the major screens at the same time. There is a constantly changing display of data flashing across each display.

"Twenty-two minutes ago." The stream of data continues to fill the screens. "A rogue object glanced off the hull of the main platform amidship and impacted dead-on into module three." The other observatories were shut down to protect them from any debris during jettison. "We never saw it coming." Murdock curses himself for ordering all the observatories off line to protect them from flying fragments during the release of module three. Had they been up and running, one or the other would have detected the incoming rock in more than enough time to direct the shipboard lasers to disintegrate it before impact.

"Is there much damage?" Murdock inquires.

"Not to the module itself. The deflectors absorbed most of the impact, but the module is oscillating more than we can control. If we don't release it right now, it's liable to break free on its own and breach M.A.B.U.S.'s hull integrity," the deck command informs him.

Meteor impacts are a fact of life aboard any space station. Most are only minute particles of space dust and go unnoticed, deflected back into space by the shielding.

The sensors installed onboard M.A.B.U.S. are designed to single out any large chunks of rock and, when detected, they are either destroyed or fragmented by lasers so they will do no harm. This one would have been no different had it been discovered in time. A meteor the size of a beach ball grazed the outer hull of the M.A.B.U.S. platform just aft of the central observatory and impacted solidly with the precariously perched module number three.

The resulting collision, although mostly absorbed by the deflectors, caused the observatory to resound like a bell. The vibrations continued to increase in frequency and magnitude until the entire structure was threatening to rip itself loose from the main station, held in place by only eight small, fragile explosive bolts.

"Standby to jettison!" Murdock orders. "Is everyone off and clear?"

"Everyone is clear and the shuttles have been launched," replies the CO.

"Just before we detonate the explosive bolts, fire the forward thrusters. That should give the module a stable, constant pull against the hull of the platform. At release, the module should move away without causing any damage. The onboard thrusters should move it a safe distance from us. Let it get far enough away but not too far out, and then fire the reverse thrusters to stop it. When it has had time to settle down, we can send a trio of shuttles out to retrieve it later. The safety of the platform comes first, the module next. That's only hardware and alloys!" Murdock orders.

The groans from the tensile flexing of the last remaining hold-downs are heard throughout the entire ship. The module is now beginning to sway even more on its delicate mountings. The massive observatory rocks back and forth—slowly buckling the plates around the fastenings.

"We can't wait any longer!" the CO exclaims.

"Fire forward thrusters," Murdock orders. "Standby to activate the explosive bolts!"

The thrusters ignite—the sound of buckling metal grows louder. "Fire the bolts, now!" In the vacuum of space there is only silence as the eight explosions occur simultaneously. Glittering sprinkles of reflective metal expand outward in all directions. Tiny sparkles of fragmented titanium glitter around the space platform.

Inside the M.A.B.U.S. station, the loud, thunderous sound accompanying the release of the observatory is almost deafening. All eyes watch—the freed module moves slowly at first, then with quickening speed away from the main platform.

"Fire reverse thrusters!" The order echoes through the bridge. The module begins to slow and eventually stops at a distance of seven and a half kilometers from M.A.B.U.S.—still pulsating—beginning to slowly rotate as it hangs in the weightlessness of space.

"It should be safe there for a while," the CO remarks with a sigh of relief. "Have the shuttles rendezvous with the module and report on its condition. I want a damage report on the outer hull of the platform right now."

"We'll need to bring the module back in a lot closer as soon as possible," Murdock states. He scans the numerous data screens. "It's totally unprotected out where it is now. The sooner we get it back into an area we can scan and cover with the lasers, the better."

The atmosphere in the control room slowly begins to relax with the immediate danger now passed. Murdock turns to Ensign Morgan, who is looking extremely worried, standing off to the right, doing her best to remain out of the way. "Sorry you didn't get a chance to watch all this from outside, Ensign. Maybe next time."

"After what I just saw on the screens, I'd rather be back on Earth hiding under a bed!" she replies.

"Send me your full report as soon as possible," Murdock commands the CO. "And let's get the other two modules back on line. We don't want or need any more surprises today. I'll be in my quarters if you need me." Murdock realizes now that the sensors will have to be moved from the other observatories onto the main station itself before any more external reconstruction is undertaken to prevent a reoccurrence of today's scenario. "We can't afford to open up any more blind sides to the cosmos at this late stage in the game," he says aloud to himself.

He and Susan return to the main passageway—he notices she is walking in silence, and at a much slower gate than her usually springy pace. Murdock, sensing there is something troubling the young ensign, glances over toward her. He watches her alternating one foot in front of the other in quiet contemplation. Her body rigid. Her head down. Her eyes looking not at where they were going but at the steel decking they plod upon, one step at a time. He wants to speak to her but doesn't quite know what to say.

They walk on for several moments in silence, when suddenly she stops. Turning to look at her—Roy Murdock is faced with a look of fear—a look of fear that now replaces the look of wonderment he has always seen in the features of the lovely Susan Morgan. The look in the woman's eyes makes him draw back—this unexpected revelation is something he cannot at this minute comprehend. He is at a loss to grasp the thoughts tearing at her mind.

He cannot help but observe tears—tears mingled with a frightened look in her beautiful brown eyes. "The..." She swallows hard. "The world is really coming to an end—isn't it?" she asks with a trembling in her voice. "It's not just a rumor! Not some silly exercise! It is really happening! Isn't it?"

He could not help but notice she is shaking all over. "Not for many years to come." He tries hard to reassure her. "Not for a long, long time." He takes her in his arms, and she willingly follows. He pulls her close to him, stroking her glossy, silken hair. She begins to sob against his chest. He holds her close to him. She trembles in his arms, crying more openly. He kisses her where her lovely chestnut hair meets the smooth soft skin of her forehead. She continues to weep.

He holds her tightly. "Not for a long time, my darling, not for a very, very long time," he whispers to her. She turns her tear-streaked face up toward him, her beautiful brown eyes wet with her tears, her supple mouth still slightly trembling with fear. He gently places his palm against her soft cheek and greets her lips with a long, deep caress. Fully expecting her to push him away, he instead feels her arms entwining around his neck, her sweet lips press harder against his own, parting ever so slightly.

Chapter 17
The Most Tangled Webs
Are Often Most Frail

"Good morning, Georgia," Jensin says, entering the lab, looking more asleep than awake. "What'd I miss?"

"Morning, Robert. Oh, not too much. Just a near catastrophe on the M.A.B.U.S. platform. Nothing that would concern you, though," Georgia Simone chides him. "How was your day off?"

"What?" he exclaims. "What happened?" he looks at Georgia Simone, not sure if she is joking or not.

"They took a meteor hit of sizable proportions, just as they were readying the smallest observatory for jettisoning. They almost lost it. Damn near came close to losing the whole ball of wax, too," she replied.

"Is everyone all right?" he asks in earnest. "Is the platform still OK?"

"Everybody's fine and the station is still intact, Bob. They will have to tow the jettisoned module back to M.A.B.U.S. from several miles away. The meteor didn't penetrate, but it sure made a mess of things. They'll be busy for a while gluing everything back together," she tells him.

"I take it from your overt display of concern and remorse that things are really as okay as you say," he sarcastically adds. "What else has been going on?"

"Well, Murdock is jumping up and down like a kid waiting for his birthday presents, wanting to get his hands on those transponders we're holding in ready for your new program, and the people down in the deep space lab want several sets for their exploratory probes. We've been running around like chickens with our heads cut off while you were relaxing in the sun all day yesterday."

His face fell. He feels delinquent for taking a day of rest that he truly needed. Georgia Simone, for the first time in the many years she has worked close to Robert Jensin, saw the frailty of this young man's spirit, and she suddenly experienced a wrenching, heartfelt guilt because of her careless ribbing of Jensin. She was watching his thin shoulders slump. She knew she had gone too far with this sensitive young man.

"I'm just kidding you, Bob! I'm just riding you. Don't you know when somebody is making light of a bad situation?" she says, seeing that it didn't make much difference. "You needed the day off, and you deserved it." She walks over and gives a motherly hug to this sullen figure. "You really did need time away from all of these problems, Bob! You know this place can't run right without you, and we need you. We need you up to snuff. We can't have somebody like you running around on only two cylinders. We need you at full bore! The short time you were away was well spent, if you unwound only just a bit!"

"What about you, Georgia? When are you going to take some time off? You need it too, and you deserve it more than me," he needles her back.

"Oh, I burned out a long time ago. It's the fresh, young minds like yours we have to protect from meltdown," she says, placing her hand on top of his head. "Come on, we've got work to do. And for Pete's sake, Robert—comb your hair!"

"Yes, mother," he jabs back, brushing his hair to one side with his hand. It is rumored that Robert Jensin has never owned a comb in his life.

The lab techs and others busied themselves, twenty-four hours a day, assembling the banks of QT transponders Jensin and Simone requisitioned. Each bank of transponders sits unprogrammed at Georgia Simone's order. Jensin had stated he wanted to update the programming to eliminate any possible errors and that statement alone was sufficient for her to set aside all further programming and delay any further work past the present stage of the probes until Jensin completed the program he was working on.

Bob Jensin sits at his virtual computer keyboard, sorting through the millions of lines of code needed to operate the transponders and other peripherals in conjunction. His eyes constantly fixed to the displays of his console, diligently searching for the slightest error or omission. It will take him most of the day, but again, he needed to be absolutely sure.

"That's it!" he finally exclaims. "No gremlins hiding inside. I made a few minor changes to speed things up a bit; nothing drastic, though. We're ready to go now. Let's program those babies!" The linkups complete, they begin to download the refined program to each of the transponders. The lab is suddenly a hum of activity!

"Murdock will be happy to get his mitts on these," Georgia states. "I'll bet he's been pacing like a mad man since he left—waiting for them." She moves over to behind Jensin now, sending the final data to the last of the QT packs, gently resting her hands on his thin shoulders, her fingers slowly moving in circles as if to reassure him she was still there.

These elementary probes they are readying to send up to the platform are only the beginning of the advances that are to come in the next few months. In addition to the communication arrays being installed on the space platform for their own experimentation, there is also a series of transponders that are going to be installed into the complex structure of a number of deep space probes. These are specifically designed to be launched from M.A.B.U. S. when the probes are deemed fully operational.

All thirty-eight sets of two are going up to M.A.B.U.S. as soon as they are fully programmed. The deep space probes are designated to be released from the space platform as soon as they are fully assembled. Dr. Roy Murdock intends to send each of them out in wormholes, each toward a distant galaxy, each one in search of a new home for the voyagers on the M.A.B.U.S. *Star Traveler*.

The probes can be more easily launched into the deep reaches of space from onboard the platform. In the weightlessness of space, they are free from the atmospheric drag and gravity of Earth. The probes are loaded aboard shuttles and ultimately transported up to the waiting platform. In the weightlessness of high Earth orbit, completely free of gravity, they will be able to send the probes out into the far reaches of space unhindered by the gravitational pull of the planet below, thus saving immense quantities of fuel needed to break free of the Earth's gravitational attraction. When ready to launch, the probes are placed immediately into wormholes and sent on their way while still inside the space platform.

They will launch the probes as soon as feasibly possible. Once the last of the two remaining observatories are shut down, there will not be any more information coming in and they will only have the older data to go by so they are pressed for time.

"They need to find somewhere to send M.A.B.U.S. very soon, if it's going to go anywhere at all," she says to Jensin. "They are going to send out probes to explore the eleven closest star systems that we know definitely have planets."

"What about that new one they discovered a couple of years ago?" Bob asks. "The one obscured by Proxima Centauri. Ah, what the heck was the name? The one that they theorized for decades should be there. Ari something or other. They said they think that system might have planets."

"I know the one you mean. Arilium, no, Arilias. Yeah, that's the one. The Arilias system. However, it's more than forty-five light-years away. I don't think they're even considering that one," Georgia replies.

"I was just thinking out loud," Jensin says. "It's probably way out of our reach anyway."

"Come on, Wonder Boy, we have work to do," she says, placing both hands on his slim shoulders from behind him. Squeezing gently, she turns to leave.

"Georgia?" he says.

"Yes, Bob."

"Have you thought about it?"

"About what, Robert?"

"The end. About what you're going to do when the time finally comes."

"By that time I'll be in my eighties, and by all rights I should be sitting in a rocking chair on my porch, watching the sun set for the very last time."

"Bull!" he says, and she sees he is truly upset. "You'll only be at the midpoint of your life. You would still have many more years ahead, if only…I thought a lot about it yesterday, and I…we…I can't…I don't…I won't give up yet. There is so much more I need to do. So much more I want to do. So much…I want…but…I'm going to keep going for as long as I possibly can, but when the time comes…I…I…I just don't want to be alone."

"I'll always be here with you, Bob. You know that!" she says, placing her hand softly on the back of his neck.

"That's not what I mean!" he growls, turning away from her. She hears him mutter something under his breath. Something about "never have" or something about "probably never will." He falls back into the envelope of his work. Georgia Simone walks slowly back to her office. She has never seen Robert Jensin this distraught before, and it worries her. This whole project has been pivoting around that brilliant mind of his, and they cannot afford to have it unravel now. Not at this crucial time.

She is about to turn and go back to him, back to the young man she has come to look on as the son she could never have, and thought it was better to let him be alone right now. Her fondness for him has increased over the years they have worked together, and she has come to be able to read much into his actions and moods. He has also grown very close to her, trusting her more than anyone else he has ever known.

She believes she knows what is really at the seat of the problem, but there is nothing she can do about it. Not now, probably not ever. "However, at this time, he needs to get away from here," she says to herself. "He needs to get away very soon before we lose him completely."

The first of many assemblages of the transponders are loaded aboard the shuttles, bound for the M.A.B.U.S. space station. Also aboard along with the transponders are several deep space probes ready for launch and, in addition to the hardware, one unkempt lab technician by the name of Robert A. Jensin, with the full blessings of Georgia Simone.

Georgia Simone had cleared everything with Dr. Roy Murdock before issuing the orders for Jensin to join the M.A.B.U.S. station. Explaining Jensin's state of mind, Murdock was in full agreement that Bob needed a change in venue. "Couldn't you just give him a job cleaning lab rat cages over in bio-med or something? I can't say that it will be a pleasure to see him again. You know how much he gets under my skin. However, as you have stated numerous times, we really need him. I think I will be able to force myself to put up with him for a little while. Frankly, he's the brightest star we have in this abyss of uncertainty," he communicates back to her.

Dr. Roy Murdock and Ensign Susan Morgan return from one of their many routine meetings, neither one of them wanting to discuss what happened in the passageway last week, although Murdock wishes it would happen all over again.

Murdock breaks the silence. "The latest reports are in from the bio-labs concerning the live experiments with wormholes. All the tests were successful with no signs of after effects. They have sent hundreds of animals into the wormholes and retrieved them all without problems. The three human volunteers sent in a number of times, each for a longer duration limited only by the stored air available inside the probes they occupied, showed no ill effects. With M.A.B.U.S. making its own air, there is no limit to the duration."

"I'm glad to hear that," Susan answers. "That's something I never even thought about. How crossing the dimensional barrier into a wormhole might affect life."

"We didn't make too much noise about that fact, in order to keep everyone's spirits up, but it was a great concern," Murdock adds. "If only inanimate objects could cross the barrier, all our planning and work would have been in vain. Now we know living organisms can cross over and return without problems."

"By the way, we're going to have a guest," he announces to Ensign Morgan. "You'll need to prepare yourself for this fellow. He is unlike anyone else you have ever met in your entire life. He is one of the most brilliant minds the world has ever spawned, but he's definitely…how should I put it…different. He's…well, you'll see when you meet him. Mere words just cannot cover it."

The shuttle docks inside the M.A.B.U.S. platform's hanger. Dr. Roy Murdock and Ensign Susan Morgan wait at the hatch of the air lock for the arrival of Robert Jensin. As the hatch opens, they are suddenly confronted with a one hundred and sixty-two pound living projectile careening over their heads, bouncing off the bulkhead behind them and heading straight back at them again. Murdock frantically grabs Jensin's clothes before he smashes into the rapidly closing air-lock hatch.

"Where the hell are your gravity boots?" he asks.

"Right here, sir," Jensin says, pulling the pair of boots from under his armpits.

"Robert! Boots…feet. Feet in boots. Boots on deck with feet in THEM!" Murdock turns and sees Susan Morgan doubled over in laughter, trying her best not to wet herself.

"Robert, I would like you to meet Ensign Morgan, my liaison." Murdock starts to break up. "Susan, this is Bob Jensin," At that, Murdock totally loses it and joins her in laughing. Bob Jensin, realizing the comedy of what had just happened, joins in with them both.

"Welcome aboard, Bob," Murdock says when he was finally able to speak again. "Welcome!" Susan repeats, wiping the tears from her eyes and extending her hand to Jensin.

"Hi, it's a pleasure," he says slowly, rotating within the confines of the air lock, continuing to struggle to get his gravity boots fastened. Susan is suddenly gone again, wrapped up in a total fit of hysterical laughter.

"Well, Bob, I guess you made a good first impression," Murdock says. "We'll show you to your cabin. Where's your stuff?"

"Stuff? I was supposed to bring things with me?" Jensin asks. Susan loses it for the third time.

"Never mind," Murdock says. "We'll find whatever you need someplace aboard." Continuing in their laughter, they make their way to Jensin's quarters, Murdock takes Susan's arm and whispers in her ear, "If you ever teach him how to fly, I'm going to kill you very, very slowly!" Once more, Susan cracks up.

"He's precious! Where on earth did you ever find him?" she says as she and Murdock leave Jensin's stateroom. "I can't believe he actually survived down on Earth!"

"Don't let him fool you. That young man is one of the greatest minds there ever was. He might forget to tie his shoes, but he knows where every single piece of whatever is needed to fit together to make everything in the universe happen, and knows in what order to pick up those pieces so they will fit. Without him we would be nowhere—nowhere near as far as we have come in our outreach to the stars. He's given us the push we needed to go forward."

"Wow," is all she can think to say. "That nerd?"

"That nerd, as you so inappropriately put it, has done the most to further our endeavors to find a way to escape the devastation to come as well as having to live with the realization that he was the one who discovered it was going to happen in the first place, so cut him a little slack…please!"

"Him? He was the one? I'm sorry, Dr. Roy, I didn't know. I really didn't know!" Murdock continued to fill Ensign Susan Morgan in on the story of the nerd, Robert Jensin, and the magnitude of his accomplishments in the scope of the mission facing them all.

Later, Susan Morgan finds Robert Jensin struggling desperately to get the door to his cabin to stay closed. "Here," she says. "The hinges have springs so that the hatch is either open and against the bulkhead or shut all the way. Just pull it straight out and listen for it to latch and it will stay closed."

"Thanks," he says, unconsciously moving to push back the glasses that have not slipped down his nose in the weightlessness of the space station since he arrived. "I'm on my way to find Dr. Murdock. It's that way, right?" he points down the passageway. Susan extends her finger in the opposite direction and smiles.

"Come on, I'll show you where he is," she says. "So, you're the one who came up with the vital communications link we so desperately need? I hope you'll let me see how it works sometime. Here we are," she says to him. They briskly enter the work area where Murdock, Lieutenant Southern and numerous technicians are busy setting up the deep space probes for launching. Jim Southern is to be working side by side with Robert Jensin on the communications end of the probe network.

"Hello, Robert, Susan," Murdock says without stopping the work he is in process of completing. "You all settled in and ready to get to work, Bob?"

"I'm always ready for a new challenge," he answers. Susan motions to Lieutenant Southern to join them.

"Bob, I'd like you to meet my brother," Susan says. This is Communications Specialist James Southern. Jim, say hello to Robert Jensin, the man that put the system together that you're working on. You two should have a lot in common."

"Your brother?" Murdock interjects, more than just a little bit surprised by her statement.

"Yeah," she states matter-of-factly. "Actually, my half-brother. When Jim was just an infant, his father was killed in an accident. Four years later, our mother married my father. I was born two years after that. I thought you knew we're related!"

"Actually, I didn't. I see now why he seemed so protective of you." Murdock felt like a real jackass. His dislike for Southern—although he kept it completely hidden—was totally unfounded all along. *This bit of news will make it a hell of a lot easier to work along side this young man*, he says to himself.

Lieutenant Southern and Jensin hit it off immediately. They were both engrossed in the innards of one of the probes when Murdock said, "Hey, Jim." Nothing but the butts of the two men were visible above the probe. "Don't let Jensin drop anything. He's probably figured out a way to make things fall in zero G's."

As if on cue, Bob Jensin pops his head out from the belly of the probe. A spanner slips from his hand and heads directly for the deck, bouncing once ever so slightly before resting motionless on the steel plates. Silence prevails while the eyes of the other three stare fixed on the wrench. Jensin reaches to retrieve the tool, laughing. "I magnetized it on one of the servo coils." He chuckles.

"I told you, Susan," Murdock says to her, standing there with her mouth open. "Don't ever underestimate him! About anything." He joins Jensin in laughing.

Georgia Simone crosses the lab complex, leafing through a stack of requisitions on her way to her office. She pauses momentarily, passing Robert Jensin's now empty chair in front of the computer. She sighs deeply, saying to herself, "Oh, Robert! I hope you are going to be all right up there.

Heaven knows you had enough trouble getting around down here."

Not very much to her surprise, she discovers she really longs to have him back where he belongs—here in the lab—and she does miss him terribly. She stares at his empty chair for a few seconds longer before proceeding to her office—feeling like she is going to cry. "Take good care of my boy, Dr. Murdock. Please, just take care of him," she whispers to herself, continuing to make her way into her office. Waiting on her desk is an envelope from Dr. Roy Murdock, chief administrator of the M.A.B.U.S. platform, security level 1. The envelope said "eyes only" supervisor, astrophysics lab: Georgia Simone.

Her heart falls. "He gone and gotten himself hurt, or worse!" she says aloud, tearing open the communiqué with trembling hands. "Why else would Murdock send this to me under security 1 cover. She begins to sit down, opening the pages of the letter, and commences to read the horrible news she knows those pages will contain. An instant later she is wrapped in a fit of hysterical laughter. The message to her described Bob Jensin's arrival on M.A.B.U.S. and his following antics in the work bay. Murdock had sent the communiqué via security so as not to embarrass Jensin. "He really does like you, Robert. As much as he pretends differently, he really does like you."

Breathing a sigh of relief, she begins to laugh all over again, thinking, *Only you, Bob! Only you could pull something like that wrench shtick on Murdock and get away with it. You're going to be all right, son! You are really going to do fine.*

The following weeks aboard the M.A.B.U.S. platform are fraught with work. The grueling fifteen-hour workdays are taxing on everyone. Jensin turned out to be a real dynamo, tackling each new challenge with a vigor that most, outside of Dr. Roy Murdock, had never seen before. Bob Jensin and Jim Southern had become the best of friends. Murdock, with his positional demands and constant meetings, had been able to see very little of Susan, and it tore at him. He really missed having her around. The revamping of the M.A.B.U.S. platform was proceeding at breakneck speed. The new hyper-sleep chambers were installed and tested, as well as the preliminary work started on the massive hydroponics garden designed to supply vegetable food for the journey. The last of the deep space exploration probes arriving with Robert Jensin were launched, and they were awaiting more probes to be sent up from Earth.

Murdock was just finishing up the last of the day's paperwork when he hears the melodious laughter of Susan advancing down the passageway. "I guess she's not alone," he thinks to himself. "Probably has her brother with her again. Oh well, you can't have it all."

A lovely voice calls through his door, following a gentle knock. "Dr. Roy! We're going down to put on the feedbag. Want to come along?"

"Be right with you," he replies. Opening his door, he expects to be met by the lovely ensign. To his surprise, she has already advanced several steps down the passageway. Instead, he is greeted by Lieutenant Southern. Taking a place beside her brother instead of next to the beautiful young woman he had expected to be walking with, he turns to follow after her. Up ahead of them, she is walking with Robert Jensin. Their hands clasped together, tightly holding on to each other. Jim leans over to him and whispers, "I think those two are becoming quite an item!"

He stole her away from me! he says to himself. *Jensin has actually stolen my Susan away from me!* He breaks into a broad smile when he at last realizes what a fool he has been. *I'm old enough to be her father.* This was the one shattering revelation he had been blind to—although she had been foremost in his mind day and night, she had only looked on him as a friend, a father figure.

That one delightful kiss had occurred in her time of need. A fluke. He just happened to be in the right place at the right time.

Damn, he thinks. *How can an old man like me feel this much desire and passion for someone he's only known for a short time, someone who is actually a stranger? Moreover, finding myself thinking more about her than even the work I have to do. Maybe there is a slight glimmer of hope for this species. Maybe the need for each other is strong enough to give us the sufficient drive to do what is necessary to see us through this mess. Way to go, Bob!*

He turns to Lieutenant Jim Southern and says, "Between you and me, Jim, as chief administrator, I'm entitled to bend a few rules. After chow, why don't you come back to my stateroom? I have a couple of un-gelatinized soupers filled with 86-year-old scotch. We can toast your sister's newfound romance."

A half a million miles above its surface, Dr. Roy Murdock, Ph.D., came back down to Earth. Walking behind the two young lovers, watching them march along hand in hand down the main passageway in front of him, his eyes continued to gaze upon the lovely Ensign Susan Morgan, still admiring the view as much as ever, but with a completely new perspective on what he was viewing.

"Way to go, Bob!"

Chapter 18

The torrential rain was falling in heavy sheets, whipped by the wind. Georgia Simone is finishing the last of the day's paperwork. Without the constant, invaluable assistance of Robert Jensin, her workload has increased greatly. Exhausted beyond the point of being able to think clearly, she prepares to head home for a long overdue sleep. In the pocket of her coat is a new relaxation chip cartridge she plans to play once she gets in bed. After such a long day, anything out of the ordinary might help to ease the tensions of the work-a-day world.

Ducking quickly from under the overhang of the lab's entrance, she rushes to her vehicle. All attempts at trying not to get soaked are useless because the incessant rain is blown at her almost sideways. Her umbrella is useless. Once inside her transport, she struggles to remove her sopping wet outer garment. Feeling the audio chip in her pocket, she removes it to keep it as dry as possible. "For what they charge for these things nowadays, I don't want the rain to ruin it now," she says aloud. Starting the turbo-motor, she places the chip on the dashboard and her drenched topcoat on the seat beside her. She shivers and waits for the heater in the transport to warm her enclosure as the rainwater drips onto the carpeting from her drenched overcoat.

Her vehicle is an older model, one of the first in a series to be equipped with auto-drive. It was all she could afford at the time, buying it secondhand. It has served her well for the last few years, taking her back and forth to work each day with the occasional shopping trip for groceries or clothing. It may not have been meticulously maintained, but it started each time she needed it, and it always got her where she had to go. She can now well afford a newer model, but why? "This one still works just fine," she would say.

Leaving the parking area, she turns onto the main artery and heads toward Highway 73, the road home, and to her warm bed. She heads up the on-ramp, reaching for the auto-drive switch, flipping it on, something that is not recommended for such adverse weather conditions like tonight. Her vehicle accelerates. The sensors onboard her transport detect the poor road conditions and engage the governor, which prevents the vehicle from traveling any faster than 130 miles per hour, about half the usual highway speed limit of 250 mph. Her vehicle is traveling at a speed that is still unsafe for tonight's terrible weather.

Her transport vehicle settles into the center travel lane and she leans back in her seat. At this rate of travel, it will take somewhat longer for her to get home. She will still be there in about thirty-five minutes. The rain obliterates her windshield. It does not matter, there is almost no one else on the road this time of night, and with auto-drive she doesn't need to see anyway. The transport has full vehicle avoidance, and it will also alert her when she is approaching her pre-programmed exit, automatically change into the slow lane and decelerate. She will then switch off the auto-drive and take manual control of her transport and drive to her home.

She looks over at the audio chip she had just purchased today. Curious as to what it sounds like, she slips it into the vehicle's sound system. Pleased by what she hears, she rests her head back against the seat's headrest and closes her eyes. The quiet strains of white sounds blended with soft background music soon lull her into a deep sleep. Her vehicle travels its straight path down Highway 73 at 130 miles per hour as the rain continues to pour down.

Twelve miles away, a bolt of lightening strikes an unmanned substation providing the signal for the auto-drive cables buried several inches below the highway pavement. A transformer shorts out and sparks. The breaker controlling the power to this stretch of road upon which Georgia Simone is traveling trips out, cutting signal to her transport. For the half second her vehicle searches for a signal before beginning emergency breaking, she continues at 130 miles per hour, sound asleep. The automatic breaking system engages and the danger alarm sounds. The transport continues straight, hydroplaning along the road, which curves slightly to the right. The left wheels of her vehicle contact the soft shoulder of the highway median. Her car continues to break—the tires on the left side begin to slide even faster on the wet grass, skidding sideways. The alarm still sounding, Georgia opens her reddened eyes in two slits. Instead of seeing the highway directly in front of her, she sees the roadway passing sideways through the front windshield.

Suddenly wide-awake, the last thing she sees through the driver's door window is the bridge abutment of the overpass for Highway 168, three miles from her home.

Georgia Simone will not have to worry about the long, arduous hours at the lab anymore. Her vehicle wraps itself around the immovable concrete pillar of the overpass at almost 100 miles per hour. Georgia Simone will no longer need to be concerned about the ever-expanding sun.

Dr. Roy Murdock sits somberly at the desk in his stateroom with his chin pressed down against his chest, eyes closed. In his hand he still holds the emergency communiqué from the home office. With a tremble in his voice, he clicks open the key on his intercom to summon Robert Jensin.

Chapter 19

The shuttle approaches near Earth orbit, readying for its three orbital fights skirting the atmosphere as it steadily slows in preparation for re-entry. Its four passengers sit in silence. Susan Morgan sits to Jensin's right, holding his hand tightly. He sits with his wet eyes closed. Murdock, on his left, has his hand on Bob's forearm. Jim Southern is sitting to the other side of Roy Murdock.

"I never got to tell her," Bob sobs.

"Tell her what?" Susan asks.

"About you. About us." He continued to breathe deeply between sighs. "I wanted to surprise her!" he said. "And about a lot of other things too! How much she meant to me. She was…was like…like family. Like a second mother to me! I never got to tell her." He began to sob anew.

Murdock squeezed his arm gently. "She knew, Bob. She knew how you felt about her," he said in comforting. "She knew about Susan also. I told her about your relationship a few weeks ago. Nobody had to tell her how much you cared for her, and one would have to be blind not to see how fond she was of you. She was as heartsick as a mother sending her only child off to summer camp the day you left for M.A.B.U.S. With every communiqué from her there was an eyes-only packet asking about you," Murdock continued. "I've kept them all and brought them with me. You can have them if you want."

"I…I would like that very much," Jensin sighed. "But not yet. Not till after…" Susan placed her head on his thin shoulder…he began to weep again.

The transport ride back from the funeral was again in silence. Although she had never met Georgia Simone, Susan felt she had come to know her very well from all Jensin had told her, and she felt his pain and sorrow all the time she clung to his arm. Murdock tried hard to summon up the courage to touch on the important subject he had been wrestling with since they left the platform.

"Bob, there's something very pressing which we have to discuss right now. I know the timing stinks, but I must leave for M.A.B.U.S. tomorrow," he began. "We...all have to leave tomorrow. We desperately need a replacement for Georgia, and no one knows the workings of the lab better than you do. Would you consider picking up where she left off?" he asked. "We really need someone we can count on!"

"What about—" he asked, turning toward Susan Morgan. "What about—"

"She has to return to M.A.B.U.S. tomorrow, and Jim also. I know how much you two mean to each other, and I can't give you any guarantee, but I will promise to do all I can to get her assigned to a complex nearby. That is, if she has no objection to ground-based work and doesn't mind leaving her brother behind," Murdock says, turning toward her brother. "With what you've has learned about the QT's from Bob, you're much too valuable upstairs where you're needed most. Susan, what do you say?" he says, looking over at the young woman. Susan gazed deeply into Jensin's eyes, tears starting to show in her own.

"Working in outer space was always my life's ambition. I could think of nothing else, until I met you, Bob!" Turning to Murdock, she asked, "Do you really think you can swing it? I do love Bob so much!" Although he knew she did, it was the first time Murdock had heard her say it. It was also the first time Jensin had heard her use those words in the presence of anyone but himself. He kissed her.

"Do you really think you can get me assigned to a base near Bob? Where we might be together?"

"It may take a little while, but I think I have more than enough pull," he said, assuring her. He knew it was as good as done. With his authority in the program he had the power to send anyone wherever he wished. He could order Jensin to the position if he really had to, but preferred to give him the option. "What about you, Bob? Will you do it?"

"I guess so, if you really think I can handle it!" he replied with a tone of apprehension in his voice, still holding Susan close to him.

"After watching you work up on M.A.B.U.S., I have no doubts

whatsoever," Murdock answered. "I know it will seem like an eternity for you two young lovers, but it shouldn't take more than a couple of weeks and you will be back together again. I just want you both to promise that you will not elope. I want to be invited to the wedding!" He looked into Susan's deep brown eyes and said, "I want to get to kiss the bride." Her eyes lowered for just an instant before she smiled knowingly.

The shuttle taxied out to the launch area. Susan Morgan sat with her head back against the seat, her eyes closed. A single tear slid down her lovely cheek. Roy Murdock, doing some last minute sorting of the documents he would soon have to stow away for the flight, could not help but notice it. "It's only been ten minutes and I miss him already!" she sighs.

Murdock takes her soft hand in his and pats gently with his other. "It won't take long, my dear. I promise!" he says, releasing her hand, and then begins to pack up his paperwork. "You two will be back together before you know it. Or my name isn't Dr. Roy!" At his saying that, she laughed for the first time since the news about Georgia Simone arrived, and it made his heart feel glad again.

Lieutenant James Southern holds his sister's other hand, gazing out the window. The shuttle, gaining speed, lifts off from the Earth spaceport. This would be the last time he would see this sight.

Chapter 20

The mammoth amount of work needed continued unabated aboard the M.A.B.U.S. platform over the next several years. All endeavors centered mainly on making the station completely self-sufficient. When the time comes for M.A.B.U.S to depart, there would be no more provisions arriving from the dying Earth. The platform was nearing the point where it needed no outside supplier. The hydroponics gardens produced more than was needed for food and at the same time produced more oxygen than was needed for the more than ample crew.

Murdock would find himself spending less and less time aboard the space platform. He was needed more often back on Earth once the reports from the first deep space probes began to arrive. He continued to make numerous trips back to the platform as time progressed, overseeing the work in progress. Occasionally he was accompanied by Mr. and Mrs. Robert Jensin.

Murdock did get the opportunity to kiss the bride. Tenderly, on Susan's right cheek, while shaking Bob's hand in congratulations. Unfortunately, Susan's brother, Jim Southern, who was also Bob Jensin's best man, would not be returning to the M.A.B.U.S. platform. He would be joining Georgia Simone. The shuttlecraft he had boarded for his return to the platform shortly after the wedding had crashed on takeoff. There were no survivors.

The initial reports from the probes so far have not been promising. Of the eleven reachable star systems that have planets, the closest six solar systems had been explored. Only one had a planet that might harbor life. The small rover-landers are dispatched to the surface for further study. It would be two weeks before the information could be retrieved. Everyone wished the earlier probes had the more refined and improved QT communications systems that evolved over the past few years. The data from the rovers needed to be transmitted to the mother probe via normal radio signal and processed. The main probe could only receive data when it was overhead in its orbit of the planet.

At last, the data began to arrive. Surface median temperature 106 degrees F. A little high, but doable! Atmosphere 16 percent oxygen, 30 percent nitrogen, 12 percent carbon dioxide, 13 percent methane, 20 percent ammonia, 9 percent inert gasses, no water detected. Another washout!

It would be another seven months before the next series of probes were due to return to real space and begin exploring two additional star systems in search of a safe haven for M.A.B.U.S. The search continued for additional solar systems that might harbor planets using the combined resources of all the earthly and lunar observatories as well as the last remaining operational one docked alongside the M.A.B.U.S. platform. The largest of the three, separated from the platform would remain in service until a final destination is determined.

Additional probes are dispatched, implemented solely with equipment to do a broad search for any star systems with planets beyond the thirty light-year distance. It will take almost two years for these three stage explorers to reach that point, traveling at eighteen times light speed. Two long years before there will be any news if the remaining five series of probes, which are still traveling in wormholes, find or fail to find a suitable planet.

The sets of probes launched in groups of six allow for any failures once the mechanical explorers return to real space. Traveling at near half-light speed in real space, there have been instances of collisions with natural objects in space. Some of the other probes ceased to function for unknown reasons.

One series of probes was sent to explore the region beyond Proxima Centauri. The probes would take five long Earth months to pass this near star and would not begin reporting until a year and a half later. Until that time the only news from the probes would be status reports from the onboard equipment as each traveled through its separate wormhole.

Reports begin to arrive from probe series seven and eight. No inhabitable planets found. Only three of the eleven original sets of probes remain in wormholes, streaking toward their distant star system destinations. Only three more chances of finding a place close enough to be even slightly sure they might be reached by the M.A.B.U.S. platform traveling at four and a half times light speed. That is, getting to the star system while the crew was still young enough to set up a colony. The first of these three is due to break out of its wormhole in eleven days. There is nothing more to do now but wait.

The work continues on the space platform. Day by day, M.A.B.U.S. is becoming increasingly self-sufficient. The hydroponics garden is now supplying 100 percent of the food base for the onboard crew, producing more than is being consumed; the surplus is freeze-dried for later use.

Number nine probe set is breaking out of its respective wormholes. There is no star system in the vicinity. A slight miscalculation has sent the probes more than six billion miles off course. The probes do not have the necessary equipment on board to return to the wormhole, and even if they did, there was no way to direct the wormhole's path accurately without the extensive computers needed to calculate the alignment of the e-matter electrons.

Traveling in real space at the maximum safe speed, it would take the probes more than eight years to reach their intended solar system. Far longer than it would take a new set of probes to arrive using wormholes. Number nine probe configuration would be left to wander the cosmos long after the Earth is gone.

Preparations got underway to launch a new set of probes to replace number nine just as the reports from the tenth series began to arrive. Again, to everyone's disappointment, no inhabitable planets are found. Only one last set of probes remained, and another new set is being readied to launch. These are the last two chances to find a new home among the nearer star groups. If these last tries prove fruitless, the entire success of the mission will be in jeopardy. The nearest star system thought to possibly contain planets after that is more than forty light-years distant. If the Arilias system does indeed have planets and one is suitable, it will take M.A.B.U.S. over ten years traveling in a wormhole to reach it.

The reports from probe eleven and the replacement for probe nine arrive within a week of each other. Both prove negative. There are no planets within a distance of thirty-five light-years capable of supporting human life. All that is left to do is wait on the probes that are still searching farther out and to continue to ready the M.A.B.U.S. station for a much longer journey.

The idea of equipping M.A.B.U.S. with additional boosters to enable the platform to travel faster is broached. Years of study and countless experiments conclude this to be infeasible. The immense mass of M.A.B.U.S. would require several boosters of extreme size to accelerate the platform beyond terminal velocity. Such sizable boosters—the mass of which, when jettisoned into and subsequently re-entering real space and time, would create a devastating shock wave beyond calculation. Even if only a small portion of the resulting shockwave is vortexed into the wormhole—with the cataclysmic force propelling it and nothing to slow it down, the chances are better than 60 percent it would have enough energy to overtake the platform—totally destroying M.A.B.U.S. and all aboard before it dissipates. M.A,B.U.S. is limited to its initial terminal velocity of 4.5 times light speed.

There was a certain amount of trepidation in sending the probes to the Arilias system. For the wormholes to reach the central part of the Arilias system, they will have to pass directly through Proxima Centauri itself. The same path M.A.B.U.S. will have to take if it is to travel to that distant star system.

No probe had ever intentionally been sent directly through the heart of a star. No one knows if the wormholes are capable of surviving such an encounter. One additional probe is sent along, with the six parallel probes. This last one will travel at a speed equal to the maximum speed of the M.A.B.U.S. platform. Its sole mission is to see if a probe traveling at the same speed as M.A.B.U.S. could withstand the massive pressures inside the nuclear furnace of a star for that longer period of time. If the other six probes survive, this one would see if traveling at a much-reduced speed made any difference. If the others make it through, this last one would reach the surface of Proxima Centauri almost two years later. At about the same time, the six previous probes will begin to report their findings, if they do indeed survive.

The first signs of climatic changes have begun to reveal themselves. The mean temperature of the entire globe has risen by seven degrees. There are already signs of the polar ice caps melting. The numerous glaciers throughout both polar areas have begun to move at alarmingly increased rates. Massive sections of the Antarctic ice shelf are breaking free and floating northward into warmer waters. Sea level has risen more than three feet, inundating many low-lying coastal regions. What was once New Orleans is completely under water, as well as much of what was once the state of Florida.

Mighty rivers such as the Mississippi, the Nile, Ganges and Yellow Rivers have all but stopped their flow due to the encroaching seas. Widespread flooding is rampant over the entire globe. With the stagnant rivers comes a more devastating enemy…disease.

Outbreaks of pestilence, long thought to be eradicated, such as cholera, dysentery, typhoid and other water-born maladies, as well as the dreaded ebola, lassa fever, Marberg virus, Bolivian hemorrhagic fever, and a slew of new hantaviruses begin to rear their ugly heads from the microbial soup that the air and water have become. The widespread flooding contaminating many of the water supplies is accompanied by the breakdown of most of the world's sewage treatment facilities due to the tremendous increase in earth tremors.

The vast number of unburied corpses in the ruined cities is compounding the ever-growing threat of pandemic outbreaks. Along with the increased incidence of disease came another threat that would prove to be a blessing in disguise.

The sun began erupting with monstrous solar flares, prompted by the now huge solar storms on the surface. These immense flares would regularly reach out into space to distances much greater than any previous distance recorded. The solar eruptions toward Earth have thus far been minor. Some of the solar flares have reached tens of millions of miles out into space.

Following each massive solar flare is a subsidence of solar activity and a slight reduction in the expansion rate of the sun's surface. The expulsion of such a massive amount of solar matter causes the sun to calm slightly after each explosion. Normally a solar flare will fall back into the sun, but these new storms are of such a magnitude that the energy continues out into space. As these solar storms persist, the reduction in the sun's expansion rate adds a little more time for the preparations to leave our doomed planet. However, if a large magnitude flare should erupt directly toward the Earth, all endeavors to leave will be in vain. The planet would be reduced to cinders in a matter of minutes.

These solar storms also wreck havoc with worldwide communications. Normal radio transmission became an impossibility with the increased solar activity. Quantum teleportation is the only reliable form of communication left that is not affected by the heavy magnetic pulses from the solar storms. The increased solar winds and higher-than-normal radiation levels make space travel even more dangerous. The M.A.B.U.S. platform was fortunate to be shielded from these solar winds by the Earth. If it had been in any other orbit, the platform might well have been rendered useless by the radiation.

The shuttlecraft ferrying personnel and supplies to and from the platform are forced to forgo the three orbit reentry and instead use a spiral inbound flight pattern on the night side of the globe to utilize the protection of the Earth's silhouette. The craft drop into the atmosphere blanketed by the earth's protective shadow.

Chapter 21

September 17, 2042

The sets of probes sent into the far reaches of space have all reported back with negative results—except one. The last series of six probes were sent toward the Arilias system. All six explorers passed through the center of Proxima Centauri without any problems. The slower-moving, trailing probe is creeping along at the snail's pace of only 858,000 miles per second, nearing the star's surface. When the probe enters the segment of its wormhole that passes through the center of the near-earth star, it will spend an eternity of just over thirty seconds in the bowels of that inferno. Considerably longer than the eight and a half seconds the previous six probes endured as they passed through unscathed. If the probe survives, it will relay vital information back to Earth concerning conditions inside the wormhole as it passes through the fiery innards of the star.

The other probes dispatched to additional distant solar systems failed to find any star systems with habitable planets any closer than nearly one hundred light-years from Earth, and even in those they did find, few were up for speculation. If there is nowhere to go in the Arilias system, the project is finished, and so is humankind.

The final probe approaches Proxima Centauri. All eyes are on the telemonitors as the probe—traveling in its wormhole—begins to enter the fiery celestial innards of this neighboring flare star. Sensors onboard relay information to the QT transmitters. There is no change detected within the wormhole. Even the colossal pressure and astronomical temperature of the heart of this huge star are not great enough to cross the dimensional barrier of the wormhole. If the M.A.B.U.S. platform is to follow this same path, it will be able to pass directly through the center of a star and not even singe the paint on its name.

The Arilias probes begin to report—one by one. Of twelve planets, six are too cold for human life, and five are too close to the central star and far too hot to endure. The sixth planet orbiting the distant star is examined. This last orb is found to be thirty percent larger than the Earth and shows some promise. All the probes are brought into the proximity of this one planet for extensive exploration. This is the last hope for the M.A.B.U.S. expedition. The landers are sent down to the planet's surface. A total of twelve auxiliary probes gently set down in various sections on the surface below.

The sixth planet from the star named Arilias is the last chance for a place to land a colony. The report reads: Oxygen 30 percent, nitrogen 51 percent, carbon dioxide 9 percent, inert gases 10 percent, abundant liquid water and water vapor, no toxicity detected. Surface mean temperature 82 degrees. M.A.B.U.S. has a target at last.

Chapter 22
Time for Me to Move On

Seismic activity reached an unprecedented scale at a time when Dr. Roy Murdock was preparing to address the World Scientific Committee for the last time. Massive earthquakes and smaller tremors have become an everyday occurrence. The sun's surface grows closer to the Earth, increasing the gravitational pull on the tectonic plates around the globe.

"Good afternoon," he says, placing his celluloids on the podium. "I'm sure by now you all have been briefed about the discovery of Arilias-6, the intended target for the M.A.B.U.S. platform. Unfortunately, once the platform departs, it will take more than ten years for it to reach the Arilias star system. We here, all of us remaining behind, will never know if the mission is successful. It will still be several years until the platform is fully manned and all testing is complete. We should, however, learn if it survives its passage through Proxima Centauri. With the recalculated time period, we plan to send M.A.B.U.S. off in a maximum of nine years from this date—sooner if conditions on Earth deteriorate as time progresses or the station is completely ready ahead of schedule. Based on that date, the Earth will no longer harbor any life long before the platform breaks out of the wormhole."

"It is with that thought in mind that we must now turn our attention to selecting and training the crew for this historic journey. The platform will support a maximum of eighteen hundred crew members. We will need to train at least twice that number to insure we have a complete crew as the departure date draws near. Selection of the candidates will commence immediately. All nations will be screening prospective personnel based on their previous training and experience, and most importantly, their immunity to the diseases that have become rampant. These people are going to be very green as far as space travel experience. The maximum cut-off age at time of departure has been agreed upon as no more than thirty years old."

"You have in front of you the criteria for selection. When you return to your respective countries, please give much thought to your choices. Those you ultimately choose are going to be all that is left of the human race. All prospective crew members will be trained as though all are to be going. When the launch date nears, it will be up to you to decide who of these highly trained personnel goes and who stays behind. This will not be an easy task. Nationalities and politics will not be a factor in this selection. The best and most qualified are to be selected to man the space traveler when the time comes to leave."

"Dr. Murdock, you state that it will be up to us to decide on the crew," the chairman of the standing committee asks, "but surely you will be playing a major part in that difficult decision?"

"I'm afraid that will not be possible," Murdock replies. "My work on the M.A.B.U.S. platform is finished. The project is in the hands of much younger and more capable people now."

"You will still be able to add some insight to our final choices?" the chair continues.

"I'm sorry!" Murdock adds. "My health is rapidly deteriorating, and I may leave this life long before the selection is completed and training has even begun. I believe I will be fortunate enough, at least, to have passed on before the actual end of the world arrives. My physicians have informed me that I will most likely not be of any additional use to you, the platform, or the world for very much longer. I'm afraid I will be leaving you all behind in a very short period of time—my doctors say less than one year."

"Dr. Murdock, Dr. Murdock!" the voices echo.

Waving their raised hands aside, he says, "I will continue to assist this project for as long as possible, but I feel it is necessary to remove myself as head of the M.A.B.U.S. project—effective immediately." A new wave of pain shoots through every fiber of his body. "I cannot continue in my present capacity due to the fact I am becoming less able to endure any physical activity, and I have reached a point where I am no longer able to be completely sure of my judgment."

THE WANDERERS

The years of constant shifts between weightlessness in space and Earth's gravity have taken their toll on the aging Dr. Roy Murdock. The ground begins to shake beneath the feet of those present in the conference room. The lights sway—a heavy oak table slowly skitters along the floor, pressing several delegates tight against the far wall. It is only a mild tremor, something everyone has become used to. The vibrations add more to the pain Murdock is feeling, severely aggravating the agony in his leg joints; he struggles to keep his balance as the building sways.

On his last trip up to the platform, Roy Murdock had an extremely difficult time adjusting to the conditions onboard. Upon returning to Earth, he saw his doctors. His heart is dangerously enlarged. All his joints have begun to deteriorate, wracked by arthritis. He is also bordering on renal failure. One more trip into space would probably kill him. His mind and spirit are still willing, but his body has totally quit on him. The doctors have given him eight months, at the outside, before complete heart failure if he continues at his present pace. A fact that, until today, he has kept hidden from even his wife.

A multiple transplant—heart and kidneys, is one option offered to him, but with the tremendous amount of disease and infection rampant in the world today; he would most likely die a more horrible death a short time later. He might gain one or two weeks, maybe a couple of months of life, but he would never be able to leave the hospital before some microbe attacked, totally destroying him. No, the transplant road is one devastating path he would, by choice, not travel. That option was definitely not in the picture. He would not put his family through that ordeal.

He knows he must tell Jannene what the doctors have informed him. He did not know how he was going to tell her, but it would have to be tonight. She has the right to know, and she should not have to hear it from someone else! *If only the pain would go away for just a little while*, he thought. The ground shook once more beneath his feet, and the pain increased.

Only the newer buildings, those built after the massive earthquakes of 2033 and built to new seismic standards, have survived intact. Most of the other older structures have been reduced to nothing more than rubble. Even these super-strong scientifically designed buildings are showing signs of weakness and fatigue after years of constant shifting and shaking. The world is becoming a massive outdoor arena. People are afraid to enter any building still standing for fear it will collapse in around them at any moment.

Roy Murdock left the science conference with a heavy burden. He must confront his wife with the news he has kept to himself. The stark revelation that he will not be around much longer weighs heavily on his mind. Even more important, he must meet with his eldest son-in-law, or better yet, with both sons-in-law, to discuss the times ahead. It is necessary that they do something for him before the final time approaches. He has a small key in his pocket, a key to unlock the door of a special compartment in his desk at his home.

He had a chemist friend concoct these painless but lethal adhesive patches he keeps securely locked away, after it became indisputable there was no way he and his family were going to be able to escape the final devastation. One of these small patches placed anywhere on bare skin would begin to work immediately. The body's own heat would cause a release of a strong sedative that is immediately absorbed into the skin. Within three to five minutes, the person wearing the patch falls into a deep, comatose sleep. As the person continues to sink deeper and deeper into the arms of Morpheus, a deadly poison is released—also absorbed through the skin—slowly and painlessly stopping the beating of the heart. You peacefully slip into oblivion.

Murdock is thinking to himself that he might need to use one long before the others choose to if his pain continues to increase at the rate is has been of late. He will hold out for as long as possible, as long as he can be of some use to the project, as long as he is capable of tolerating the constant pain. Jannene would never know of its use until it was time for her to use one of them herself.

She would only assume he had simply died in his sleep. She has seen his deteriorating condition, knows about his constant pain. Tonight she will learn how ill he really is and how little time he has left. If the time comes when he can no longer function, he will consider using one. For now, he will bravely endure the pain, taking it one day at a time, doing whatever little he is still capable of doing to aid the project to its completion.

Chapter 23
Eenie, Meenie, Minie, Mo

Mother Nature made the job of selecting candidates for the M.A.B.U.S. voyage somewhat easier. Diseases that have been ravaging the entire globe have become a natural selector. Every possible crewmember is tested for antibodies to all the plagues rampant through out the world, and retested as new ones developed. Originally chosen based on their training and experience, strength and apparent health—the field of over eighty thousand possible choices is selectively narrowed down to a minuscule number of only six thousand two hundred by the smallest organisms on the planet.

Each of the prospective choices has to be immune to the illnesses taking such a devastating toll on the rest of the population. Blood tests narrowed the field dramatically in a very short period. There could be nothing left to chance. If even one of the prospective crew carried a microbe in their system that could possibly surface later, there would be disastrous consequences. Immunity became one of the most important, if not the most crucial, of the prime requirements for selection.

The best of the best begin their training, a rigorous regime designed to weed out many more from the selected group. The continuation of the human race is at stake. Extensive physiological evaluations, a multitude of medical and physical tests, psychological screening, as well as extended periods in hyper-sleep are all used to narrow the field even more. The group of candidates is now down to a paltry two thousand eight hundred. When the final day comes, one thousand of these superb specimens of the human race will remain behind to die along with the rest of the world.

Roy Murdock managed to hang on long enough to see the final selection of all the trainees. Up to the time he was reduced to a total invalid, he was active to the best of his physical limitations in aiding the M.A.B.U.S. project. Now, in his extremely weakened condition, he has been diagnosed with drug-resistant tuberculosis. Another devastating disease thought to be only a memory. He made his decision and called for his eldest son-in-law, Greg, Linda's husband and father of his only grandchild.

Totally bedridden, he speaks in whispers to his oldest daughter's husband. "I…I cannot let this condition spread to the rest of you. I need your help, son. You know what to do. Promise me you will not tell Jannene until it is time for all of you. It will go easier for her now if she doesn't know. I would do this myself if only I had the strength to get out of my bed. And I want you to tell Bob Jensin…please make sure he and Susan are set for that event, if you know what I mean?"

"I understand," Greg says, holding the dying man's hand. Turning, he proceeds to Murdock's desk, clutching the small key his father-in-law entrusted to him only weeks before.

Chapter 24

July 8, 2043

The family and friends of Dr. Roy Murdock gather in his home, waiting for the authorities to come and claim his remains. There is a quiet sadness mingled with a sense of relief that his suffering is finally over. Jannene Murdock sits in her chair, wiping the tears from her eyes, comforted by her two daughters. Robert and Susan Jensin stand talking with Murdock's younger son-in law while Greg quietly slips away to the great man's bedroom.

Roy Murdock lay in quiet stillness, his son-in-law taking hold of his hand for the last time. "Goodbye, Pops," he says, carefully removing the small adhesive patch from the inside of Murdock's upper right arm. "We'll all be joining you soon. Until then," he says, laying Murdock's arm gently back down on the bed beside him. Lois joins him, clutching him tightly—they hug. Greg carefully rolls the small patch into a tight ball, making sure he only touches the outside surface.

Chapter 25
Death Pangs

The sun continues to pulsate, its surface growing closer and closer to the Earth, now causing dramatic climate changes over the entire Earth's surface. The fluctuation in the sun's gravitational pull on the Earth, combined with the seismic activity, is causing numerous tidal waves—some minor—others of catastrophic proportions devastating entire coastal regions. Whole cities are inundated. The loss of life is inestimable. Cities are awash with the swell of the oceans. The people flee inland, but there is nowhere to go.

Areas where the tidal fluctuation was once only a few feet between high and low are now experiencing tide surges of over thirty feet. The global temperature of the world has risen another several degrees. The ice caps continue to melt at an alarming rate, raising the sea level even higher. The earth's climate is in complete turmoil. There are heavy rains in desert areas, drought in tropical rain forests.

The continual changes in the diameter of the sun's surface caused the moon to shift its orbit around the Earth, deviating by thousands of miles from its normal path, causing additional pull on the Earth's surface. This increased pull, along with that of the sun, is causing the tectonic plates to break free of the last locking points holding them in place for the past millennia. These new, more frequent earthquakes make anything recorded before seem like a gentle fluff of the bed covers.

What had been previously recorded on the Richter scale could not even begin to compare to the pangs the Earth was now undergoing. The violent movements of the Earth's crust being felt at this time could not even be calculated at the levels registered on that low scale. The Mississippi River began to flow northward, a mixture of fresh and saltwater surging as far north as Missouri, flooding the entire region along both banks. All the major rivers throughout the world are experiencing the same inundation by the seas and oceans, their direction of flow reversed. There is widespread flooding everywhere.

With the slipping of the earth's plates came the increased and devastating tremors, the likes of which have never been felt before in the history of this world. Entire cities slipped into the rising seas. Buildings previously considered earthquake-safe disintegrate like a house of cards. Almost no manmade structures remain standing.

No one feels safe inside their homes, and no one is really safe outdoors. The Earth is splitting wide open in random fissures that rival the Grand Canyon, but with molten magma seething at the bottom instead of a river of water. The world is rapidly tearing itself apart at its seams, and its people have nowhere to run. There is rioting and looting everywhere, but it does the looters little good. The world is dying and there will not be time to enjoy their spoils. Famine is prevalent in every place on the globe. People are willing to kill for a small piece of dried protein supplement. Those fortunate unfortunates who manage to survive the storms, quakes, disease and other devastations are destined to endure the increasing temperatures and suffering that is still to come before the sun finally expands and snuffs out what little remains of humanity.

The lunar bases have now been abandoned. The major concern was that at any time the moon would be ripped from its Earth orbit and eventually pulled into the expanding sun. This fact forces all those remaining to abandon the protective moon bases, return home to Earth, and wait for the final days. M.A.B.U.S. must leave soon if it is to ever leave at all!

The crew for the platform—their training complete—is ready to begin boarding the one vessel which might be able to save them from the devastation and destruction surrounding them. The unanimous international decision of all governing bodies of the doomed planet Earth was to have the final selection of the crew done by lottery. Two main groups, one male and one female—divided into numerous sections, each comprising the various necessary fields of expertise needed aboard the *Star Traveler*. There would be an equal number of men and women aboard. If the human race survives, procreation will be left up to the remaining people on board, without the outside influence of nationalities or politics.

Much of the training needed was ultimately done aboard the platform itself, so through attrition, everyone left onboard the spacecraft was already a selected candidate for the voyage. The last of the final crew is chosen, and they begin boarding the transport shuttles taking them to the M.A.B.U.S. *Star Traveler*. The new "ark." The last hope of all humanity.

Launchings are delayed on a continuous basis because of earth tremors. Groups of twenty at a time are leaving on space transports, modified to hold the larger number of passengers as well as supplies. Some transports returning with relieved crew personnel who had not yet been selected to be part of the final departing members are disabled by hard landings on the shifting runways—never to fly again. The launchings are aimed for a rendezvous with the massive Earth orbiter as often as every forty-eight hours, or whenever the tremors subsided enough to allow the shuttles to get off the ground.

The urgency of the crew's departure is hastened by the continually growing riots of the general populace. No one wants to be left behind to die, but there is only so much room on the ship designed to take this small number beyond the cataclysm soon to inundate the Earth and the rest of the solar system. Those selected to depart board the shuttles waiting to take them up to the platform.

Although the *Space Traveler* is an immense ship, there is only room to accommodate eighteen hundred people and the needed supplies for the many years' journey out of the solar system and on to Arilias-6.

Much of the travel time will be spent in hyper-sleep, a form of suspended animation where body functions are slowed down to only ten percent of what they are when you're awake. Hyper-sleep has its limitations in that—as with regular sleep, the body is still functioning, but at a much slower rate—and it still has its needs.

Once the transports are unloaded, the supplies and equipment properly stored, most of the new arrivals are put immediately into hyper-sleep to conserve the ship's resources. The crew is replaced at a rate of thirty at a time now, and will continue to be replaced on the same schedule throughout the voyage. There might be cases of some of the crew having problems coming around after a long stretch of hyper-sleep.

Waking from such a deep comatose state is much like being awakened from dreamless sleep. The last thing to function properly is your mind. With hyper-sleep, however, it takes several hours for your brain to waken completely, and your motor functions are vastly impaired. The "new walkers," as we call them, would spend their first waking day ambling along the passageways, bumping into walls, objects and each other.

Everyone needs to be awakened after every twelve to fifteen days of hyper-sleep. Their semi-detached bodies still need nourishment and exercise. The waking process takes almost a full day in itself. This is an awkward full-time job for the skeleton crew of ninety people overseeing the ship's systems while we are stationary and, unfortunately, we will have to continue with this regiment for the duration of our long flight.

The crews will be rotated on three-month shifts, sleeping normal sleep during this twelve-week period. Half of the ninety would be on duty, and the other half sleeping or entertaining themselves as best they can, usually by helping the "new walkers." Those on duty will take over the tasks of maintaining the ship, doing whatever repairs are needed, tend to the gardens and wake the different groups of people as scheduled.

Aboard the space platform, we have modified our way of tracking time. We have saved some of Earth's time to use as guidelines. We still have twelve months, but with only thirty days each. Each day has thirty hours, divided into two fifteen-hour shifts. Months are numbered instead of named. It would be very strange to have a February 30th, but no December 31st.

Some individuals tolerate hyper-sleep better than others; a few are even able to pass the twenty-day mark. Including the two days they would be awake every two weeks, each of the crew would spend almost five years asleep between duty tours when the voyage starts. Upon resuming a fully awake status, most people have no recollection of the numerous times they were awakened during their stay in hyper-sleep.

Between one hundred and one hundred and fifty people need to be brought out of their sleep every day for a literal two-day stretch and allowed to move around for the needed exercise. During this time they receive nourishment before they are returned to hyper-sleep. A number of the newly awakened members of the crew would be required to replace others who have completed their three-month tour of duty. Those individuals are watched over more closely, assuring they have fully awakened before relieving their standing crew members.

At any given time, there are between two hundred and two hundred and fifty "semi-zombies" wandering around the ship. The off-duty crew is never at a loss for something to occupy their immediate attention.

In addition to herding the new walkers around, there is also the need to tend the massive onboard gardens. The green plants growing in this immense agricultural complex continuously replenish the oxygen for the ship as well as removing the carbon dioxide and, more importantly, recycling all the waste from the crew. This vast amount of vegetation will provide fresh air and food for the long and arduous journey ahead. Seeds from these plants will give the new settlers a good start on the distant planet they intend to make their new home.

The purified moisture given off by evaporation from the plants is reclaimed by scrubber dryers and returned to the drinking water supply for the crew. Nothing is wasted. Non-edible parts of plants are biodegradable and the nutrients returned to the new plantings.

Everything is grown using hydroponics. There is no soil. The plants grow in a three hundred and sixty-degree configuration along huge tubes of fibrous cellulose used to transfer the nutrient-rich "soup" to their roots. This vital ecosystem—though taking up much space in the ship—will increase the chances of the crew surviving the long and arduous voyage ahead.

As the departure date for M.A.B.U.S. approaches, the inevitable happens. The powerful politicians and the super rich begin clambering for a place on the platform. Offers of vast riches are made to anyone who will give up their station for a member of one of the world's richest families. Money, no matter how much, is now worthless. All it could buy is more money. The politicos also try to use their power to press for room aboard. One delegate, taking an adamant stand, threatens to suspend funding if his family is not allowed onboard. Funding of any kind is something that has fallen by the wayside several years ago. He was laughed out of the conference.

There are other threats. Threats which are taken very seriously—threats to destroy the platform and all on it if certain people are not among the departing crew. Threats coming from powerful people—not only those with wealth and influence, but from the average joe on the street knowing they are going to be left behind.

The main launch bases for the shuttles are, out of necessity, sealed off. Orders are to shoot first and ask questions later. The M.A.B.U.S. space station is put on full alert. No craft of any kind is to be allowed to approach the platform without specific authorization and not without strict code verification with encryption that is changed hourly. If any craft continued to approach without clearance, they are to use the powerful lasers, designed to disintegrate incoming meteors, to vaporize any unauthorized vehicles approaching the space platform—without hesitation!

In addition to the unrest growing among the remaining world was the nearly one thousand candidates who had trained long and hard, sacrificing the past several years of their lives to be aboard the space platform when it leaves. These men and women have just heard the devastating news—they will not be going back to the platform. They will have to remain behind to die with the rest of the world. This is a thought that does not sit well with the majority of them.

When they started their training, every one of them knew that not all would be going. They knew this was inescapable. Yet each feels they should be on the platform with someone else left behind to die. A few resigned themselves to their fate and offered to do whatever they could to help. Most of the rejected crew is joining in the mutiny rapidly brewing all around the main base. There have been numerous armed conflicts, leaving hundreds dead.

Hours pass like days, and conditions worsen on the planet below. The decision is made unanimously by the ground base below and by those on the platform that M.A.B.U.S. would proceed into the wormhole. At least there the space station would be safe from any outside attack.

The platform had been in and out of the wormhole hundreds of times, so there was no immediate concern about the procedure. Ready to leave or not, the station could remain just outside the dimension of time and space indefinitely—totally impervious to any outside interference, including the exploding sun. Calculations for the alignment of the e-matter electrons to project a wormhole through Proxima Centauri, toward the center of the Arilias star system, are finally completed. "Stand by to influx e-matter." The control was switched over to the computers for the exact instant of alignment. The massive structure shimmers and is immediately gone—vanishing from the physical universe. The platform materializes in a wormhole—just as a squadron of military type shuttlecraft come into range, opening fire on the giant space platform. Lasers flash at the sudden emptiness of space....

"M.A.B.U.S., this is ground control, do you copy? M.A.B.U.S., this is ground control!"

"M.A.B.U.S. station here, what the hell was that all about?"

"We're not sure who it was or who was behind it! They were using stealth. We did not pick them up until they were right on top of you! Stay in the wormhole until further notice. Worldwide air forces have been dispatched to intercept the attacking craft. It could get nasty out there. You are safe as long as you are in the hole.

"Roger, ground control. We didn't know they were even there until they were within visual range. I think they wanted to get close enough to take out the e-drives without damaging the rest of the ship. We just made it into the wormhole with our underwear hanging out and flapping in the breeze!"

"Stay in the wormhole! I repeat, stay in the wormhole until you hear from us. We will keep in contact as long as possible. Things do not look very good down here right now. You are cleared to leave whenever you are ready. If we stop transmitting, it's all over and you will be on your own. Out!"

Chapter 26
The Voyage

Events continue to deteriorate on the planet's surface. Widespread civil unrest—the masses demanding they have access to the space station and the growing mutiny add to the problems the base is facing. There is political infighting in all arenas. Word is sent up to the *Star Traveler*, resting safely in the wormhole, "It is time to get underway."

Due to growing unrest, the main command center for the M.A.B.U.S. project is hastily moved to the abandoned N.O.R.A.D. facility in the base of Cheyenne Mountain. There, they would not need to defend their new base; they could simply lock everyone else out. The heavy steel blast doors are tightly shut for the last time.

The M.A.B.U.S. *Star Traveler* readies to depart. The last testing of all systems are complete, the order is given to prepare for thruster firing. The platform is now leaving forever. "Fire thrusters!" The massive space station accelerates forward, one hundred thousand miles per hour, six hundred thousand miles per hour, three hundred miles per second, two thousand miles per second! The speed increases exponentially until the ship is nearing one hundred and forty thousand miles per second. Approaching light speed! "Stand by to engage E-Drive." The ship continues to accelerate. "Engage!" The massive space platform streaks ahead. The drive activates ten more times in as many seconds—the giant space ark is traveling at more than four and a half times the speed of light away from the small planet soon to meet its doom.

"Base, this is M.A.B.U.S. We are on our way."
"Godspeed, M.A.B.U.S. Godspeed!"

The weeks pass, and M.A.B.U.S. sails farther and farther away in the wormhole on its way to the belly of Proxima Centauri, and then on to the Arilias system. Conditions on Earth continue to deteriorate. Inside Cheyenne Mountain—the new home of the project headquarters—the staff keeps M.A.B.U.S. informed of all the developments. It is winter in the northern hemisphere, but you would not know it. Temperatures as far north as Toronto are in the constant eighties or higher. Most life in the southern latitudes has vanished due to the intense heat.

There are no longer any recognizable coastlines on any of the continents. What were once the great plains of North America are now a shallow inland sea. Except for a few uninhabited patches of higher ground, what was the previous state of Florida is gone—awash beneath the undulating sea. The sun is increasing its expansion rate, growing ever faster.

Earlier this month, the moon at last broke free of the Earth's pull and spiraled off toward the sun. The last remaining observatory serving as an outside base during the earlier tests to send the M.A.B.U.S. platform into a wormhole followed soon after. Ripped away from the dark side of the Earth by the combined gravitational forces of the passing doomed moon and the ever-expanding sun—carrying with it the last remaining souls who tried to keep the observatory operational—hanging on to that last thread of visual contact to where the platform is destined.

It is now estimated there is less than four months before conditions become intolerable over the entire globe.

Water has become very scarce, in all of the coastal regions fresh water supplies have become brackish, polluted by the influx of the seas. It has not rained anywhere in the world for almost three months. Wildfires are rampant through all the land areas.

Even in the bowels of Cheyenne Mountain, they are not spared the effects of the constant earthquakes. Cracks and fissures develop almost everywhere, prompting minor cave-ins. Some sections need to be abandoned due to major collapses. The temperature inside the maze of massive granite caverns is now constantly above 90 degrees and rising. In their quarters deep inside the immense complex of intertwining tunnels, Robert and Susan Jensin lie in each other's arms, rapidly sinking into a final deep sleep. Each wears a small adhesive patch over their jugular veins.

Two months earlier, the extended Murdock family hugged each other one last time before applying Roy Murdock's "gift" to spare them the final agonies.

"M.A.B.U.S., this is the base! The sun has drastically increased its expansion rate. Solar flare activity has gone beyond measuring. We have not had any contact with the outside for five days. Readings indicate a very large flare heading directly at us. We do not have much time left. Good Luck on your mission! Remember, all of…"

The photons in the earth-link quantum teleportation transponders begin to rotate at an ever-increasing rate of speed. One by one, the transponders are switched off. Earth is gone.

The platform is silent for most of the remainder of the ship's day. Recorded in the ship's log is one short paragraph.

Ship Time: Year 1, Month 4, Day 8. Earth equivalent date: March 6, 2047. Communication with Earth base terminated. Transponders rendered useless. God rest your souls! Farewell!

Still far ahead of us is Proxima Centauri. No one on Earth will know if we reach it or not. If we are successful in penetrating this flare star, will the massive platform survive? Despite the glowing accomplishment of the earlier probes passing unhindered through the impending inferno, there is still the nagging doubt in the minds of many. M.A.B.U.S. is thousands of times larger than those previous probes. There is still so much about wormholes remaining shrouded in mystery. A way to measure the thickness of a wormhole's walls has never been discovered. Are they uniform regardless of size? On the other hand, are they like a toy balloon, stretching to accommodate the volume inside with the walls becoming thinner and weaker as the mass it contains increases? We will soon find out. There is no turning back! There is nowhere to turn back to—Earth is no more….

Our calculations place us less than eight hundred million miles from Proxima Centauri. We will know in a little over fifteen minutes if we are going to survive. There is nothing special to be done on our approach to the surface of this giant star. All the calculations have been worked out and we are streaking toward the surface of this massive fire ball. We will either survive or be destroyed. M.A.B.U.S. rushes toward Proxima Centauri. Our *Star Traveler* approaches the outer reaches of this distant sun. The sensors onboard detect no change in the wormhole.

We begin to penetrate the outer reaches of the surface of this celestial giant. M.A.B.U.S dives deep into the fervent hell of this massive holocaust, traveling deeper and deeper into the inferno. All sensors reporting no change in the wormhole! Thirty-four seconds later, we might emerge on the other side and head away from the fiery furnace, or we may not... Those in hyper-sleep are the fortunate ones. If our wormhole collapses, they will never know about it. But if we do survive, we will be headed onward toward the Arilias system.

Everyone holds their breath—the space platform slips silently through the fiery center of this inferno and now outward...breaking clear of the star's outer surface—out from the bowels of hell! We watch the readings—the massive star recedes behind us. Ahead of us is our new home! The Arilias system. We are still alive!

Chapter 27
The Arilias Star System

I am awakened from hyper-sleep along with a large number of additional crew members—nine days before the scheduled breaking is to begin. It is extremely crucial that all command personnel as well as each and everyone necessary to effect the proper running of the ship while it is in physical space be out of hibernation and fully functional before the breaking process commences.

We are awakened in an order based on the length of time we have been in hyper-sleep, beginning with the longest duration down to the shortest. All hands will need to be fully acclimated and functional long before the crucial moment of breakout back into physical space and time. We need to have all the cosmic cobwebs swept away before the crucial time arrives. The longer someone is in hyper-sleep, the longer it takes before they re-gain their full faculties.

"Oh, man! I am so stiff! My head just doesn't want to clear up…everything is still foggy…I don't know if I am up to being really myself!" Captain Richards, one of the officers in charge of logistics mutters.

"Stow it! We don't have time for one of your panjandrum complaints right now." Turning his attention to the other newly awakened "zombies," Commander Ralph Miller, the medical officer in charge, sets about putting the "new walkers" through their paces—exercises designed to re-awaken all the senses, especially those which tend to become stale after months of hyper-sleep. A certain captain's equilibrium is foremost among those he targets.

Commander Miller's task is not an easy one—getting everyone ready to assume his or her required position aboard ship for our final breaking as quickly as humanly possible.

"Let's go, people! Let's pretend you're still half human! Come on—let's all move together! Bend and stretch, bend and stretch! Right foot forward! Bend and stretch!"

It is no easy job. After such a long ordeal in space with lengthy durations of weeks in hyper-sleep—all of us have become complacent and greatly influenced by apathy. He has his work cut out for him. More than a hundred still dazed and un-willing subjects....

Nevertheless, he is a determined taskmaster, and although we all know why he's doing what he has to do, we grumble and groan—bitch and moan—but we follow his instructions to the letter. We are soon fully awake, functioning at peak efficiency—alert again. Up and running in a fraction of the time usually allowed the new walkers to get back to normal.

Once everyone is awakened and has time to regain their "space legs," we began the preparations to leave the wormhole. All ship systems are go! All personnel on station! It is now time. Everyone and everything is ready!

We are now set to begin the first of the procedures necessary for us to complete in order to slow our speed to a point where we will be traveling slow enough to safely engage the e-matter pulse drive and open up the forward end of our wormhole.

"Get ready, people. Ten minutes until reverse thrust," Commander Jackson, the senior officer in charge of the shift on duty, announces over the intercom. The command officer of the current shift remains in command and has complete control of the ship until the end of his tour of duty.

"Secure all free objects. We are going to be coming out of the wormhole at a much greater distance from the Arilias system than originally planned. The last probes we sent out have indicated several rogue comets in the area, and we don't want to become a permanent part of one."

"Stand by to commence breaking." The command is issued from the main control room. Everyone throughout the ship prepares for the rigors of breaking and exiting the wormhole. The process of returning to physical space and time is about to begin.

"This is one of the few occurrences where we have enough time to test fire the thrusters before the actual breakout," Commander Jackson says to the officers next to him at the command console.

"It's been a number of years since the thruster engines have been used at all, so a major testing is in order. We'll give the thrusters a two-second firing in eight minutes and refigure the calculations before the extended firing."

We have at last reached the region of the planet selected for our new colony. All hands stand ready. We are still more than a billion miles from the Arilias star system, with millions of miles passing by us each minute. We all hope and pray that the star system will be there, where it is supposed to be when we break out.

"Fire thrusters!" The command is issued and the ship shudders—the forward engines spring to life for two brief seconds. The speed of the M.A.B.U.S. *Star Traveler* drops immediately to just under four times light speed.

"OK," he says. "Now let's get the calculations for the main firing and all the way down through the final initiating of the e-drive." The staff immediately begins carrying out his orders. "I need the exact instant for reverse ionization. We only have one chance, so let's get it right!" he adds. "We don't want to become nothing more than cosmic dust this late in the game."

The new data in, he gives the order, "Stand by to fire reverse thrusters on my command…execute!" The massive star ship, traveling at almost 4 times the speed of light, is slowed to a little more than half its speed. The thrusters fire for just over one minute. "Stand by to fire thrusters!" The second firing will slow the immense ship even more. Yet, there is no sensation of slowing.

All calculations need to be precise. Breaking a millisecond too soon or too late could prove to be catastrophic. Now traveling at a speed just over twice that of light, the ship and everyone aboard is ready to slow again, waiting for the unfelt backward push of the thruster engines. "Fire thrusters."

The engines respond, and the ship slows to just about light speed. "OK, people, get ready."

"We have two more ignitions, the first one coming up in 20 seconds, and then we break out of the wormhole. Everybody strap in!"

"Stand by to fire thrusters. Fire!"

The ship has now slowed to a snail's pace of a little more than 140,000 miles per second. The engines ignite once more, slowing the station to an even lesser speed. "Stand by for reverse ionization."

There are many white knuckles, grasping the seat arms—the crew awaits the final break out. It has been almost eleven years since the ship and its crew has been outside the wormhole and once more traveling within the confines of real space and time. When we break out of the wormhole, our speed is going to drop from almost 250 million miles per hour to just under 900,000 miles per hour. The inertia that has been absent for the last eleven years is about to become a frank reality once again.

"Let's get those helmets on and tighten all cinch-straps," the Commander orders. "Two minutes and counting!" The crew don their protective helmets and face plates—pulling tight and re-checking the harnesses on each of their seats. The helmets they wear will protect their heads from impact. Not from what they will hit, but from what might hit them. Even after a thorough checking, there are bound to be items that will fly loose as the ship decelerates. Forgotten items that will become deadly missiles once the ship enters physical space.

"4, 3, 2, 1. Reverse ionization!" The ship is at once surrounded by the blackness of empty space—each of the crew is thrown forward against the safety harnesses, the straps digging into their flesh—the massive structure drops dramatically in speed. The wormhole is gone—the *Star Traveler* is back in the physical universe.

All eyes watch the holographic monitors—the wormhole shimmers and disappears. We are back—back in real space. The eleven years of traveling inside the wormhole are finally over. We have arrived and we are still alive! "Engage forward e-drive now!" The ship slows to almost a complete stop.

Ahead is the Arilias star system. Twelve planets, all unique, orbit a star twice the size of our own dead sun. Twelve planets so different from anything we have ever known—except for one. Our objective is the sixth planet from the star. The only planet in the system determined to be capable of supporting human life—Arilias-6.

"On your toes, people! Let's get every thing back on line. We don't want any unnecessary surprises when we approach the Arilias system," Commander Jackson states amid the brouhaha of backslapping, handshakes and hugs. "We need a whole new set of coordinates and calculations before we proceed any farther. We don't have the wormhole protecting us anymore, so stay sharp!"

From this point on, the e-matter drive will be used to propel and direct the path of the M.A.B.U.S. *Star Traveler*, conserving precious hydrogen fuel for the shuttles. As long as we are traveling through physical space, we can collect more e-matter atoms to supplement our engines. This is something we have not been able to do for all of the eleven years we have been inside the wormhole. We move on toward the Arilias system.

We are rapidly approaching the orbit of the ninth planet in the system.

Spectral analysis presents more questions than answers—the composition of the huge globe is made up of elements unknown to us. It is a large, gaseous giant, much like the planet Jupiter that once orbited in our own solar system. It will remain a mystery for now—our objective is to use its massive gravitational pull to slingshot us toward the inner planets—sending us on our way for a rendezvous with our ultimate target, the sixth planet.

"Standby, people, this could get a little hairy!" Commander Jackson announces. "Everyone strap in and be ready for at least a three-G pull once we start to go around Arilias-9. Let's hope the ship holds together!"

All hands assume their respective seats and begin to tighten their restraining harnesses. This will be a force greater than the breaking effect of exiting the wormhole and will be at an angle to the position of the ship as it enters the gravitational pull of Arilias-9. This will not be a straight pressure from head-on, but from one side with a constant changing force and direction—changing as the ship careens past the immense giant below. An unfamiliar gravitational force surrounds the crew once the star ship begins to swing around the planet. A force not felt in many years.

We are approaching Arilias-9, a blue-green, colossal orb much larger than any planet we had ever known; almost ten times the size of Jupiter. Our assumption is Arilias-9 is completely gaseous, with no solid core. The sensor readings we used for our bypass calculations indicate a lesser gravity than should be exerted by such an immense planet. Given its size, it could have become a small star in its own right. Our now dead sun was composed of mostly hydrogen, and this lightest of elements was pulled close enough together to flare into the beacon that provided life for the world until just a few short years ago.

At this crucial moment we have no time for much scientific study. During our fly-by, additional cursory scans are still unable to ascertain the planet's exact composition; spectral analysis remains negative. Arilis-9 is composed of one or more unknown elements. What these are, unfortunately, we will never know. The ship shudders once the effects of the massive planet's gravity begins to be felt. At a speed of over 872,000 miles per hour, the *Star Traveler* takes a curved path around the colossal celestial body on the port side. The ship groans under the pull of Arilias-9. "Hold together, old girl, you can make it!" is the sentiment on everyone's lips.

The intensity of the gravitational pull and accompanying g-forces come as a surprise to many. Although expected, after almost eleven years in their absence, the sensations accompanying having weight have long been forgotten. The slingshot effect causes our speed to increase as we round the massive planet below us. Once clear of the gravity of this titan, we will use the e-matter engines to slow our speed to a much safer velocity.

Our trajectory changes by 50 degrees and we start heading into the inner reaches of the Arilias solar system. Anything not properly secured and items that did not fly loose when we exited the wormhole now become dangerous missiles, flying from where they were to a location in a direct line opposite to our new direction of travel. We have our hands full, ducking and retrieving all the forgotten loose items accumulated over the last eleven years. Fortunately, no one is hurt and our free-floating chaff does no significant damage.

Murdock and his crew did their job well! The ship survives the tremendous pull of the planet below and breaks free of the huge orb's gravity. M.A.B.U.S. performs exactly as it was designed. Our next stop: Arilias-6. We should reach its orbit in less than two weeks. From our scanners, we observe only a minuscule image of the shimmering blue spot projected on our monitors. The small spec in the cosmos before us is our destination. We are finally reaching our goal after nearly eleven long years in the wormhole. Our new home!

"I wish there was someone left back home we could tell about this," Lieutenant J.G. Gueimaldo says to the crew companion seated next to her—her fingers digging into the arms of her seat. "It would have been nice to let somebody know we made it this far…" she trails off. "This is the first time…first time since we left that I feel we are truly alone! There is no one left back on Earth to tell about this or…or go home to," she states. Her voice starts to flutter with the strains of sentimentality.

The next two weeks are going to be demanding on everyone. We prepare to close in on the new planet far ahead of us. The image on the view screens grows larger each hour.

Bringing a craft the size of the M.A.B.U.S. *Star Traveler* into a safe orbit around this distant world is going to require the full attention and efforts of all the crew. There is going to be no room for error. The ship must be slowed enough to obtain a proper orbit, but not too quickly. We must do this right the first time. There will be no second chance. If we are traveling too fast upon approaching the planet, we will continue on past Arilias-6—eventually be caught in the gravitational field of its immense star and pulled into the fiery fury of the Arilias sun. Our e-drive engines do not have enough power to overcome the gravitational pull of this giant star, and there would be insufficient time to put M.A.B.U.S back into the safety of a wormhole. Even with the e-matter drives at full power, we would be helpless to break free from the star's pull.

If we slow too much or begin to decrease speed too far out from Arilias-6, we might find ourselves trapped in a decreasing spiral orbit, crashing into the planet below before we would have the time to increase our speed enough to stabilize. We only have one shot....

At a distance of 380 million miles from Arilias-6, we begin to again slow the ship. Each hour, the forward e-matter engines release one single pulse. Each pulse slows the ship by nearly one thousand miles per hour. One minute before each pulse, an announcement is made. Everyone stops what they are doing and straps into the nearest seat. With each pulse, we again are exposed to inertia. There were a few minor injuries to some who did not get strapped into a seat in time, but nothing serious. A few bumps and bruises here and there from banging into bulkheads or protrusions.

After five days the pulses come every thirty minutes, delicately slowing the massive structure to a little over 115,000 miles per hour, nearing the speed calculated to obtain orbit around the fast approaching planet. We correct our angle of approach with side thrusters so that M.A.B.U.S. is converging at the proper attitude, insuring it will be caught by the planet's gravity and continue around the new globe and not pass by—going back out in space and toward the Arilias sun.

There are only forty hours until the final slowing, which will take us into orbit around our new home. The planet looms before us on the video displays. We see oceans, mountains, clouds and abundant landmasses. The excitement and anticipation builds as we approach ever nearer our goal. The planet grows larger on our view screens. More and more detail becomes visible as we close in on this new world. Two uniform ice caps, lush green areas below and above a wide band of equatorial desert. Flat lands and mountain regions, forests, oceans and deserts—a profusion of terrain to explore.

We approach closer to our objective—the ship has slowed almost to our pre-determined speed. One last firing of the breaking engines once we are in the gravitational pull of Arilias-6 should put us in orbit around our target.

When and if our orbit is stabilized, we will begin the tedious task of mapping the planet's surface and begin the arduous process of selecting what we plan to be our landing area. The adverse anticipation and thought of having to spend weeks or possibly even months before setting foot on our new home is tempered by remembrance of the long eleven years it took us to get here. Still, everyone can't wait to get on the ground.

The ship is starting to react to the pull of the planet below. Less than an hour left before we attempt to attain orbit. The engines are fired the moment we start to swing around the planet. M.A.B.U.S. settles into a near circular diagonal orbit, crossing both hemispheres once every two and a half hours. The beautiful blue and green planet streams by beneath us, looking very much like what earth must have looked like thousands of years ago—awash with pristine waters and covered by virgin forests—a virtual Garden of Eden with none of the pollution caused by modern day industry.

Our orbit is stable. We have arrived home at last. Numerous landers and airborne probes are going to be launched over the next several weeks and commence the exploration of our new planetary domain. There is a definite excitement in the air as the probes are made ready. It has been decided to forgo the immediate exploration of the vast equatorial desert regions. The lack of detected water and high temperatures found there make those areas far too hostile for any colonization. It will still be some time before the first human being plants a foot on the surface of this planet—a planet in another star system far different from our own lost world.

A flat region in the upper temperate zone is selected for our first landing on the planet. The terrain is rolling, but not mountainous. There are dense forests as well as vast open areas. It is in one of these open sections of terrain we will first land. The shuttle crew makes ready to depart for the planet's surface.

The shuttle slowly backs out of the hanger deck. Onboard along with the five crew members is a vast array of sampling equipment. Before the first space helmet is removed on Arilias-6, atmosphere, soil, water and vegetation samples will need to be completely analyzed. The collected samples will be brought back up to M.A.B.U.S. for intensive study.

Braking slightly, the craft clears the station and begins its decent to the planet's surface. Hearts pound—they fire the thrusters, sending them into a spiral re-entry. Something the crew had much practice doing during the final several months the platform was in orbit back on Earth, protected from the fierce solar winds—sheltered on the night side of the globe.

Full orbital re-entry was decided against due to the larger size of Arilias-6 and the possibility of having to use too much fuel to reach the landing zone once inside the thicker atmosphere.

Hitting the outer fringes of the planet's ionosphere, the craft begins to vibrate—the outside titanium skin begins to heat up. The rate of descent is now greatly reduced to prevent overheating the protective outside layer of the shuttle.

At an altitude of twenty kilometers, the retractable airfoils on the craft are deployed—giving an added degree of stability to the shuttle, slowing it even more.

Now, literally flying through the atmosphere of Arilias-6, the craft is directed toward its landing zone. "Eight minutes to touchdown!" Captain George Roberts announces to the other four members of the landing party. The alien sensation of constant gravity is felt for the first time in years. The craft drops lower and lower. Everyone on board has eagerly awaited the almost forgotten feeling of being pulled down into their seats. "Landing zone in sight!" Roberts exclaims. "Fire the reverse thrusters."

The craft is now hovering, slowly descending straight down at a modest rate of fifty meters per second. The engines increase thrust, stopping the descent the moment before the craft is about to gently settle on the surface of the new world surrounding them.

"M.A.B.U.S., this is Shuttle One. We are on the ground." Cheers echo throughout the entire massive space platform.

Chapter 28
Arilias-6

The shuttle sits silently on the planet surface. There is the sound of clicking as the remaining heat from re-entry is slowly dissipating from the titanium hull. "I feel like I can't move!" Science Specialist Peterson says in slow, almost slurred words. The unfamiliar gravity holds all five passengers prisoners in their seats. "I forgot what it's like to have any weight."

"We can't do anything until the outer skin cools," Roberts states. "Take your time and get used to being on the ground again, but be careful! We don't want any injuries that will cause us to scrub this mission." They spend the next several hours relearning how to stand, move and walk under the influence of gravity, which proves to be a hard task.

Compounding their situation is the fact that Arilias-6 is about one-third larger than the former planet Earth. If a person weighed 180 pounds on Earth, on Arilias-6 he weighed in at around 240 pounds. Everything else—every piece of equipment—is instantly more than thirty percent heavier than it was back on Earth. Everyone is accustomed to handling equipment onboard M.A.B.U.S., where it was weightless. Hundreds of kilos could be moved with the fingertips—now it takes superhuman effort to lift your own hand.

The time it took the crew to regain their equilibrium was not a serious factor. The craft had landed in the early dawn hours of the planet's day, and Arilias-6 rotates once every ninety-four hours. There will still be sufficient time to collect all the needed samples, lift-off and rendezvous with M.A.B.U.S. long before the Arilias night sets in.

"Look! There is something out there! I saw it move!" Science Specialist Li Iamoto exclaims. All eyes turn to the view ports. "There it is again!" she says. "Over there! To the right of that large brush clump."

An animal with a rounded back—about as large as a medium-sized dog, with fur a dark brown in color, was digging at the base of the bushes. "There's another one!" she excitedly exclaims.

Arilias-6 supports life. However, will it support *their* lives? They began feverishly sorting through the various sampling equipment, readying the more important sensors to be deployed first.

"We now know that we're not alone here," Roberts states. "When we get outside, keep your eyes open. We don't know how these creatures are going to react to our presence."

They commence to load the two small carts brought with them with the various sensing apparatus. Some of the equipment will be left behind on the planet's surface to monitor weather conditions and temperature fluctuations through the long Arilias night.

"I'm glad we don't have to carry all this stuff!" says Morg Grundon, microbiologist. "I'm having enough trouble just carrying myself!"

"OK, let's get our helmets on and check your packs. Once we open up it will be at least an hour before we can go back on the ship's systems again. All of us, as well as the entire inside of the shuttle, will have to be decontaminated before we can come off the packs. Make sure your lasers are on and ready." They each lock down their helmets and don their air packs.

"Gads, that's heavy!" Navigator Broswedo grunts, hoisting the breathing pack up on his back and connecting up. The equipment is ready, the crew is ready, and the hatch begins to slowly open. There is a slight rush of Arilias air into the shuttle. The pressure outside is slightly higher than that inside the craft. They are about to step out onto the surface of a place no man has ever seen before, let alone walked on.

The five pioneers stand in silence, gazing out over the landscape. The wind gently waves the tall grasses nearby. "We have work to do, folks," says Roberts, breaking the silence.

"Hey, Cap! Say something to commemorate this moment," Grundon states.

"Why?" Roberts questions. "There's nobody here but us, and we all see what's happening?"

"For history! Armstrong said, 'One small step…' and this is a bigger step than any man ever took!"

"There is no history. Earth is gone."

"Five minutes from now this will be history. The new history of the human race!" Peterson adds.

"We're all going to be history if we don't get a move on," Roberts replies. "Let's get about our business."

The gear that is to be left behind has to be placed far enough away from the shuttle so that it will not be damaged by the thruster blast when they lift off.

Peterson, Iamoto and Grundon collect various vegetation and soil samples as the party moves along. Roberts and Broswedo stand at ready with their lasers, scanning their surroundings.

The preliminary sensing equipment is all in place, and all but one of the sample vessels are filled. The only chore left is to collect some liquid water for analysis. They spotted a stream just before landing—over the rise to their left, down in a small ravine. Upon clearing the top of the rise, they are confronted with three of the creatures they saw through the shuttle view ports.

The animals' heads are round, with small ears like a beaver, but with a much longer snout. The three animals look up at them in unison, sniff the air a few times, and return to grubbing in the ground, oblivious to the five much larger creatures standing on two legs not more than twelve feet from them. There were five individual sighs of relief in unison once the crew is able to cautiously move on past the strange quadrupeds they accidentally stumbled upon.

Reaching the streambed, they spot small creatures swimming in the water like fish, but not exactly like fish. "I wish we could catch one of those and study it," Grundon states. "I've never seen anything like them."

"No one has," adds Iamoto. "There will be other opportunities to do that if things check out. You might get to do a little sport fishing in a few weeks. You never know what you might catch."

"Or what might catch you!" adds Roberts. "It's time we head back to the ship. We still have some wait time before going back on the shuttles life support, and these packs won't last forever."

The five turn and begin to climb back up the ravine. Although the slope is quite gradual, with the increased gravity and weight of their heavy packs, all five need to stop at the top and catch their breath. Collecting the two sample-laden carts they had left at the top of the rise, they head back in the direction of the shuttle.

Not more than thirty meters from the shuttle, Li Iamoto's foot tangles in the underbrush, and she starts to fall. After such a long time in the weightlessness of space, where you cannot topple, her self-preservation reflexes are dulled; she does nothing to stop her fall. She unconsciously thought she would simply right herself again as she would normally do aboard the platform. She falls toward the cart and strikes the faceplate of her helmet squarely on the corner of one of the specimen cases.

Falling to the ground, she is unhurt, but there is a two-inch jagged hole in her faceplate. She pulls the remaining loose shards away and looks at the other four in terror. Li Iamoto is the first human to breathe the air on Arilias-6.

The other four start to rush her to the shuttle, leaving the sample carts behind. "No!" she hollers. "Stop! I'm not hurt, and if there is anything here that is going to harm me, it's already too late. We came here to get these specimens, and we're not leaving without them!" She starts toward the craft under her own power.

"The air is sweet," she says. "Very sweet." She unlatches her helmet and removes it, tossing it into the cart she fell against. "Besides, if it's going to kill me, it is better that it does it quickly." She walks toward the shuttle with her head upturned, letting the Arilias sun shine down on her face. "Yes, the air is sweet, like a new spring day."

The expedition reaches the shuttle, and the hatch is opened. They start to load the precious collection of specimens aboard. Captain Roberts leans his back against the shiny titanium hull. "What's wrong, Cap?" asks the navigator.

"We have a big problem," Roberts replies. "I don't think we can go directly back to M.A.B.U.S. Li is contaminated. We will not be able to disinfect our suits and equipment. Without her helmet, the procedure would definitely kill her. There are no spare helmets aboard—the one item no one thought we would ever need. There is not enough air in our packs to get us all back to the platform if we do not go on shuttle life support. To go on ship's life support before decontamination, we will all have to be exposed to whatever, if anything, Li might have contacted. In addition, we cannot leave her here alone—especially now that we know she would not actually be alone. We don't know what else is out there. The way I figure it, we have only a few options...."

Broswedo looks at him with growing concern. "By my calculations, right now, if time is the same on the surface as it is on the platform, M.A.B.U.S. is headed for the other side of the globe, so it will be quite a while before they can launch another shuttle to come for us with extra packs. We will have run out of air by then."

"I'm well aware of that," Roberts adds. "As it stands now, we can all go on ship's support and all go into quarantine. Or two of us give up our packs and only three will have to go into isolation."

"Or die with her! Couldn't we just give her one of our helmets?" Broswego asks.

"As soon as you take yours off, you're exposed to what ever she has been exposed to," Roberts replies. "No, we have to decide what we are going to do and do it right away."

"You're in command, sir."

"This is one time I wish I wasn't," Roberts mumbles.

Closing the hatch and latching it firmly, the five settle into their seats, exhausted. "I need one other volunteer to be exposed to whatever Li Iamoto may have contacted," Roberts says, turning off his air pack and removing his helmet. "There is enough air in four packs for two people to get back to the platform. Li's pack was contaminated when her face shield was broken. Mine is still clean. I turned it off before I removed my helmet."

Peterson turned his pack off and unlatched his helmet before any of the others could respond. "If there is anything out there, what better way to find out than with three live guinea pigs?" he says.

"M.A.B.U.S., this is Shuttle One. We have had some contamination. No injuries. Three for quarantine. Let us know when you are set to isolate us on our return. Our maximum time frame is seven hours, nine minutes. We will be lifting off immediately. Send us word when you are approaching overhead. Rendezvous set for four hours, plus or minus," Captain Roberts contacts the platform. "We will dock, but remain in the shuttle until all is ready. We will need two replacement air packs if the time goes over seven hours before decontamination begins."

"Roger, Shuttle One," came the reply. "We will be waiting for you." Li Iamoto sits in her seat, looking off to the side, with fear still showing in her eyes. If she was going to have any problems with contamination, at least she was not going to have to go through it alone.

"Grundon." Roberts breaks the silence. "You wanted some words for history. Turn on the ship's recorders."

"They're on."

"What better words could be found than those stated by Li Iamoto after her first breath of the Arilias atmosphere… 'The air is sweet, like a new spring day.' Let our new history record those as the first words ever spoken on this planet's surface. Recorders off."

"But that is not what was first said…" Li replied.

"As far as history is concerned, considering how little there is of it—those words are the most appropriate anyone could derive. Subject closed. Stand by to lift off. M.A.B.U.S. is coming into sensor range," Roberts orders. The engines spring to life and thrust increases. Slowly the craft rises vertically, steadily gaining altitude. At two thousand meters, the shuttle noses up and the aft thrusters send the craft flying ever higher—up and out of the atmosphere. Less than an hour latter they approach the station and settle delicately in the hanger deck. The five sit in silence once the engines are shut down.

"I'm sorry!" Li says to the other four. "I'm sorry for causing this mess."

"It's not your fault, Li," Roberts assures her. "The same thing could have happened to any one of us." Broswego and Grundon proceed to the airlock to ready the specimen containers for decontamination. The outer surfaces of the containers will be bathed with a strong disinfectant, as will the two men while still in their space suits. The collected specimens will be safe in the airtight containers, but the disinfectant is too strong to use on human flesh. There is no way to treat any internal contamination of the remaining crew except by isolation.

When the airlock next opens, inside are the necessary replacement air-packs for the remaining three, and a new helmet for Li. Broswego and Grundon have been decontaminated along with the specimens and have left the far side of the containment area. Roberts, Peterson and Iamoto will have to remain in the shuttle until the isolation area is set up. They will go through the same external decontamination process while still inside the shuttlecraft before entering the platform, but will leave their space suits on until they are in safely in quarantine.

"How are you feeling, Li?" Roberts asks. "Feel any ill effects at all?"

"Just sick with fear," she replies.

"Same here," Peterson adds.

The news arrives informing them the quarantine station is ready. The three don the air packs and replace their helmets. The heavy disinfectant begins to fill the inside of the shuttle. Several minutes later, after the air had been exchanged and scrubbed, the airlock opens and the three are escorted along the way to the isolation area.

The sensing equipment left behind on the planet's surface transmits data continuously to the orbiting platform. The nighttime temperature drops only about ten degrees. There are no adverse weather changes brought on by the extended period of darkness. The mass of the planet is enough to sustain a uniform temperature throughout the long Arilias night.

The hours pass as the three wait for some horrible malady to strike. The days pass. They all feel fine. How long has it been? How much longer until…

The hatch to the isolation room opens. Inside the airlock, separating their confinement area from the rest of the ship, stands their medical technician, Sven Yoder. He is not garbed in any protective isolation clothing.

With a clipboard under his arm, he enters the room wearing a broad smile. "Ve couldn't even find anyting dat resembled da common cold in all da samples you brought back mitch you as well as all da udders dat have been brought up afterwards. All yer medical tests are negative. The only ting dat showed up was fatigue from yer exertion under increased gravity. I guess ve can let you out of yer cage now!"

Li jumped up and hugged both Captain Roberts and Science Specialist Peterson. "Thank you! Thank you!" she said with tears in her eyes.

"Thanks for what?" they both ask.

"You put your lives on the line! You could have left me down there alone. You could have decontaminated, letting me take my chances with the chemicals. You chose to give your air packs to the others and see this through with me. If I had to go through this waiting alone, I think I would have lost it days ago. Thank you!" she says, kissing them both.

The shuttle expeditions continued to explore the surface of Arilias-6. After numerous flights over the vast terrain of the huge planet, a sight about two thousand kilometers from the original landing area was selected as the main base for the colony. The location had abundant water, large open areas that would not have to be cleared for farming, and plenty of forests to supply the needed materials for construction.

The first expedition to set foot on the planet without the cumbersome space suits and air packs is on its way to touch down at the new sight. Hovering several meters above the surface, it lands in the middle of a large expanse of grassland. Onboard are Captain Roberts, Li Iamoto, Jeff Peterson and seven others. They will be remaining on the surface for five Arilias days and nights. Their shelter will be the cramped quarters of the shuttle while they explore and map the immediate region. This will be the first time any human stayed on the surface through the long Arilias night, and for five Arilias days and nights it will be, by far, the longest that anyone has stayed on the surface.

Several hours were spent clearing away the high grass and detritus to a radius of fifty or so meters around the shuttle, using lasers and plain old physical strength. A perimeter was established around the craft in all directions so the sensors could pick up any movement unobstructed by the growing vegetation. The last thing they wanted was to open the hatch in the morning and find a menagerie of curious creatures surrounding the shuttle.

Another necessary reason for making a sizable clearing is to give subsequent landing craft a visual target when they approach the landing area. One of the main objectives of this particular expedition is to set up experimental horticultural sites to determine if the seeds from Earth plants would germinate in this new environment. The thrust engines of a descending shuttle landing too close to the newly planted seed beds might destroy the seedlings if they germinate—an additional reason to clear such a large area located far from the intended fields.

The new visitors to the planet were piling up the twigs and windblown branches from the cleared area when it was suggested that as a way of celebration of the first night on Arilias-6, they have a bonfire. Maybe one possibly detected from overhead when M.A.B.U.S. passes miles above. "They're always watching," was stated. "It might spark, so to speak, a bit of interest onboard the platform." There has not been a visible fire such as the one they have planned for the first dark hours they will be spending on the surface for more than twelve years.

Everyone agreed and amassed a sizable stack of kindling for later in the evening.

With the surrounding perimeter cleared, their next task was to locate several areas for experimental plantings. The soil has to be well drained and as level as possible. Soil tests to determine the chemical and nutrient content are conducted. The suitable sites are then flagged and numbered. Just about everywhere they test comes up ideal for growing Earth plants. The backbreaking task of clearing these small garden plots is still ahead of them.

The lasers used to clear the landing zone are too strong to use on a garden area. The lasers sterilize the soil and fuse many of the minerals together. The laser cleared ground would not be able to support plant life for years to come.

When the time comes to actually set up the small experimental gardens on this trip, the tilling is going to have to be done by hand; not literally, but with small mechanical devices designed to churn the soil and bury the existing growing vegetation below the surface, where it will decompose and enrich the ground.

The long Arilias day is deceiving to their biological clocks, and soon the crew finds they are totally whipped. They have been toiling for almost twelve hours under the increased gravity of Arilias-6 and decide now they need a break and head back to the shuttle. The hatch is secured, and each one plops down into their respective seats, completely worn out. There will be no gentle drifting in sleeping sacks like the ones they are accustomed to on board M.A.B.U.S. They will have to do their best to rest in their seats, remaining as comfortable as possible—the planet pulling them and one-third more of their Earth weight against the backs of their perches. The outside ventilators are turned on to preserve the shuttle's air supply for the return trip back to M.A.B.U.S. They all fall in to exhaustion-induced sleep.

The first awake is Captain Roberts. Stretching, he experiences a stiffness he has not felt in many years. Working the kinks out of his neck and joints, he struggles out of his seat. "Man, I forgot how tough it is to sleep lying down!" he says to himself, trying to get all the parts of his body to work together.

"OK, folks! It's time to get back to work," he says, unintentionally plopping back down in his seat. The others stir and grumble; slowly they begin to awaken from their fitful sleep. One by one, they struggle back to the world of the living. "Ma, I don't want to go to school today!" is muttered and is met with chuckling. Little by little, they all rise to face the continuing tasks before them.

They awaken—not to a new sunrise, but to a continuation of the one they closed their eyes on hours ago, just later in the same day.

"We have to pace ourselves a little bit better than what we have been doing," Roberts states. "We don't want or need any early burn outs. We still have almost twenty hours of daylight left in our first day here. Once night comes, that time is our own. No one will be leaving the area of the shuttle when darkness sets in. Until then, let's see what we can accomplish with the time we have left before the sun sets."

Amidst grunting and groaning is heard, "Time left before the sun sets? That's two shifts for normal people!" The rest of the crew forces their way out of their seats. A new day has dawned for the crew, but it is still the same day they arrived and worked hard. The forty-plus hour days on Arilias-6 are going to take some time getting used to.

The crew set out in two groups of five to begin clearing the designated seed plots. Earth seeds were successfully sprouted in Arilias-6 soil onboard the platform, but this was done under ideal conditions and using Earth atmosphere and Earth water. Now they would discover over the next few weeks if our plants can withstand the different make up of the planet. Once each small plot is prepared, it is enclosed with fencing to keep the numerous small creatures prowling the region from disturbing the newly planted seed beds. The warmth of the sun, the moist, rich soil, and the long Arilias day should make for rapid germination. How the long night is going to affect the new sprouts, if they do indeed sprout, is still to be determined.

The Arilias sun is sinking lower to the horizon, and the crew makes their way back to their base. Everyone is anticipating the evening campfire while each gathers more pieces of firewood on their trek back to the shuttle. Back at the shuttle, they eat and watch the twilight slowly fade. The first stars begin to twinkle in the night sky.

There are, of course, no recognizable constellations. Most of the crew gazes up at the darkening skies, looking for distinct star groups to give new names. It is not often one is afforded the opportunity to name a never-before-seen constellation. They scan the heavens, picking out groups of stars that, in their imagination, resemble something. On that particular early evening, hundreds of unknown constellations were named after animals, household appliances, acquaintances and some even after unmentionable objects.

"How 'bout that fire?" Captain Roberts suggests. "Anybody know how to build one?" They just look at each other, realizing…

"I'll give it a shot," says Peterson, grabbing a handful of twigs, beginning to make a small pile with the sticks. "How are we going to light it?" he is asked. He stops dead, looking at the pile of twigs. He suddenly realizes matches are not part of the usual shuttle equipment, or even found aboard the space platform. There is no need for open flame onboard any spacecraft. Induction igniters are used as a source of ignition in the hydrogen-fueled engines, but they are not exactly portable.

"No problem," chimes in Fergison, a technician. "Stand back!" He sets his laser to its lowest setting and aims it at the pile on the ground. In seconds, the sound of crackling can be heard and the first flames lick upward. The fire begins to glow brightly. They each toss a few more pieces of fuel on the now brilliantly glowing blaze.

"I wish we had some marshmallows to toast," he says.

"What are marshmallows?" Li Iamoto asks.

"I don't know," he replies. "I just remember hearing something about toasting marshmallows over a campfire and thought it would be interesting to have some, whatever they are." The fire burns brightly, and the night proceeds to become darker.

Just out beyond the cleared perimeter, they suddenly become aware of hundreds of eyes reflecting the fire's light, giving each of them an uneasy feeling. They all move closer to the fire, each one unconsciously scanning around at the glistening specks surrounding them.

The higher oxygen content of the planet's atmosphere unfortunately causes the small pile of collected firewood to be exhausted in a short time, and the fire begins to die out. The last embers diminishing, they choose to make their way back into the shuttle for the remainder of the evening. They would sleep now, doing cataloguing and other various chores later in the night upon awakening, while they waited for the dawn of their second day on the surface.

The dawn brings with it the threat of rain. The early morning daylight reveals an overcast sky. The air is cooler today than yesterday. The filtered sunlight is slower to warm the morning air—the first drops of moisture strike the view ports on the shuttle. They had been hoping for some rain during this stay on the surface, and they are about to have their hopes more than exceeded.

"This is our first chance to get a sample of Arilias rain water," Roberts states. "We have to get wet sometime, so let's get the collecting apparatus ready to be set up. We don't know how long this shower will last." It turns out it lasted all forty-plus hours of the day and on into the night. The newly planted seedbeds and the crew got a good watering that day. A little rain was not going to keep them from the necessary work they were there to accomplish.

Peterson pipes in, "It's only water—I think! I know we need it for testing, but why do we have to get all of it at once?"

The collecting equipment attached to the long sloping side of the shuttle, using its smooth, inert titanium skin as a collector and the storage tanks as a catch basin, retrieves the runoff. All ten of the forty-liter containers were full and overflowing in less than an hour. They have all the rain samples they would ever need, and it is still pouring down.

The long day is again broken up by a period of sleep. They are disappointed upon waking to find the chilly rain still falling, and they will all have to get wet again. At least they would have plenty of extra water to wash up without having to go very far to retrieve it.

The five day's progress and the mapping of the main colony area almost complete, the crew prepares to return to the platform. With the long days of sunshine and the rich, fertile soil, the newly planted seeds are already showing signs of sprouting. Increasingly, Arilias-6 seems like the ideal planet to set up our colony. The atmospheric conditions are supremely suited for human existence, higher in oxygen than earth with none of the pollution and smog. The increased oxygen level, after a short period of adjustment, made it easier to cope with the fact that the planet was considerably larger than Earth, with higher gravity. Observations from the platform determine Arilias-6 rotates on a perpendicular axis to its sun, so there are no seasonal changes as were on Earth. The axis varied by only two degrees. Hence the cause for the vast, torrid equatorial desert region and uniform ice caps.

The desert, tropical, temperate and arctic regions remain constant all year. There is a gradual blend of any adjacent two regions in between. In that there are no changes of seasons like those on Earth, the new settlers would have the option of moving to whatever climate suited them.

Arilias-6 only rotates once every ninety-four hours. The long daylight lasts for forty-seven constant hours, unlike the varying times on Earth, and would allow us to grow more plants for food. There was also the concern we might have to supplement the plants with artificial light during the forty-seven hour night until they adjusted to this change in the photosynthesis cycle. The plants seem to be doing well without outside interference. We will know more once the seed beds are fully established and the first experimental Earth plants are up and growing on their own. If they adapt and thrive, we will be able to establish much larger growing areas around the compound without any difficulty.

The region we select for our main colony base is an area between the tropical and temperate regions. There is no sense in trying to create a settlement somewhere where we would also have to fight the elements to survive.

Arilias-6 seemed like a new Eden, complete with lush forests and grasslands, plenty of fresh water and a vast number of edible plants. There is an abundance of wildlife everywhere.

The animals all evolved short legs due to the high gravity, which at first we thought would make hunting them for food very difficult, but their lack of fear of man and natural curiosity made them easy to trap. We would at last have the occasional fresh meat. Something we have all missed for the last eleven years. We have been living on freeze-dried foods and synthetically manufactured dietary supplements, along with whatever vegetables we were able to grow during the voyage.

When we first arrived on Arilias-6, everyone was amazed at the vast variety of fauna and flora we encountered. Hundreds of different plants and creatures as dissimilar from anything seen on earth as could be imagined. None of the animals we encountered were much larger than an adult beaver or medium-sized dog. The semblance of this large variety of creatures is only slightly similar to many of those previously found on Earth; most had four legs, with a few oddities having six. Almost all had fur or hair of some kind, but the similarities end there.

There is an abundant mixture of carnivores, omnivores and herbivores. The shy creatures keep a safe distance from us because of our comparatively larger size, but show no real fear of man. Mostly because they have never seen one of us before, they are as curious about us as we are about them. Occasionally their curiosity gets the best of them and one approaches far too close to where we are working and has to be shooed away before someone trips over it. These slow-moving creatures offer no threat.

We found nothing on the planet capable of flight, probably because the increased gravity compared to Earth has kept the evolution of a flying species from developing. Creatures you might call insects are also very sparse. The most common is a nine-inch long invertebrate resembling a millipede. The main difference between the Arilias-6 millipede and one from Earth, besides size, is the outer plates of the Arilias organism are as hard as granite. When threatened, it curls up in a spiral, becoming impenetrable.

If one of the predatory animals is lucky enough to catch hold of one, attacking the soft underbelly before the armored creature has a chance to coil up, it would make a tasty meal for the hungry animal. If not fortunate to strike before the creature rolls up into a spiral, the hungry predator spends its wasted time trying to penetrate a skin that is like iron, and eventually gives up in frustration.

The next most prevalent insect type can best be compared to the ever-present cockroach. These, unlike their Earthly cousins, are as large as a man's shoe, and much slower than their counterparts. They emit a sweet, pungent odor when surprised or threatened. This strange combination of smells repels some animals, but interestingly attracts others. This is a mixed blessing that turns the large ground-clambering insect from a repugnant quarry for one of the creatures into a sought-after delicacy for another of the other small animals. Life is full of surprises!

Chapter 29
Home Base

Our landing areas are enlarged to accommodate the increasing number of daily shuttles landing with personnel and supplies. Each shuttle returning to the M.A.B.U.S. platform carries with it a quantity of Arilias water, equal to the weight of the craft itself. The fuel generating plant onboard the platform is in operation around the clock, manufacturing hydrogen fuel and oxygen from the water for the numerous shuttles. The stronger gravity of Arilias-6 results in the craft using more fuel for each landing and return launch than would have been needed on Earth. Even with the constant production, the craft are using the fuel from the reserves faster than it can be manufactured. However, the remaining supply, though slowly diminishing, is sufficient for quite a long time to come.

The temporary structures to house the crew who will be remaining on the surface indefinitely are brought down in sections aboard the larger shuttles. Erecting these structures in the increased gravity is backbreaking work. With the arrival on the surface of machinery to aid in lifting heavy objects, the harvesting of timber is begun. The thick, strong trees are selectively cut and sorted for lumber for the more permanent construction projects. The laser saw mill uniformly slices the trunks into identical pieces of usable lumber.

The first structures erected are initially nothing more than roofs with open sidewalls. The consistently mild weather and lack of annoying insects allows us to take advantage of and enjoy the open air during the time the permanent housing is being constructed. After such a long voyage in the confines of the space platform, it feels good to be out in the open again.

The crew of two hundred eighty remaining on the M.A.B.U.S. platform is rotated down to the planet's surface at ten Arilias-day intervals. This allows all the benefit of the open areas and to acclimate to the increased gravity. The two main tasks of those still up on the station are the manufacturing of the fuel and the maintenance of the hydroponics garden. For the time being, the majority of the food supply for the new colony is still being produced on the platform in space. We have found many edible plants on the surface to supplement our diets, as well as our catching and butchering a number of the many diverse, small creatures for the occasional banquet of meat.

It has been so long since we had any animal protein that most of us have forgotten how difficult animal flesh is to digest. After our first meal of Arilias stew—followed by frequent rushes to the latrines—many are content to remain with the bland diet provided from the platform. The bland food is something we have become accustomed to over the past eleven years. The onslaught of intestinal problems is not worth the discomfort caused by fresh meat.

We soon discover a new visitor to our surrounding area. They appear only at night. We would first see them as the Arilias sun was just sinking below the horizon.

At first we gave little thought to these lizard-like creatures. They vary in size from one to three feet in length. Each has short, stubby tails. They are a mottled green in color, having the ability to change the shading of their skin to blend in with their surroundings, much like the Earthly chameleon. Their forelimbs have an opposable digit, like a thumb that enables them to grasp objects as you would with your hand.

Their rear feet possess three formidable claws. The pads on their feet are covered by a fleshy surface enabling them to cling to even the highly polished titanium surface of the shuttle's outer skin. Their wide, upturned heads look much like a snake. They make no sound and can remain motionless for hours at a time, blending in with their surroundings.

Where these creatures came from, or why it took so long before we discovered their presence, we may never know. It is possible they are a migratory species similar to army ants. Traveling to where the food supply is most abundant and devouring whatever they find until they are forced to move on again to find more to feed on.

We have seen only an occasional individual of these lizard-like creatures since being on Arilias-6 for several weeks, and the quick reptilians always scramble away when approached.

The number of sightings has increased until these small- to medium-sized reptilian-like beasts became a nuisance around the compound. They are beginning to get into everything at night, especially as the dawn approaches. They are looking for a place to hide from the bright Arilias sun. The creatures never appear during the daylight hours, and our outside activities during the night are very limited, due to concerns for safety.

The first indication there is something definitely amiss is the diminishing numbers in the previously abundant wildlife. We have begun to observe fewer and fewer of the fur-bearing visitors to our compound through passing time. As the wildlife becomes more scarce, "they" have been turning their attention to us.

Until now, we have had no problems with the lizards we encountered. This is changing. We observe many of these lizard-like predators hunting on the outskirts of our compound. They move slowly toward an unsuspecting prey—silently stalking the unwary animal—or they often remain motionless—crouching within feet of their intended meal without the animal knowing it is there, waiting for the unlucky creature to move within attacking distance.

Striking without warning, they latch on to their prey and use the three long claws on their hind feet to rake and tear into the bodies of their captured victims. They possess bone-crushing jaws with short fangs, which inject venom, instantly paralyzing their prey. Once they immobilize their victim, other lizard creatures converge on the kill with lightning speed. The smaller ones bite on the extremities and begin to drain the prey's body of all fluids, leaving behind a desiccated corpse. The larger creatures attack the internal organs of their paralyzed victim, devouring it from the inside out.

We were soon to find out how dangerous and deadly these creatures were. Our newly encountered callers soon lost their fear of us slow-moving bipeds. The first direct attack occurred while First Lieutenant Pete Arthery was routinely patrolling the perimeter of our compound and approached one of the larger reptiles early in the evening—assuming the lizard would be easily frightened off.

To his fatal surprise, the creature struck, instantly paralyzing him. Even as he was falling to the ground, the reptile leaped at his throat, tearing into his innards with its rear claws. The creature was joined by several others who were lurking in the shadows—ripping large chunks of flesh from his helpless body, still alive, but unable to cry out for help.

The two distinct types of predators in the group attack different parts of his body. The smaller and, we assume younger, of these creatures seem to specialize in draining fluids from a victim, and the larger ones attack the soft internal organs. Tearing into his body cavity, their feeding frenzy rivals that of the Amazon piranhas. They ignore the tougher muscle areas of his body where the smaller ones latched on to him. Draining his body of all moisture, they continue their attack.

Only a few seconds have elapsed, and what is left of Peter Arthery's muscles when the fluid gatherers are through draining him resembles tightly bundled straw, and nothing remains inside his torso. He was rendered immobile before he could utter a scream, and he was dead before the others in the compound who witnessed the attack were able to run to his aid. The creatures turn from their fallen prey and confront the attackers advancing on them. They fanned out to defend the bounty they had just obtained.

Unfortunately, just a few of the crew were armed, but those with weapons began firing on the creatures. Their lasers cut into the beasts, severing them in half. Unfortunately, our weapons make no sound and do not have any kind of impact disturbance. There is nothing in our firing that might frighten these creatures away, no twang of an arrow, no bang of gunpowder, only a silent, deadly, almost invisible light beam.

These creatures strike down two more of the crew before they are finally driven off, and although not directly attacked by other creatures, both crewmen are dead in less than a half-hour from the venom.

What is left of the lieutenant is difficult to recognize as ever having been a human being. His skin, or what is left of it, looks like shriveled, parched leather, his body ripped open and hollow. Whole pieces of him are missing.

Retrieving the remains of Lieutenant Arthery, we retreat to shelter inside the main camp. The frightening discovery of how dangerous and deadly these unbelievably swift creatures can be prompts us to establish a "shoot on sight" policy, saving us some additional loss of lives.

From the carcasses of the reptiles we killed, we are able to synthesize a crude anti-venom. Unfortunately, it has to be administered within the first few moments after a bite, and by someone other than the victim. The bite of even the smallest of the reptiles causes instant paralysis. If one of the larger creatures bites a person, the quantity of venom injected would be fatal even if the anti-venom is administered immediately.

We mount an all-out effort to drive the creatures away. They had, in this one attack, acquired a taste for human flesh. Becoming quite brazen, actually coming out into the open, they stalk human prey. We outfit our lasers with ultrasonic noisemakers, assuming these creatures might be deaf, as they have no external ears. If nothing else, they would feel the vibration given off by our lasers each time they are fired. The creatures will soon learn we are not without defense and we can harm them. Many of these lightning-fast reptiles manage to escape our laser fire with only minor wounds, while many others end up nothing more than charred fragments.

We increase our fortifications to prevent them from entering the areas where we spend the night. Before completing the safe enclosures, we lose one of our crew when a smaller one of the lizards manages to get into the sleeping quarters. The bitten crew member never made a sound. His heart was stopping as the others around him slept.

These insidious creatures lurk all around us, and as the smaller, quicker animals became less numerous, we seem like easy prey for them. We are slow and do not flee, but to their undoing, we also fight back.

We perceive later that these small monsters are the forerunners to a more advanced descendant. As monkeys and apes are primates to us, these smaller lizard-like organisms are the same equivalent to the next life form we are to encounter. In our conjecture, they are much like something we might have evolved into had not the cataclysm that wiped out the dinosaurs on earth occurred.

Chapter 30
Intelligent life on Arilias-6

Ship's Date: Month: 6, Day: 9, Year: 11

We are surprisingly successful in driving off the night predators. There is a definitive decrease in number of these insidious creatures from when we first encountered them three months ago. Whether or not it was because we have destroyed so many, or they have just decided to move on to look for an easier prey, is unknown. We have killed hundreds and wounded scores of others. Now we only see the occasional night predator lizard, usually one of the smaller ones lurking around the edges of our camp, but still just as deadly and just as short-lived if we are within laser range. Unfortunately, we are now about to encounter a new visitation. It seems that by eliminating the threat of the night predators, we have opened the door for a new menace.

Since leaving Earth orbit more than eleven years ago, we have lost ninety-three of the crew. Seventeen were to the night predators alone. Four were to hyper-sleep chamber failures; eleven were suicides during the long, arduous voyage. We had hoped the exhaustive battery of psychological tests we all endured should have eliminated the chance of suicide.

Years of lonely space travel and the remembrance of all of our loved ones who died back on Earth can have a way of affecting the psyche of even the most stable-minded person. All the others except five were killed in either shipboard accidents or mishaps here at ground base, including the shuttle crash that claimed the lives of ten brave souls during early exploration of the planet's surface. The remaining five disappeared during a scouting mission after the original base was established. Those five vanished together, and searches from the air and ground failed to locate any sign of them. With what we were about to discover, we have a fair idea what might have happened to them.

"Boarski!" exclaimed Jamison. "Stop what you are doing and don't make any sudden moves! Look to your left about twenty degrees, over by the large tree near plot seven. To the right of the tree…in the bushes!"

Alexis Boarski turns and hollers, "Holy shit! What the hell is that?"

Standing erect, almost seven feet tall and grasping a crude, spear-like weapon with one of its front claws with the opposable appendage, is another lizard like creature. This one is out in broad daylight, a time when we did not have to be concerned about the night predators—and it is huge! It watches the progress in the compound from the surrounding brush, silent and motionless. When it realizes it was detected, it slowly crouches lower into the bushes. It shows a semblance of intelligence in realizing it was spotted. It hid itself, still holding a crude weapon at ready.

Although it made no threatening actions, we are very cautious, owing to what we previously discovered about its smaller cousins. Alerted, the sentries slowly advance toward the new visitor, but it vanishes as suddenly as it appeared.

It bore a striking resemblance to the other lizard-like creatures, although more muscular and many times larger. It had the same mottled green to brown coloring, with the ability to alter the shading of its skin to allow it to blend in well with the surroundings. Its skin was more knob-like than scaled. It possessed a broad, flattened head with a wide mouth, reptilian eyes and no visible ears. Its tongue was like that of many Earth lizards. It was not forked like some, nor like that of a snake, but short and stubby. Its forearms were considerably longer in proportion to its body than the smaller creatures. It also stood upright and seemed to prefer that posture. Its tail was much shorter than the smaller lizards, more of a rounded stub than a tail.

Two Arilias-days later, the creature returns. But this time it does not come alone. A second one is observed, and movements in the brush indicate there are at least three more. Armed sentries take up positions surrounding our enclosures, and all crew are called in to safe areas. The creatures watch us intently for several hours and then quietly disappear as silently as they had come.

The number of visitors increased as the days passed. They would always keep to the surrounding cover, silently watching us. We had much opportunity to study them also. They exhibited no verbal skills and made no movements that could be interpreted as signals or sign language. We did, however, discover they could communicate with each other using various scents, some of which could be detected by us. They had developed a language of odors, which they could control as well as we do our words. This communication, although primitive by our standards, is quite elaborate. Using scent alone, they could alert others to danger, or coordinate the movements of the group.

We were able to obtain a sample from the air of the particular scent emitted when the lizard men suddenly withdrew. We managed to synthesize this aroma, and when we were confronted by a band of these large lizard-like creatures in the surrounding brush of the compound, we released the fragrance. To our surprise and delight, the lizard men moved off. Unfortunately, this only worked twice. The third and successive times it was tried, they remained in position and seemed to grow increasingly agitated by this false scent. They learned to tell the difference between their natural communication and our manufactured odors, and they were not very fond of our "Eau de Go Away."

They would watch us day after day, spending most of the time in an upright posture, seeming to prefer that position instead of crouching in the brush. If the sentries approached and they felt speed was needed to escape, they would revert to all fours and move with tremendous rapidity—like nothing we had ever seen before.

Because they show signs of intelligence and the ability to communicate with each other, we are hesitant to take any direct action against them. Still, we keep our guard up because of what their smaller counterparts taught us about sudden deadly surprises. We post sentries continuously throughout the encampment just in case. If these creatures do turn out to be friendly, we did not want to start off on the wrong foot with our neighbors by killing some of them.

They begin to accept the idea we are aware of their presence and take less effort to conceal themselves from us. They still keep a safe distance from anyone who tries to approach. They too, like their smaller cousins, seem to be warm-blooded, but these larger creatures appear to have a greater tolerance for the daytime temperatures.

They also feed on what remains of the once abundant smaller animals.

We were able to observe several of them catching their prey and feeding on them. It is evident that they also possess powerful venom, like their smaller relatives, although from what we observed it is much more potent. Anything bitten dies immediately, again giving us concern as to how dangerous they could become. They hunt mostly during the day but will occasionally hunt at night if they are hungry enough.

Their favorite method of hunting seems to be the same as the smaller lizards, patiently waiting motionless for their prey to wander close enough for them to strike with their poisonous jaws. If they fail at the first strike, they grab a stick or log to use as a club or spear, or even a stone, using its sharp edge as a weapon or hurling it at its intended victim with deadly accuracy.

We have observed one of them grasp a branch of a dead tree and, with its muscular forelimbs, rip it completely off the tree trunk and use it as a club—bludgeoning its prey to death. The thought of how easy it would be for one of them to grab an awning pole or drainage pipe and do the same thing inside the compound gives us something to be concerned about. Almost all of the lizard men we observe carry various sorts of primitive weapons, all the while walking erect, but no threatening movements are ever displayed.

The fact the night predators had consumed or driven away most of the wildlife from our area gave us much additional trepidation. The devastation to the animal population caused by the smaller lizards left very little in our region for these larger creatures to feed on. These new individuals had the ability to cover a much wider range and at a much faster pace in less time to find food than their smaller counterparts, but they needed much more to sustain them because of their greater size. Could this be why they were so interested in us? This one thought serves to keep us constantly on our toes.

These new visitors would also approach the compound at night, but in lesser numbers. The majority departs as the evening approaches. It seemed their eyes, just like ours, are better suited for vision in daylight. Whenever the creatures approached, it was only to the outmost edge of our compound, never any closer.

We tried sending armed parties into the thick forest surrounding us to follow these creatures when they would leave in an attempt to discover where they dwelt, but we were no match for their speed. We were unable to get more than a hundred meters beyond the perimeter before we lost all traces of them.

After several of our attempts to follow them, their visits became less and less frequent. They all but disappeared, seeming as apprehensive of us as we were of them. We only spot one every three or four Arilias-days for a while, but they keep on returning. We keep our security measures at maximum level, ever wary of the return of the night predators, or worse.

The apparently intelligent lizard men still visit our compound and watch us as silently as before. There is not a single day when at least one of these huge denizens is sighted. Why are they so interested in us?

Attempts to communicate with the few remaining watchful creatures are in vain. If anyone approaches within vocal range, the lizard men flee. Communication via scent has already proven impractical. They did not like our manufactured odors. Any attempt at using gestures has the same effect as approaching too close. The creatures simply vanish into the surrounding cover.

We even left food at the perimeter to see if one of them would accept our offering. This was argued against as being the same as feeding a stray cat. Once you do, you will never get rid of it, and did we really want these poisonous creatures becoming a permanent fixture around our settlement—intelligent or not?

The creatures ignored the gesture of the gift of food. The lizard men were like earthly neanderthals, except that they were not hunter-gathers, only hunters. If they did not kill it, they would not eat it!

The majority of the lizard men appear to have moved on to where food is more plentiful, leaving us to wonder how intelligent these creatures really are, and if it is possible to ever communicate with them at all. Moreover, would they return?

All our endeavors to establish a means of communication with these extremely large reptilian beings was fruitless, because they always fled when we approached, until one day.

"One of our friends is standing over by plot fifteen," remarks Joe Galgota. He and Lorraine Davis are unloading the equipment from the shuttle that just landed fifteen minutes ago. Once the hull of the craft cooled below the point of being dangerous to the touch, the supplies are immediately off loaded and more water loaded back on, bound for the hydrogen generators on board the space platform. None of the shuttles leaves the surface empty. The faster they can be reloaded and launched, the less hydrogen needed to reheat the engines.

The large green and brown creature stands in full view of the compound, not trying at all to conceal its presence. The two crew members, ever mindful of the potential danger of these venomous behemoths, could not resist the urge to wave at this motionless, silent, omnipresent figure. To their total surprise, the creature raises its arm in a return gesture. Stopping in their tracks, staring at each other in disbelief, they wave to the lone lizard man again. The strange figure raises its forearm one more time in response. Galgota lifts his arm up and holds it in place. The visitor raises his arm up and holds it momentarily at the same angle—mimicking the gesture.

"Son of a bitch! Did you see that?" Joe Galgota exclaims. "That, whatever it is, just waved back at me!" There is a flurry of activity. The word spreads quickly through the compound concerning what had happened. There is no doubt that Galgota and Davis are not hallucinating. There are several other witnesses. With the sudden increase of activity and noise, the visitor melts into the underbrush.

"Damn!" Davis yelled. "I think that one wanted to say hello or something! You people scared it away!" The activity dies down, and the two return to the job before them. "I hope that one comes back," Galgota stated. "He seemed like he was a friendly sort."

The eyes of all the crew continually scan the perimeter for the remainder of the Arilias day. There is no sign of the lizard man who just might have waved back to Lorraine Davis and Joe Galgota. "What will we do if this happens again? What will we do if that solitary creature returning a friendly gesture should decide to return?" was asked.

All attempts at communicating with these strange semi-bipeds had been fruitless until today! Today, instead of fleeing immediately, this alien life form acknowledged our presence. We must be ready if there is a next time. We must not react in haste and frighten this creature away again. We must form a bond of communication if we are to begin a new life on their planet. They were here first. This is their home. We must show them we come in peace and mean them no harm.

The Arilias dawn presents a new surprise. The creature present yesterday has returned. It is not alone! With it are two others. The first creature advances several yards inside the compound perimeter. Its two companions remain outside the boundaries of the cleared area, partially concealed by the brush.

The lone creature stands erect, more than seven feet in height, its head held high. The three massive, razor-sharp claws on each of its feet nervously click against the laser-hardened soil of the compound. Its two companions shelter themselves in the undercover. The one out in full view raises its arm in the same gesture as yesterday. The wave is returned by several in the compound viewing this strange sight.

A group of delegates selected the night before begin to advance toward the creature. Seeing the large number coming toward him, the lizard man starts to back away, ready to disappear once more into the thick cover. The crowd halts, and so does the visitor. One lone person moves forward, but the lizard man remains perfectly still. As Captain Stuart Carthen advances toward the unprecedented guest, he extends both hands to show he is not carrying weapons of any kind. The lizard man stiffens at his approach, spear still clutched tightly in his claw. His companions sink deeper into the tall grass.

Captain Carthen advances to within four feet of the giant creature. The reptilian goliath lowers his head as in a greeting. Captain Carthen mimics the gesture, but before he is able to bring his eyes up again, the creature swings his spear around and down on his bowed head, splitting it open like a ripe melon. The dead captain is still standing upright when the massive creature spins his spear around again, impaling him through the chest and out his back. Hoisting him up like a side of beef, the creature tosses him over his shoulder and speeds away through the brush, taking the lifeless body of Captain Carthen with him. His two companions let fly with their spears to cover his escape.

Before any lasers could even be un-holstered, the three creatures are gone. This whole ruse was bait, and we took it—hook, line and sinker! They are more intelligent than we had ever imagined, and a lot more dangerous. There would be no more attempts at communication. From here on, we need to concentrate on defense if we are to survive on this planet.

After the incident this morning, an urgent staff meeting is called. "We know now that the large lizard people, and I use the term 'people' loosely, are far from friendly," said Commander Itogeshi to open the session. "All personnel are to be armed at all times. No one is to wander anywhere near the outer perimeter alone. A setback zone of fifty meters from the outer edge is now in effect. Inside that restricted area there are to be two sentries for each worker. All other immediate duties except collecting water for the platform fuel plant are suspended until complete fortifications are constructed.

"We've seen how fast these creatures can move, and we are no match for their speed." He continues by saying, "It is unfortunate that we now have to implement the same 'shoot on sight' policy we used on the smaller lizard creatures."

There was a considerable amount of murmuring through the assembled group. "Silence, please, people!" Itogeshi continues. "Any movement, by any of us, outside the cleared area of the compound will be undertaken by groups of no less than twenty fully armed crew. There will be no exceptions! Half will do the jobs necessary, the other half will keep their eyes peeled, ready to fire. These creatures are masters at camouflage, and I don't intend to lose any more of our number to feed these monsters!"

Captain Roberts, one of the first humans to set foot on Arilias-6, arose to address the assembled group of over one thousand. "Quiet, please! We have already seen what these creatures are capable of doing. They are able to coordinate as a unit without our ability to intercept what they happen to communicate to each other—as was demonstrated by the two other lizards in the brush, throwing their spears to delay our advance and give the primary attacker time to reach the cover of the underbrush.

"It is also apparent they possess phenomenal strength, judging by the distance they threw their spears. The best any one of us could manage throwing their massive shafts is one-third the distance they hurled them. We have to assume they are capable of throwing their weapons a much greater distance and with more accuracy than what we saw today.

"Their action today was only a way to gain a few seconds of time for their escape, and it worked very well! The lizards' weapons, as primitive as they are, are very effective. The two spears recovered after the three lizard creatures fled into the surrounding bushes are extremely well balanced. Although they are nothing more than tree branches that have been rubbed to a sharp point and smoothed to great precision, they can be directed at a target with great accuracy."

"We can only assume that they will be back," injected Commander Itogeshi. "I don't think we've seen the last of them. If and when they do return, I want all of you to be ready! We don't want to give them another chance at taking even one more member of our crew for their food.

"In the meantime, all efforts will be concentrated in making this compound secure from any further attacks. We are to kill on sight! Anything that resembles these creatures is to be vaporized at the first sign of movement.

"We will begin immediately to clear the perimeter an additional one hundred meters in all directions. Until we have a means to keep these creatures out, they will be forced to cross a much wider section of open ground before they can reach us. In addition, remember the lasers we use to clear the ground brush can also be used very effectively as weapons if necessary at close range. If one of these brutes should show itself unexpectedly, make him feel like the burnt grass. It may not kill the beast, but it will definitely make the rest of his day very uncomfortable."

That same Arilias afternoon, the work on widening the perimeter began in force. Wide swaths of vegetation are vaporized away. The region surrounding the compound became increasingly larger. Any standing trees, which had been spared previously for shade, were quickly harvested for lumber to add to the stockpile earmarked for the fortifications now urgently staged to be built, clearing all the land around the compound.

The work continues long into the Arilias night, the surrounding area lit as bright as daylight by the hundreds of halogen floodlights now scattered throughout the entire compound. The order is given to fire on anything that moves outside of the camp's perimeter, and it is carried out. There would be quite a few of the small Arilias-6 animals never seeing the next sunrise. No lizard men—at least none were seen or shot—approached the work parties toiling through the night and into the next day.

"The central command has come up with a possible way to fortify the compound," Commander Itogeshi says as he addresses the meeting of the senior officers. "Put your heads together and see if you can improve on what we've come up with." He lays the sheets of plans out before us. The main enclosure would be a series of three walls, one inside the next—each set at an angle of forty, thirty and twenty degrees respectively.

"We know from observing these lizard men that a straight wall of any reasonable height will not deter them. They can climb on almost mirror-smooth surfaces. The trees do not reach sufficient height to give us the boards of the length we need to construct walls high enough to keep them out. They can jump tremendous distances and heights. We do not have the time or means to construct a wall more than one board length high. The outermost wall would necessarily have to be made the most difficult for them to scale. Canted outward by forty degrees, it could not be readily climbed, but they still might be able to leap to that height. The top needs to be honed to a state or point where there are no footholds. If they manage to leap over the first one, the smooth surface should cause them to slide down between the walls. There they would be left with very little room between the first and second wall to get any running start to leap over the next. They would have to leap straight up and actually backward to reach the next enclosure. Each wall should delay their assault enough to give us time to man our defenses."

After examining the preliminary plans, the suggestion is made to place two grids of low frequency lasers between the outer, middle and inner walls. "We should be able to grind the optics in the time it will take to erect the walls," Science Officer Metsopolus comments. "The low frequency fence will use very little power compared to our stronger defense weapons. It will not kill anything, but it will definitely give them something to think about while they are dancing around in it. These would only have to be activated if there is a threat of an attack. Our sensors should pick up anything moving in the cleared perimeter long before they reach the walls, giving us enough warning beforehand to be ready."

"That's a good idea," Itogeshi remarks. "We can place them right across the four gateways in and out of the compound. Our people will know they can run quickly through them in an emergency without any harm done to them. It won't be a pleasant experience, but when you consider the alternative…"

The construction of the first of the three walls began immediately. An occasional lizard creature is sighted, observing the building of the walls. The sentries advance on the menace, and the lone reptile flees before the armed group reaches effective laser range. Those few that did not scatter immediately are either wounded or cut down where they stand. Fortunately, the effective range for our hand lasers far exceeds even the strongest of their spear arms.

Our supply of usable timber is rapidly dwindling. We would need to secure more materials, and our crop fields need tending. The first of the three walls is only three-quarters completed. The next two surrounding fortifications would each be larger and require more material than the first, innermost wall.

The following dawn, a large work party of three hundred and seventy heavily armed crew, with the machinery needed to lift and cart the harvested trees, leaves the compound for the dense forest less than two kilometers from base. They make their way into the tangle of trees—the eyes of the motionless, deadly creatures watching with interest. Almost invisible, blending in perfectly with their surroundings, the work party sees none of them.

The trees on Arilias-6 do not grow as tall as the trees used to on Earth. Most never reach the height of thirty feet, but the trunks are massive, providing an ample supply of lumber from each tree. With modified lasers to use as saws, the trees could be limbed from the ground, the resulting debris cleared, and then the trunk neatly severed with the laser, the wood quickly carted off to be made into lumber.

One crew member, Eva Cuomo, is using a laser to cut the outgrowth from one of the trees selected to be felled. She aims first at one lower branch, and as it drops, takes aim at another. To get a better angle for the shot, she moves close to a clump of bushes off to the side. A mottled, green-brown head shoots out from the base of the bush—for less than a second its jaws clamp on her calf. She stands motionless in her tracks, still aiming at the next branch she was going to cut with a startled look on her face. She then fell dead to the ground. Lasers fire into the bush and surrounding area, but the creature is gone.

Twelve other members, lasers at ready, prepared to carry Cuomo's lifeless body back to camp. None of the twelve make it out of the forest alive. They are ambushed, unbeknownst to the rest of the party not more than five hundred meters away. The attack is swift and deadly. All thirteen bodies are later discovered—some ripped apart by the razor-sharp claws on the feet of the monsters, two others pinned to trees by heavy spears. Several died from the venomous bites of the silent killers.

It is now apparent these creatures do not just kill for food. They seem to kill for the sake of killing, and even seem to enjoy doing it. None of the bodies of the slaughtered group showed any signs of being bitten more than once, and all thirteen corpses were left behind with no signs of any feeding. These diabolical beasts kill just to kill. The returning work party is about to make this gristly discovery.

The remaining work group, unaware of what just happened, continues with their chore of cutting and harvesting the needed timber. The transports are fully loaded with the needed logs and they began to make their way back to base camp. As Phyllis Doyan steers the tractor pulling the load of logs through the trees, a massive wooden shaft shatters the windscreen of the vehicle, impaling her and pinning her to the seat. A flurry of spears and other projectiles drop several more of the crew. Again the sentries open fire, and the forest falls quickly silent. Fortunately, this time they find two of their horrible attackers sliced to ribbons by the powerful lasers.

The horrifying discovery of the bodies of the group that had left the main unit not more than twenty minutes prior causes the crew to start randomly firing into the surrounding area, looking to avenge the devastating attack. Realizing we only have a finite amount of power reserves left in our lasers, we cease firing, reserving the remaining charge in case we happened to find a genuine target on which to vent our revenge with our hand lasers. We had those opportunities before we emerged from the forest. The lizard men launch two more devastating attacks against us.

THE WANDERERS

Three hundred and seventy people went into the forest...two hundred and ninety-one live souls emerge. We manage to bring all their dead out with us. No one wanted to leave any behind for these monstrous villains to snack on later. We have lost seventy-nine people and are sure of only killing six of the attackers—two in the first attack, and only four others that we know of in the later ambush.

Chapter 31
A Smaller Base Camp

    We know now it will be difficult and dangerous to venture into the surrounding forests to gather timber in the future. It is extremely risky to be in the thick cover of the forest when your enemy has the ability to look like the leaves surrounding you. For now we will make do with the wood we have been able to glean on this last trip into the glen. Unfortunately, there is not even enough to finish the first fortification wall to the size originally planned.
    We will continue the construction work with the materials we have on hand, but we will begin by moving the wall inward to enclose the main compound. The enclosure will have to be made considerably smaller, a much tighter circle and farther inside the perimeter we first mapped out. The newer design will make for more cramped living, leaving barely enough room for two shuttles to land at the same time. The construction material supplies from up on the M.A.B.U.S. platform have been just about exhausted.
    There is not much left on M.A.B.U.S. that can be sent down to us, so we must turn to scavenging lumber from our own living quarters. Primarily at this time, we need to construct at least one secure wall to protect us from these creatures. We will endeavor to acquire more timber as the urgent need arises, but not before. The number of armed sentries in relation to each worker will be doubled. No one, at any time, is to let themselves be separated from the main unit. If they do, they may never return.
    Through all this, we continue to care for the garden plots containing the newly growing Earth plants that are now standing several inches tall. The

plots, located in open areas far removed from the dense growth of the woodland, allow us to do so in relative safety. Still, we remain ceaselessly on guard against any sudden rushes by those creatures. The grasslands surrounding each plot are kept cut down to stubble to remove any cover for these quiet ground-creeping attackers.

Even in the open fields, we are not immune to attacks. There have been several over the past few weeks causing us more casualties. The number of lizard creatures seems to be increasing. When they are sighted now, instead of the usual solitary figure, they are frequently gathered in groups of several or more.

The remaining supply of cut lumber is now exhausted. We must again venture into the timberland to gather more wood to complete our stronghold. This next tree cutting work detail will comprise almost half our total group. Every piece of lifting and carting equipment will accompany the nearly eight hundred into the thicket. Two hundred will be doing the cutting and loading, while the remaining six hundred guard the perimeter. We are hoping that our sheer number will deter the creatures from any attack.

Reaching the stand of trees selected, we began the process of clear cutting, which we have avoided doing until now. It will take many years for the depleted forest to re-grow, if it ever does, but right now, every piece of timber is precious and the less time we spend in the dense woods, the better.

The sentries are posted at arms'-length intervals around the work party. We begin to cut from the center outward. The loading of the logs will be safely done in the cleared region. The sentries fire at any movement or sound whatsoever in the surrounding woodland. As the trees are cleared, the circle moves outward, resulting in the space increasing between the armed guards. There is now a distance of about twenty feet between the guards, which is becoming more dangerous. There is brush between them and also behind them.

These lizard-like monsters, as large as they are, are capable of blending in perfectly with their surroundings and moving undetected along the ground through the brush. Moving ever so slowly, they remain undiscovered. Five of the sentries are dropped by lethal bites once the first rush of the creatures occurs. They number only about forty, but take a devastating toll.

Only a few wounded ones manage to escape, but not before they take a distressing toll of eleven more of our people. It is time to get out of the thicket—to a place where we can see what we are fighting!

Pulling back to the cleared area, the last of the cut timber is loaded on the transports. Each vehicle is filled to capacity, making the going slow over the rough terrain. Unknown to us, up ahead, over the rise in front of us, an ambush is waiting. More than a hundred of these creatures wait motionless and silent in the underbrush.

Our saving grace is crew member Adrian Rasmussen's keen nose. He senses the faint odor of one of the lizard men's communications. The scent must have been emitted very strongly, aimed at reaching all of the creatures who were hidden and waiting for us. Rasmussen was able to detect a slight whiff of a strange alien smell.

"Those bastards are nearby!" he exclaims. "I can smell them, I tell you! I can smell them!" The convoy halts and the forward sentries advance to the top of the rise. Even now, others can begin to distinguish the ominous odor. A flurry of spears and other projectiles drop three of the sentries before they can return fire and seek cover.

"Base, we're under attack! We're pinned down in a gully, two clicks from the perimeter," the commander of the work party says over the radio to the compound. The heavy transports, riding low to the ground with the massive logs, give us a substantial amount of cover. Their element of surprise eliminated, the lizard men begin advancing their position, endeavoring to encircle our convoy. The transports are moved alongside each other, giving us cover on two sides and leaving only the two ends of our column open to attack.

Each time one of these denizens attempts to advance toward us through this gauntlet, it is instantly cut to shreds by a hail of laser fire. The logs piled on the transports provided us with ample protection from any assault on our flanks. Their primitive but deadly weapons are useless at penetrating several feet of solid timber.

Many of the sentries, as well as myself, climb onto the logs of the loaded transports to return cover fire on each side. The topmost logs provide protection from their spears and rocks, effectively stopping or deflecting them. Bringing my head up over the top of the log pile to look for a target, I am suddenly face to face with one of these hideous creatures. It had climbed up on the unprotected outside of the transport to assault our people from above.

It opened its gaping mouth, revealing rows of teeth accented by four sharp, short fangs. For an instant, I stared into its alien, reptilian eyes. It was just as startled by me as I was by his sudden appearance. Before the creature could recover enough to attack, my finger pressed on the fire button of my laser.

The lizard man's head exploded in a spray of slime, its lifeless body tumbling off the pile of logs. I can still smell the stench emanating from the jaws only inches away from my face.

From the base camp a platoon of three hundred armed crew, accompanied by laser-armed shuttles, head for their trapped comrades. Word is sent to the work party to remain within the shelter of the transports. The surrounding area is blanketed with intense laser fire from the shuttles and the advancing ground troops. The few creatures not killed when the reinforcements arrive on the scene flee into the surrounding dense forest. Any wounded lizards incapable of retreating into the deep woods are dispatched with extreme prejudice. The convoy makes its way back to base, both flanks and rear covered by the hovering shuttles.

Our losses sustained during this short battle amounted to nineteen, reducing our total number to less than sixteen hundred—including the crew up on the M.A.B.U.S. platform. The lizard-man body count in this one raid exceeded one hundred. The exact number was impossible to tally, due to the large number of reptilian fragments scattered through the surrounding forest. Countless other attackers were wounded. We hoped they might learn something from this experience. They did! But not the lesson we hoped to teach them.

Our next foray into the wooded region was met with peaceful non-interference. Through the entire work detail, only three of these creatures were sighted, and all three were at a great distance from where we were working. They had learned they were no match for our superior firepower, but they had also learned that if they were going to continue to prey on us, they would have to use cunning instead of brute force.

Beyond the fields containing our garden plots is a sizable lake of clear, fresh water. We had set up a solar powered pumping station to supply water to the compound. Completely self-contained, the water is pumped through a pipe buried deep beneath the Arilias-6 soil and into our compound. During the long hours the sun shines in the sky, the pump operates constantly—shut off only by the relay circuits signaling the pump all our storage tanks are full.

During the night, the station is silent. The water piped to the compound is stored in large tanks and as much as can be safely carried is sent up to the space platform on each returning craft—water to be converted into fuel for the shuttles. The rest of the more than abundant stored water is for the use of the crew at the home base during the long Arilias night. The water from the tanks is also used for crop irrigation during dry periods, which fortunately are few. The region we inhabit has ample, regular rainfall.

The pump we installed is quite small, delivering only eighty liters per minute. It is a small quantity for that given time, but when you take into consideration the length of the Arilias day, it equates out to over one hundred and ninety-two thousand liters each day that the sun shines. More water than we could ever use.

The creatures turn out to be more intelligent than we gave them credit for. They have determined we need water. How they deduced where we were getting our water from is anyone's guess. They attack the pumping station. Whether they thought there might be some of our people in the pump house or if they somehow figured out this is the source of our water, we do not know. They attack the pumping facility with vehemence. Their attack on the pump station destroys the photo voltaic cells providing electrical power to the pump.

They pummel the collector panels with everything they can lay their claws on: spears, stones, sticks—even approaching and biting the edges of the panels. After destroying the solar array, they attack the pumping facility itself, laying waste to the complex machinery inside the protective shed. The lifeline to fuel and survival, our water supply, ceases. There will be no more water for some time to come.

The shuttles fly out to the location of our main and only pumping station, strafing the area with laser fire. There are no lizard men to be found anywhere in the area. The pump complex is totally devastated. We will have to start from scratch if we are to continue to supply water to the base camp. The construction crews move into the area to repair the pumping facility.

Deploying the shuttles overhead for observation in the higher Arilias-6 gravity uses a tremendous amount of fuel. Every second a craft is airborne in the Arilias atmosphere uses an amount of fuel equal to that derived from six hundred and forty liters of water. Nine thousand, six hundred plus gallons of our precious water need to be converted into hydrogen for every hour of flight. We send one single shuttle out ahead of the advancing work party to report on any movement of the creatures in the area. If the work zone is clear of the lizards, the party, once on the scene, will be able to defend the area that is well out in the open without much difficulty.

The shuttle will return when it is time for the work group to head back to the compound, scanning the region for any of these denizens who might be lurking in the cover of the brush. It takes us several days to repair the pump complex and set up the laser perimeter surrounding the facility in hopes of preventing another future attack.

There is no way to safely man the pumping station. A large band of these creatures could very easily overwhelm the few guards positioned there, destroy them and the pump complex, and be gone before any help could arrive. We do not have the number of personnel needed to defend the pump station, the base camp and still continue with our fortifications. All we can do is try to make the pump more difficult to disable.

We were able to obtain flowing water for three Arilias days before it ceased again on the fourth morning. The creatures had attacked the pump house sometime during the third night. Shuttle overflights showed a section of the laser perimeter had been blocked with debris, rendering it ineffective. The pumping station was again totally destroyed. We were back to square one!

The work on the walls surrounding the compound is progressing at breakneck speed. We make several more excursions into the forest to cut lumber without serious incident. Nonetheless, over the last few months, isolated attacks by the lizard men on the various work parties in different areas have claimed the lives of an additional one hundred and eighteen people. Nearing completion of the fortifications, our next challenge is what we are going to do about obtaining the massive quantities of water we need to sustain the colony. The water source is too far away to effectively defend, and it is too late in the game to move the compound closer to our supply.

"Attention, all personnel! There is a command staff meeting at 2100 hours," the intercom blares across the compound. 2100 hours is noontime on Arilias-6. This is a meeting of grave importance. A meeting to decide our next course of action. A meeting to determine the future of the human race.

The higher-ranking officers gather in the main building inside the compound. The matters discussed would be handed down to their subordinates at the close of the meeting. All decisions made concerning the settlement are multi-lateral. The lowest ranking individual has as much say as the most senior officer.

"May I have your attention!" Commander Itogeshi calls the meeting to order. "We are faced today with some very serious problems. Our water supply has again been cut off. The shuttles are capable of collecting water directly from the center of the lake, where they are safe from attack, but doing so uses more fuel than the water will replace.

"For the time being, they will supply us with the necessary drinking water, but that is all. Until we figure a way to secure the pump station against future attacks, or replace it with a portable system, we will be going on water rationing. The fields are to be left at the mercy of the weather. All rain water runoff will be collected and sent up to the platform for fuel conversion."

"What are the chances of moving the compound to a different region of the planet, somewhere far removed from these lizard creatures?" someone asks.

Captain Roberts answers, "We have collected extensive biophysical data on these creatures. This information has been sent up to the M.A.B.U.S. computers for analysis. The resulting data has been programmed into the sensors on the low orbiters. As we speak, the craft are searching for any regions that are devoid of these predators. Unfortunately, the results so far do not look very promising. Sensors show these creatures are widely dispersed through all sections of the planet, except the polar ice caps and the hostile desert region at the equator, and they are even into the fringe areas of those two regions. The only exception might be some of the larger islands many hundreds of kilometers out to sea. We are still waiting for data on most of those."

Commander Itogeshi again addresses the group. "We have to assume we will be met with the same hostilities no matter where we try to settle on this planet. Preparations are underway to send out new probes into the nearby star systems in hopes of locating another close planet where we might settle. Until then, we will make our stand here while we wait to receive information from the probes. We should be impervious to attack once the fortifications are complete. Our food supply is very much assured by the surplus of freeze-dried and fresh produce from the platform."

Captain Roberts again interjects. "Our foremost concern is going to be the supply of water. When we have constructed a portable pump fixture that we can take to the lake in the morning, guard during the day and return to the safety of the compound in late afternoon, we will have to use what water we are able to obtain sparingly."

"Bring your respective groups up to date on what is happening right now and relay back any input the others may have to offer." The main body of the group rose to leave the assembly room. Commander Itogeshi is handed a message from the communications center. Reading the message, he calls the group back to pass on this new information.

"The shuttles have completed surveying all the islands large enough to support our population. Any that have the sufficient resources to sustain us, even for a short while, also are inhabited by the lizard creatures. Our only hope is to bide our time here while we search for another planet."

THE WANDERERS

The assembly files out and Roberts turns to Itogeshi. "I don't hold much hope. The Earth probes failed to find anything closer than seventy light years from here. I don't think anyone is looking forward to a long space voyage of any extended time, let alone one of that duration."

"I fully agree with you, Captain," Commander Itogeshi says. "But when the original search was done, they were using primitive sensors compared to the advances in detection equipment we made during the voyage here. The Earth bases could only locate the larger star systems. Our probes can now detect solar systems smaller than what was once our own. Don't give up yet! We still might have a chance."

Chapter 32
Hold Your Ground!

To use an old Earth expression, we "hunkered down" in the confines of our compound, waiting for the probes to transmit back the hoped for data they might find in another solar system with another life-sustaining planet. Someplace safer. Safer than this lizard-infested hell where we are now forced to defend our utter existence against constant attacks—or become the main course at a lizard banquet. The probes continue to search for another planet where we might move our colony.

Our enclosure is now complete. Three separate, encircling walls some twenty feet in height surround us. The outermost slants away from the center of the compound, set at an angle of forty degrees to perpendicular. The base is ringed with a laser fence to prevent anyone or anything from approaching the foundation of the wall. The second or middle wall is set at an angle of thirty degrees. Spaced at only ten feet at the base, the distance between the top of the outmost wall and the top of the one in the middle is about one meter wider, a little over thirteen feet. The same spacing is found between the middle wall and the innermost fortification.

The timber, cut into uniform slabs by the laser saws, has an almost mirror-like finish. The ultra smooth surface provides no hand or foot holds for anything attempting to scale the slanted wall. Although these creatures possess the ability to leap the twenty-foot height of the enclosure, they will not be able to gain the distance needed to reach the top of the second wall. The hapless attacker would find itself sliding down the glasslike surface of the barrier, directly into the waiting laser fencing between the two enclosed areas. If one should latch on to the top of the surrounding structure and climb up to the edge, it would be an easy target for our sentries before it could leap to the next barrier.

The inmost fortification is ringed with a six-foot wide platform from which our watch sentries patrol the entire surrounds. We have the ability to move a tremendous amount of firepower to any of the various sections of the compound where these creatures, if they decided to attack, choose to front. We are secure for now, except for our water supply.

We have made several successful treks to the lakeside pump station to operate our pump manifold for as long as the Arilias sun beams down on us. There are a few minor incidents with the lizard men, but nothing of consequence.

However, unknown to us at the time, scouts from the lizard creatures group discover a section of our pipeline buried in a thick area of undergrowth about halfway between the lake and our compound. As we pump our precious water, their keen senses detect the gurgle of the lifeline to our compound.

Morning came and we were met with an awesome sight. Just outside the cleared perimeter of our compound stands a virtual army of these lizard-like creatures surrounding our enclosure. They stand there, erect, silent, motionless—each one holding a formidable weapon. Our best estimate put the number of these monsters at between three and four thousand. All during the Arilias day they stand watching us, never moving, as if trying to psychologically wear us down.

When we launch the shuttles and the craft approach the lizard men, those creatures in the immediate area simply melt into the underbrush and become invisible only to reappear again once the craft has passed overhead. The shuttle's lasers are ineffective in that the foliage and brush either absorbs or deflects the fire. The creatures just materialize in a different location, their sheer presence taunting us.

It was with this standing force confronting us we were about to make a terrible, frightening discovery. The Arilias sun began to set. We had focused our attention on our infrared detectors to monitor the movements of these creatures as it grew darker. To our horror, the devices turn out to be useless. It was true these creatures were warm-blooded, but they also had many traits of a reptile.

Their smaller counterparts, the night predators, shied away from the heat of the Arilias sun, preferring to do their foraging in the cooler night hours. Their smaller cousins had not developed the ability to regulate their own body temperature.

The larger lizard men, able to tolerate a much wider range of climate, are able to endure the heat of the day, but as night falls, their body temperature drops to equal that of their surrounding area. We watch in horror as we see on the scanners the mass of creatures slowly disappearing one by one from our sensors. As the ground temperature drops, so does the body temperature of these creatures.

At night we are blind to their movements, which is why they were able to amass such a number together before dawn to surprise us. They could move slowly enough so any of our motion detectors would miss them. We would only know they were near if one of them ventured into our laser field and caused a disturbance. We turn on all the floodlights, taxing our already overburdened generating system.

All during the Arilias night, everyone is on edge. Our lights show no movement. The shadows cast by the crossing lights make everyone jumpy. At a time like this, you see all kinds of terrible things in the distant dim illumination, but we did not see what was right in front of our noses.

The lizard men had flattened themselves against the ground, inching slowly closer to our stronghold. The mottled coloring of their skin blends in perfectly with the ground they are creeping along. Inch by inch they close in—pressing their bodies against the laser-hardened soil—totally silent. They had over forty hours of complete darkness to cross our perimeter. They were suddenly upon us!

We would not have known they closed in, except one of the unlucky creatures ventured an inch too far—contacting the laser barrier we set up. The disturbance in the field sets off alarms throughout the compound. There is a mad scramble to defend the walls. Shuttles take to the air—additional bright floodlights flash to life—armed personnel running in every direction.

"Damn! The ground is alive! They're everywhere!" The halogen lights flash back and forth. Lizard men completely surround our compound, leaping toward the walls from every direction. We open fire at random, dropping as many as possible. They scale the top of the outermost wall. A great number clear the first bulwark, only to slide down into the waiting lasers at the base, where they are subjected to painful bombardment of the low frequency light beams. Desperately struggling upward, several dozen manage to reach the top of the middle enclosure.

They have breached halfway to the inside of our fortress. Wave after wave of these formidable creatures throw themselves at the walls of our enclosure. The attacking forces are successfully repelled, except for the few individuals who manage to avoid our direct fire and escape the protecting lasers at the base of each wall. They are coming at us by the hundreds. Scores of these lizard-like creatures are cut to pieces once they reach the top of the first wall. Our lasers slice more apart in their attempt to scale the middle enclosure. Several dozen manage to reach the final, innermost barrier. They are at last inside our compound.

Eighty-six of these terrible warriors manage to gain a foothold inside our fortress. Now, in close quarters, the fighting has become even more intense. The monsters bite anyone within reach. Several of our own crew are struck down by our own laser fire directed at the creatures. Their brute strength is equal to five of our people—their razor-sharp claws and immense stature make us no match for them physically. The toll they take before we finally destroy the last of the invaders is devastating, two hundred seventy-three dead, twenty-six others seriously injured.

Dawn is breaking and the lizard men retreat to the surrounding brush. Under the cover of darkness, thermally blending in with the surrounding ground, they have the advantage. Now, in the light of day, we are the more astute. There are a few wounded creatures attempting to crawl away. They never make it to the edge of the perimeter.

"We need to get the wounded up to the platform as soon as they are stabilized," Commander Itogeshi declares. "Half of the medical staff is to accompany them. The rest will remain here. We are bound to need them, if last night is any indicator. I don't think the lizards are finished with us yet!"

The wounded are loaded onto the shuttles—frantically made ready to rendezvous with M.A.B.U.S. Because of their wounds, the shuttles would have to literally fly up into space, using much more fuel, instead of making a rapid, direct climb. The injured would not be able to withstand the intensity of the G-forces during ballistic acceleration.

"There is still a good forty hours of light left before we can expect the return of these bastards! Let's make the most of the daylight while we can and see what we can do to bolster our defenses," Itogeshi adds. "Here is the hard part. We cannot bury our dead. We do not have the time or the resources to dig graves. Nor do we have the fuel reserves to transport their remains back up to M.A.B.U.S. for disintegration. We have all lost friends in last night's battle. Some of you, I am sorry to say, lost more than just friends. I have given the order for one of the main meteor-deflecting lasers from the platform to be installed on a shuttle. We will cremate our brothers and sisters here on the surface."

Commander Itogeshi knows the meteor laser, capable of vaporizing a chunk of ferrous rock the size of a house, would not only efficiently cremate the bodies of those lost in battle, but would also give us a weapon that no amount of brush or foliage would be able to deflect. It will take more than the remaining Arilias daylight hours to complete the installation of the laser on the shuttle.

The remains of the slain crew are gathered into an area near the main gate of the compound, the first to catch the sunrise as it breaks the horizon. The covered bodies are delicately placed one next to another, awaiting their final resting place outside the compound.

"Something has to be done to protect the topmost sections of the walls," Captain Roberts states. "We have already seen these creatures get over our boundaries and a large number climb back up the first wall to get to the next and then the third. Fortunately, none that got in ever got out again to tell the others what they found. They're still in the dark as to what they are up against, but we can't press our luck!"

"Might I suggest," Science Officer Spiro Metsopolus declares in his quasi-continental manner of speaking, rising to his feet, "that we electrify the top of the blasted wall! It would only take some wire strung a foot or less above the top edge of each enclosure with a wire grid placed from the top down for several feet and left hanging. These lizards need only to touch it and find some other ground source and they will become instant reptile fricassee. We can use the extra fencing set aside for the gardens and retrieve any more we need from the fields.

"We don't have to worry much about the little furry critters getting into the gardens right now anyway! Most of them have been eaten by the lizards. Why worry about stopping the few left from eating our plants when our greatest concern is to keep ourselves from being eaten. We can put the wire fencing to a much more important use, and besides, we have already bolstered our power output. We now have the generating capacity to put enough juice through a substantial wire network to barbecue a full-grown elephant."

"Get on it," Itogeshi remarks. "Let's get it up and running before nightfall."

"I remember reading somewhere about an old twentieth-century guerilla war tactic. They would put pointed sticks in pits and the advancing armies would fall into the holes and become impaled on these sharp points," someone says. "These sons of bitches might get a good shock, drop down between the walls, get zapped by the lasers and be pissed off enough to jump over our electric fence and make it to the next wall. How about if when they drop to the ground between the walls, they meet with an array of spikes. What say we don't give them anywhere to safely land?"

"Good idea! You're in charge of that project," Roberts agrees. "Just make sure you leave the gateways open. We don't want anyone running in here in a hurry, looking like he had just met with a porcupine." It was good to hear a little laughter after the night we had just been through.

The jobs of erecting the electric fence and planting the thousands of punji stakes got underway. The stake planters followed a safe distance behind the crew installing the electrification perimeter. If one of the crew lost his balance and slid down the wall, he would look like a shish-kabob if the punji stakes were already under him.

Daylight is waning. The crew from the water detail is now returning, accompanied by one of the shuttles. Crew member Defalous pauses when passing by a thick clump of trees. The ground did not look right. It looked too fresh. She does not think any more about it and proceeds along with the rest of the column.

Nightfall approaches, accompanied by the hum of the generators. If the creatures are to come again tonight, they would get a shocking experience. The hours pass. Nothing! More time elapses, still no sign of attack. As dawn approaches, everyone gives a sigh of relief.

There would be no water detail today. There would be no work parties of any sort, other than the funeral procession to the cremation pyre. We carry the bodies of our comrades one by one to the area designated. The shrouded remains are positioned ceremoniously next to each other. All two hundred and seventy-three are brought out. The shuttle equipped with the powerful laser ascends and hovers above our gathered comrades. All the crew stands at attention, many clasping hands—the bluish light envelops the line of motionless shrouds, proceeding from left to right. All that remained of each body after the laser passes is a small strip of fine white ash quickly swept away by the prevailing breeze. The shuttle then moved off to dispose of the large pile of lizard remains that we had unceremoniously stacked beyond the walls at the opposite side of the compound.

Several of the command staff, including Commander Itogeshi and Captain Roberts, speak words of eulogy. We spend the rest of the day in halfhearted preparations for the coming night while we mourn our fallen friends. The compound should be, by all reasoning, secure from outside attack. The electric fencing is all along the top of the walls. The punji stakes are set in the ground at various angles, covering each and every possible angle of fall. If the lizard men do attack tonight, they are going to be met with some very new experiences. Everyone hopes for another quiet night like the previous evening—the sun sinks below the horizon.

About the fifteenth hour of darkness, there is a flash on the top of the outermost wall. They have returned! Assaulting the walls, one wave after another, driven back by the electric barrier we had installed the previous day. Instead of hundreds, tonight they come by the thousands. Instead of creeping slowly toward us, they rush the compound upright, in vast numbers.

The shuttle with the newly installed meteor laser takes to the air, fully armed. Broad swaths of lizard creatures cease to exist in an instant. The laser continues to fire until the power reserves are exhausted. With this weapon depleted, the remaining shuttles launch and commence blanketing the entire surrounding perimeter with additional laser fire. Nine hours left until dawn. Still the denizens keep coming.

Reaching the top of the first wall, the lizards encounter a high-voltage deterrent. Some of the dead creatures become part of our defenses. Their lifeless bodies, charged with electricity, would decimate any other lizard man who touches them. Some fall backward, off the wall to where they started—others fall down the sloping inside surface of the walls, into the waiting spikes below, their agony compounded by the laser fence between the enclosures.

The high-voltage barrier on the outer wall eventually ruptures. The cumulative weight of the electrocuted creatures is too much for the tensile strength of the wire, and it snaps with a shower of sparks. The attackers now easily scale the first wall, using the bodies of their forerunners as stepping stones to reach the next wall.

Their assault on the middle bulwark is relentless. Myriad after myriad minions follow. The second stretch of electric perimeter fails under the weight of decimated lizard corpses, also erupting in a shower of lightning flashes. All hands are at the walls, firing our lasers at any visage presenting itself. Once more, these hideous monsters might find their way into our sanctuary. The innermost wall has no electrification. We would have to defend our position without the help of the high voltage wire fence.

The remaining shuttles launch, circling the compound, firing on the advancing hordes, driving them into retreat. The creatures still close to the compound continue to advance. The returning shuttles, their lasers capable of killing, but without the power to vaporize the attackers like the meteor laser has, begin strafing the two outer walls. Still, a large number of the attackers manage to reach the enclosure. We were again face to face with this horrible foe.

Falling back from the wall, we form a tight group in the center of the compound, allowing an area for the shuttles to counterattack from above. We fire relentlessly at the advancing menace. The shuttles overhead cut many of them to pieces. Finally, the last lizard man that gained a foothold inside our home ground falls dead in its attempt to subdue us. The sun is beginning to light the early morning sky.

Later today there will be another funeral. Not as large as yesterday's, but just as devastating to the emotions and morale of the remaining crew, if not more so. One by one we gather the mutilated bodies of one hundred forty-eight of our slain crew members.

It is clear now to everyone that we cannot stay here on Arilias-6 any longer. We must prepare to evacuate the planet surface or face certain death at the claws of the lizard men. We need to immediately formulate plans to remove equipment and personnel. The meeting is held directly after the funeral for our crew family.

Chapter 33
The Search for
Another Home

We resign ourselves to the fact we can no longer remain on this planet. We are under constant attack from these creatures, who not only want to destroy us, but also wish to make us part of their menu.

The search for another planet continues. More probes are launched—reports from previous explorers are arriving. Still nowhere to go! We are forced to quest farther and farther out into the reaches of deep space, searching for that one globe that will peacefully support us. Hopefully, a planet free of anything as horrible as what we have found here on Arilias-6. For now we will remove everything we can from the planet's surface, restoring our equipment back aboard the M.A.B.U.S. platform, holding out for as long as we possibly can on the surface below.

"Your attention, please!" Commander Itogeshi says, addressing the assembly. "Effective immediately, we will begin to load the shuttles with every piece of non-essential hardware we have with us. The shuttles are to be loaded with the maximum allowable weight. If size undershadows the weight limit, such as with the transports, the additional weight tolerance is to be made up with water. The more water we can get transported up to the platform, the more fuel we will eventually have."

There is some murmuring about water supply. "Our tanks, right now, are filled almost to capacity. Any one of the six storage tanks will give us almost a week of water if we are careful and do not waste what we have. The water detail will resume tomorrow. That is, if we manage to survive the night. You are all aware that it takes two liters of water, converted to hydrogen, to give us the fuel to bring three liters of raw water up to the platform. The shuttles are going to be making many more trips into space than ever before, using fuel faster than the platform can manufacture it."

Captain Roberts rises to address the group. "Right now the electrification of the barriers is being repaired. We all saw how effective it was in repelling these creatures. The supports are now placed closer together to prevent the same kind of failure we experienced last night. Furthermore, we are not going to destroy the bodies of the lizard creatures right away. Those we pry off the punji stakes and all the parts of the remaining creatures we are going to place around the outer area of our cleared perimeter. I know this seems barbaric, but if these lizard men do decide to attack again, the first thing they will encounter are the lifeless bodies of their own kind. This might buy us some time—if they are capable of fear."

The day draws to a close—twilight settles in—and checks are made of the perimeter to reassure all systems are operational. The reinforced electric fence stands tightly strung around the top of the middle and outer walls. The lizard-bloodstained ground of the cleared area is awash with floodlights. The walls are manned with one-third of the crew. The other two thirds were either resting before their watch or were working at disassembling equipment and loading the shuttles. Everyone is armed, even the crew who are now asleep.

All through the night we wait. There is no sign of our attackers. The third watch was ending as the sun peeked over the horizon. We survived another long night. We can start to relax now. The creatures seem to be reluctant to try to cross the bare perimeter ground in the daylight. If they do try a daylight attack, we will have the advantage of seeing what we are firing at and should be able to keep all of them from reaching the walls.

The water detail departs for the lake accompanied by one of the shuttles. We keep two more of the craft in reserve, including the one with the meteor laser to defend the compound if needed. The rest are making trips to the M.A.B.U.S. platform with equipment and water. Each returns to the surface of the planet with a full load of fuel, plus extra tanks of hydrogen for the shuttles remaining on the surface.

Four days and nights pass without incident. The lizard creatures appear to have moved off. There is only an occasional view of one or two of these creatures, and they flee at the first sight of us. Our hopes are that they have given up the notion of attacking us again—at least for a while.

The water detail takes a path to and from the lake that avoids any cover where the lizard men might be able to set up an ambush. The work party passes far from the place where Defalous noticed the accumulation of moist dirt on the surface. If Laura Defalous had not been one of the causalities of the second attack on the compound, she might have told someone what she had seen.

Another week passes without the lizard men approaching the enclosure. We are beginning to feel safer. Out of necessity, we dispose of the lizard carcasses. The stench was beginning to become overpowering. Once a good part of our equipment had been moved back up to M.A.B.U.S., the shuttles ferrying water up to the platform also carry small groups of crew members whose expertise is more useful up on the platform. The remaining crew on the ground number around seven hundred and fifty, but the exact number changes daily. Some days more, some less.

The water sorties are now only every other day. We have abandoned the plants in the fields. Now we concentrate on transporting our remaining equipment back to space. The platform is our sole source of food supplies. No one ventures past the cleared perimeter except for the water detail.

The twelfth day after the last attack began like any other. We were preparing to send out the pumping party for their usual task of refilling the water tanks. Some of the crew is loading two of the shuttles with equipment. An incoming shuttle starts to set down off to the side, away from the group loading the other transport—clear away from them so they would not be affected by the thruster blast. As it touched down, the starboard landing skid sank deep into the ground, up to the hull itself. The pilot increased thrust as the ground beneath the craft started to cave in. Hovering above the now gaping hole, he looked in horror at the mass of lizard men deep inside the chasm.

The creatures had dug their way under the compound, following our shallow pipeline right beneath our encampment. Ten to twenty at a time, they leap out of the hole, scattering throughout the compound. We are again under attack. The partially loaded shuttles take to the air. The three craft circle the inner enclosure, firing at the lizard creatures as they emerge. The one craft with the meteor laser was stuck on the ground. It was waiting for the returning shuttle to bring the much-needed fuel. It does not have enough in its reserve tanks for more than five or six minutes of flight.

One of the shuttles manages to seal the hole on the advancing attackers by hovering low over the breech, the heat from its thrusters raising the temperature inside the tunnel to well over two thousand degrees in a matter of seconds. Our water line burst, sending a stream of superheated steam through the length of their tunnel, boiling the lizard creatures alive. We halted their advance, but we still have scores of the lizard men inside our compound.

We have the advantage of daylight and superior weapons. They have the advantage of speed, agility and strength. The battle rages for more than an hour before we finally destroy the last lizard man. Our losses are devastating. An additional two hundred and sixty-three of the crew are dead. Almost one hundred of the remaining crew are wounded. Some critical.

Full evacuation would have to commence immediately. We cannot afford to remain any longer. The shuttles launch with the wounded and additional medical personnel. More shuttles are on their way back down from the platform. The transport with the meteor laser is refueled. The grim task of removing our dead to the outside of the walls is in progress. There will be no solemn service as before. As much as these gallant people deserved the same respect, there is no time. As the bodies are lined up, the craft activates the laser.

We place explosives we had once used to clear large rocks throughout the length of the tunnel the creatures had excavated. In a mighty roar, the entire length collapsed, all the way back to the stand of trees where they first began to dig their way to our compound. They would not be using it again.

We estimate we must stay in the compound for at least another three Arilias days until all of our equipment and personnel are safely transported back to M.A.B.U.S. The shuttles will be flying around the clock, each one loaded to capacity with materials and people, returning with only additional fuel to add to their tanks once on the ground.

Our number on the surface is down to one hundred twenty-three. Seven more shuttle flights will bring us all back to the safe haven of space. The last of our equipment is now back on the platform. All that remains now is the last of our water, the storage tanks and us. There is no rest for the weary. The shuttles bring replacement personnel to relieve some of the crew who dare not sleep—returning to M.A.B.U.S. with the exhausted people and additional water. The generating equipment to supply power for the electric fence and lights is to the last item sent back up.

Now as darkness settles in, we huddle near the four craft on the ground, waiting for the other shuttles to return. It takes time to unload the craft and for them to be refueled. If only the creatures will leave us alone, we will be gone tomorrow. We are thankful to get our wish—the sun is creeping over the horizon. But the sight that greets us sends chills up our spines. They are back! Back by the thousands! The craft with our main laser weapon takes off, making a broad circle around the edge of the cleared area. The laser begins firing in short bursts and cuts deep into their number.

The shuttles are returning from the platform. We decide to leave the water tanks behind. Anything else that remains in the compound will also be abandoned. The crafts land and immediately start loading the people onboard. Weight sensors in the landing skids tell the pilot when the ship reaches its capacity. Some hold fifteen—some hold more. I climb in and my weight exceeds the limit by half a person.

The pilot yells for me to stay onboard, but I tell him I will catch a cab and push the hatch closed from the outside. The creatures rush the walls, leaping over our barrier as if it was not even there. Dashing clear of the craft to avoid the thruster blast, I fire at anything and everything I see that is not human. The next craft lands after sweeping the area with its laser.

The lizard men were everywhere! Two hands push me through the hatch of the next shuttle. It was Commander Itogeshi. Before he could climb in, his chest erupts in a spray of blood as the spear piercing his back exits just below his sternum. The last of the living crew lift off the ground. The shuttle with the meteor laser makes a final sweep of the compound, vaporizing the dead bodies of thirty-four more of our beloved comrades. None are going to be left behind to provide a free lunch for these hideous creatures. The craft continues to fire on the lizard men until the power reserves for their lasers give out. When the laser is no longer effective, it climbs and heads out into space.

Chapter 34
Safety

The last of the surviving crew arrive safely back aboard the space platform—weary and heartsick over the loss of so many friends during the last few weeks. The lizard creatures have decimated our company. We now number only eight hundred and eighty souls. Those we lost include our senior commander, Shinto Itogeshi, and his attaché, Captain Alan Roberts. Now with both Roberts and Itogeshi gone—I became the senior officer. It is now my duty to assume the position of commander of the M.A.B.U.S. platform.

The wounded who have been brought on board—with the exception of three—all show signs of improvement, and we are assured they will survive their injuries. The three remaining in critical condition are given the best possible care, better than could ever have been provided on the planet surface under the most ideal circumstances. All of us are hoping that they too will pull through.

With the cessation of shuttle flights to the surface below, we also halt fuel production. The remaining stored water is earmarked for drinking purposes. We have no idea how long we will have to remain in orbit around Arilias-6 until we locate another planet. We can return the shuttles to the lake to retrieve more water if and when it is needed. For now, all craft and personnel will remain safely on board.

All the returned equipment has been stored away in preparation for another long space journey, and since there is nothing to do but wait for news from our probes, we return to the regimen of hyper-sleep and our previous thirty-hour daily schedule. All the wounded crew, including the three critical patients, recover sufficiently to the point where it is only a matter of time to complete the painless healing process. They are also returned to the Hyper-sleep chambers.

The days drag on as we wait for any report from the numerous probes we have dispatched. There are twenty-six explorers streaking toward distant star systems. We have only nineteen probes held in reserve. We do not dare send any more out until the ones already on their way report in. None can be retrieved, and if we use the last of them and nothing is found, we will be totally blind in our search for a home.

We are to remain in orbit around Arilias-6 for three and one-half months longer before one of the probes sends the glad news that it has found two planets in a single solar system capable of supporting life. The two globes occupy the same orbital path around their star, located half a sun orbit apart. Both show promise.

All of the other probes so far have found nothing, but there are still eight probes on their way to more distant destinations. I am awakened from hyper-sleep to receive this news. After the necessary time to re-orient myself, the rest of the command staff is brought out of their sleep. They and the ones on duty assemble once everyone is functioning somewhat normally.

"We have found two possible targets for our settlement," I begin. "Both located in the same solar system at a distance of approximately seventy conventional light years from where we are. It will mean a journey of over fifteen years at maximum speed to reach this system. To date, there is nothing any nearer to us capable of supporting life."

"There are still a small number of additional probes searching farther beyond that star system. We will not hear from them for some years to come. I do not believe there is doubt in anyone's mind that we cannot stay here forever, and there is no chance of ever returning to the surface of Arilias-6. It is my recommendation that we make preparations to move on toward this newly discovered star system we have designated as Alpha."

Charts are brought out and passed around; reams of data discussed and dissected. After days of discussion and debate, we decide leaving the orbit of Arilias-6 as soon as possible and beginning the voyage to the Alpha system is the most prudent course of action available to us at this time.

We prepare to leave the orbit of Arilias-6 immediately. If we receive more enticing news from any of the additional probes, which are still on their way to more distant star systems, we could always move on after exploring our options in the Alpha star system. The unanimous consensus is that we prepare to leave Arilias-6 as soon as possible.

The first order of the day is to ready the shuttles to return to the surface to collect the water we will need for this long journey. The craft would not land, but proceed directly to the lake, fill to capacity with water and rendezvous with the platform to offload.

Fuel manufacturing will re-commence while the flights are conducted, and cease when the water storage tanks are full. The shuttles depart, their leaving and return times calculated to coincide with when the platform is overhead in its orbit, conserving as much fuel as possible. They will be in no danger of attack from the lizard men. The lake is large and they will be far from the shore when they siphon up the precious water.

The first shuttles returning to the planet's surface, make a flyover of our abandoned compound. The lizard creatures destroyed everything we left behind and every structure we erected. The buildings lay in shambles, the walls torn down except for one small section near the main gate. The water tanks are toppled and smashed.

A few of the creatures still wander inside what was once our home. The pilots resist, although with difficulty, the urge to open fire with their lasers in revenge for our lost comrades. They proceed to the lake. The wave of craft, all we had aboard except two, met at the lake and began to collect the water. We are holding two of the shuttles in reserve in case we need them for some outside work on the massive space platform.

Numerous trips are made. All the water storage tanks are filled. Before the last trip down, the pilots meet with the command staff to ask permission to avenge our losses. Reluctantly, we agreed. We all have a hatred for these merciless monsters. After each shuttle filled with water, it flew in low toward the shore of the lake. The creatures had gathered in tremendous number, watching the shuttles in the distance over the open water. As the craft approached dry ground, each opened a barrage of laser fire, a final salute to a foe that had defeated our attempt to land and live in peace. We inflicted a heavy toll before returning to M.A.B.U.S.

Chapter 35
Moving On

The shuttles and crew are all back onboard. It is time to make ready to get underway. M.A.B.U.S. must be moved out of orbit and into a region of space where it can become motionless while the delicate calculations are made to direct it to the Alpha system. The e-matter thrusters accelerate her speed until the velocity needed to break orbit is obtained. We leave the planet below, shedding tears for those we lost in the short months we were there. Our hydrogen fuel reserves are down below half, but our water is at maximum so we should be all right for now. The e-matter containment vessels are full—there is no shortage there.

Arilias-6 is now just a small blue-green spot on our monitors—the massive platform is slowed to a stop. News from one of the remaining eight probes arrives. Negative! The work on the calculations for the trajectory of our voyage to star system Alpha begins. M.A.B.U.S. is nudged into alignment for e-matter influx. We begin the countdown. I give the order for influx and we are again within a wormhole. The thrusters fire and the platform leaps forward. There is no sensation of movement. Our speed increases with each thruster firing.

"Approaching point seven three light. Stand by to fire e-drives."

The e-drive engines kick in with their eleven pulses, and we are on our way at almost five times the speed of light. There is the long voyage of nearly fifteen years still ahead of us. The launch crew secures from quarters, many returning to the hyper-sleep chambers.

THE WANDERERS

In a few days I am due to be placed in the deep sleep of extended space travel. Our ship hastens toward our next destination. It will be eight months before I again take my place on the bridge of the *Star Traveler*. I make my way to the hyper-sleep chambers. I cannot help but reflect on how close we came to finding a new Eden. Unfortunately, it was replete with not one, but with thousands, of serpents.

Chapter 36
Α and Ω

In the dreamless realm of hyper-sleep, time passes quickly. You dream only when going in, because you need to be in natural sleep before the chamber is activated. Most of your dreams are unremembered. I am again rousted out of my slumber. I have no recollection of the numerous times I was awakened for exercise and nourishment. During that time, my mind was still asleep, trying to forget the horrors of the last days on Arilias-6. I blocked out all the memories of what happened to us back on the planet surface. When I am fully awake I can still see the jaws of the lizard creature inches away from my face on the other side of the log transport. I can still hear the mortal thud of the spear that pierced Commander Itogeshi's body when he pushed me through the shuttle hatch.

So here I am, back at my post at the command console on the bridge of the space platform. I sit here, fingering the key hanging on a chain around my neck. It is with some sense of irony that I sit where I am with my eyes fixed on the locked panel in front of me. We are on our way to a star system we call Alpha. Alpha means a beginning. Emblazoned on the cover of the panel is the Greek symbol …Omega The symbol for the end. This simple, locked panel is something they chose to install onboard M.A.B.U.S. in the last few days before departure from Earth. It was decided that if we were never to find a secure place, the life support systems of all those remaining could be terminated quickly instead of everyone dying slowly in space. The air locks on all modules would blow open, causing total decompression and an instantaneous, swift death for all aboard.

At the same instant in time, the e-matter containment would shift out of phase. M.A.B.U.S. and all those onboard would be returned to physical space and vaporize at a thousand times faster than the neurons in the brain could transmit any sensation. In a single millisecond, all humankind would cease to exist.

This action could not be taken unilaterally. The key that I feel hanging around my neck only unlocks the access panel to the command switch, sending the order to awaken all other command personnel from hyper-sleep. There was a total of twenty when we started on the voyage from Earth, but that number has now been reduced down to only thirteen since we landed and met with the creatures on Arilias-6.

All the personnel holding the necessary keys would have to agree there was no other alternative. To activate the self-destruct mechanism requires five of these personnel acting as a unit throughout various parts of the ship. All five officers need to react in the same instant—turning their keys on command—or nothing would happen. If any one of them had second thoughts, the platform would continue on as before. If all five turned the keys in unison, we would cease to exist.

An interesting thought—we have become nothing since combining with e-matter. We are traveling through nothing at millions of miles each minute. There is nothing in front of us, nothing behind us—we are surrounded by nothing. If the five switches are pulled, do we continue as nothing or does the physical universe suddenly close in on us and for just that short millisecond do we return to being something? Thoughts such as these are what make us human.

Many times I have thought I should use my key and try to convince the others to put an end to the tedium of this long voyage, wishing it to be over. Then I see the shining face of one of the infants who has been born since we left Arilias-6. I hear their laughter and quickly tuck the key back inside my jumpsuit.

During the short time on the surface of Arilias-6, several of the crew really got to "know" each other. We have been blessed with several new arrivals since leaving the planet. Unfortunately, the poor mothers had to endure their entire pregnancy without the benefits of hyper-sleep. Hyper-sleep slows the development of an embryo to the same rate of metabolism as the mother.

Even suspended in hyper-sleep with a reduced metabolic rate of ten percent, there is not a woman in all existence who would wish to endure a seven-and-a-half-year-long pregnancy.

The weightlessness of space, however, is a definite plus in their favor. Attached to the decking by their magnetic gravity boots, they are free from the usual gravitational discomforts all the mothers on Earth were forced to endure. There is no sensation of almost always falling over forward. No problems with back pain caused by the added weight of the baby and fluids accompanying Earthly pregnancies.

With navels, you have your "innies" and "outies," with the new mothers-to-be there was another way of looking at their distended abdomens—we had our "uppers" and "downers." Some carried high and others low, some in the middle. Everything that could be imagined is done to make life as comfortable as possible for these courageous pioneer women. A new generation is fast coming into being.

We will go on. We will strive forward. We will find a new home where these little ones will learn to walk, run and play. With hyper-sleep, they will be the first teenage toddlers ever born to the human race. To hear their laughter and their cries—to see their faces and the hope in the eyes of their mothers will insure that the formidable key will stay safely where it is for now.

In our search for a new world to call our home, we have traveled more than 300 trillion miles. We are but a minuscule speck in the cosmos, moving ever onward, away from our starting point. Even if we were the largest body in the universe, the most powerful telescope ever constructed, including those on the original M.A.B.U.S. platform, would not be able to detect us from where the Earth once was. Continuing forward, never looking back—for now we will remain nomads within the vast reaches of the unknown. We continue to be…

…the Wanderers.

Printed in the United States
38588LVS00005B/319-366